CORRUPTION

CORRUPTION

A Griffin Hunter Novel

Volume 1

Parker Samuels

Other books in the series:

Relentless

Superstition

Destruction

Fennec Publishing

Fennec Publishing
P. O. Box 1708
Oak Harbor, WA 98277
www.fennecpublishing.com

ISBN: 979-8-9882615-0-6

Cover photo by Sam Williams from Pixabay
Interior images by Sedef Früh

This is a work of fiction. All characters are entirely
fictitious and are not intended to represent actual living persons.

DEAR READER

If you would like to be notified when you can download the next volume in the Griffin Hunter series for FREE enter your email address at GriffHunter.com.

Learn some of Krunch's backstory when you register for the Griffin Hunter newsletter at GriffHunter.com.

Would you like to be a beta reader for the next volume in the Griffin Hunter series? Send an email to Beta@GriffHunter.com

Would you like to discuss your favorite characters, ask questions, etc.? Subscribe to our reader forum at GriffHunter.com.

What's new in this edition?

I've added a few drawings inspired by CORRUPTION. These were commissioned as part of an effort to bring the story to a graphic novel format. Your imagination should still guide how you see the characters in your mind's eye. The illustrations are just the artist's interpretations and not necessarily how I envisioned the characters.

1

I lay crumpled on the gritty asphalt, oozing blood, staring at a soggy cigarette butt.

Only minutes ago I was in Goldberg's Delicatessen, where the aroma was a savory symphony of sausage, grease, and garlic. Good food littered the red and white checkered tablecloth. One perk of working for Benni Sokol was that he liked good food. During the last half of the fifteen months I'd been undercover, infiltrating his organization, I'd gained eight pounds.

His bodyguards, Jonah and Reuben, littered the worn chairs on either side of Benni.

"So, when are you going to propose to my daughter?" A mist of crumbs sprayed from Benni's mouth as he spoke.

I couldn't tell him that would never happen. Well, at least the marriage. "I take it that means that I have your permission?"

"Of course. Of course. You've already become like a son to me."

A lanky man with a receding hairline and a bushy mustache came in. Without looking around, he stepped up to the cashier and asked somewhat loudly for three bagels to go. It was Teddy Lawson, my case agent, or as I thought of him, my handler. His sudden, unexpected appearance meant something I didn't know about was going down. Bagels to go. I could only assume they were going to take Benni and his two bodyguards into custody.

That also meant that I would escape the ticklish position of having slept with his daughter and Benni wanting me to marry her. "I'll ask her soon."

He smiled. It would be one of the last smiles on Benni's soft round face for a long time.

That settled, Benni changed the subject and rambled on about justice.

Benni was a lieutenant in one of Houston's crime families. His part of the business was gambling and strip clubs. The clubs were the other perk of the assignment.

Most of the lunch crowd had already cleared out. So had Teddy. Benni removed the soft napkin from his corpulent lap, signaling that it was time to go. Without a word, Jonah, the bodyguard, stood and took the lead, scanning the remaining customers as he headed toward the front door. In front of him, one of the few remaining customers stood. Jonah froze. Several paces behind him, we all did the same. The customer, a pug-faced man in a blue button-down shirt, went to the register and pulled out some bills to pay his tab.

Benni appeared to be examining the rye bread in a dark, rich wooden case fronted with glass. I stood on alert next to Benni and glanced behind us at Benni's other bodyguard. Reuben, the bodyguard not the sandwich, turned to face the back of the deli while I turned my back to the deli cases in order to turn to either the front or back if necessary.

The cashier took pug-face's money, and he ambled out the door.

A few seconds later, Jonah continued his march to the

front door. We waited a couple of seconds to put a bigger gap between us just in case pug-face was waiting to ambush us outside. If he was, he would be in for a big surprise. Jonah could be violent if need be.

Donning my Ray-Bans, we made our way out into the humid Houston heat. Houston had its own smell. Three parts sea breeze, two parts oil refinery, and one part mildew. The locals never noticed the odor, but it was there all the same.

Continuing our previous conversation, I told Benni, "Revenge is a dish best served cold." He waddled through the arched wooden portal that served as the entrance to Goldberg's Deli.

Jonah slowed near the corner of the white stone facade, where the adjoining parking lot lay tucked off to the side. Our pace slowed to match his.

Jonah turned the corner into the lot next to Goldberg's and headed toward the back of the lot so that he could examine the dumpster and the alley behind the deli for threats.

Benni's fetid breath reeked of pastrami and sauerkraut as he turned to me. "It isn't revenge if it is justified."

I was distracted from the rest of Benni's rambling rationalization by a glint of light that drew my eyes to a rooftop across the street. SWAT snipers must be perched there.

Benni and I continued into the parking lot and headed back toward Benni's white Cadillac CT6. As we passed the rounded hood of the Caddy, Jonah unexpectedly pulled his pistol and aimed down the alleyway.

I glanced behind us and saw that Reuben had taken his

position in the lot near the entrance.

Jonah, an impulsive man, fired a round. Time slowed down. A brief volley of shots rang out. Both Jonah and Reuben dove between parked cars.

I shoved Benni down face-first on the oily asphalt next to his car and threw myself on top of him, not so much as to protect him, but to get out of the line of fire. My Ray-Bans skittered across the pavement.

Gunfire rained down on the parking lot as Reuben fired shots in return. I pulled out my weapon and crept to the front bumper of Benni's car. Benni, unarmed, stayed on the ground, face down, hands stretched over his head, already posed to surrender.

Jonah was taking careful aim. Just over his shoulder, I saw the two crouching cops he was aiming for. I fired a shot into the back of Jonah's head, followed up by two shots into his back. The thunderous roar of my 9mm immediately punished my hearing.

Jonah's head made an unnatural wobble, then he slumped to the ground like a sack of Wala-Wala onions. Beyond Jonah's limp corpse was a detective raising his weapon in Jonah's direction. At that moment, time stood still, and I prayed they had briefed the entire takedown team on who I was. The face of Detective Nick Lawry changed from concern to relief and a faint smile crossed his lips. I knew I would not be shot by friendly fire that day.

With Jonah down, that only left Reuben maintaining the fight. Reuben took a hit but kept on firing. I decided it was time to "surrender" and end the carnage. I tucked my weapon back into its holster and raised my hands above the hood of the CT6.

As I stood up, I was suddenly jerked to a stop. My oversized silver and turquoise belt buckle had caught on the lip of the Caddy's wheel well.

As I reached down with my right hand to free the buckle, my left shoulder jerked backward and the sensation of spattering hot grease radiated out from it. As I continued to fall backward, I realized it was more than just a pulled muscle.

I had been shot.

I yelped from the searing pain and yelped again as my head hit the car parked next to us. Instinctively, I reached for the wound and felt the oily blood.

My blood.

I pressed my finger on the wound to retard the flow of blood. The opening was surprisingly small. Like someone had stabbed me with a pencil.

I grew light-headed. The gunfire had ceased. Either that or I just couldn't hear it anymore. As my body rolled face down onto the gritty asphalt, I dimly saw a soggy cigarette butt.

Then everything went black.

2

Across the street, the sniper had watched Griff's hands appear above the Cadillac's hood. He had been waiting for that. As Griff arose, the sniper took aim and ever so gently squeezed the trigger. "Crap." Griff had abruptly stopped, his ascent pulled to the side. He knew the shot hadn't been fatal. He couldn't do anything about it now. Not without revealing himself to the various cops on every side of him.

The wounded bodyguard, Reuben Heinz, popped up one more time to return fire. A detective shot him, and the bodyguard went down with a scream. After the detective kicked the gun away from the wounded man's reach, an ambulance rolled around the corner.

Detective Lawry scampered out of his spot in the alley and looked at Jonah. No need to check for a pulse. Half his head was missing. He continued forward to check on the undercover detective who had just saved his life, Griffin Hunter.

Lawry, peeking around a parked car could see Griff's bleeding body in front of him, and a prostrate man, Benni Sokol. Sokol was motionless, repeating the words, "Don't shoot. I surrender."

Lawry handcuffed Benni. With that done, the detective bent down to Griff and checked for a pulse. "We need another ambo." Benni was roughly dragged up and walked over to a car. "You have the right to remain silent..." blah, blah, blah.

Benni looked concerned, but not for his own safety. He was worried about his men and the one that had saved his life, Palmer "Woody" Woods. He still had no clue that Woody was aka Griff, an undercover cop. "I want my attorney," was all he said as they put him into a car.

The paramedics assessed Reuben and Griff, then put Reuben on the gurney. The SWAT team arrived, having descended from their perch.

"Hey, hey, hey! The other guy goes first."

"Sorry, this man's injuries are more life-threatening. The other guy can take the next car. It should be here within four minutes."

"No. I don't think so. This guy is a criminal, the other one is a cop."

"Doesn't matter. That's not how we do it. This guy needs attention sooner than the other guy. Doesn't matter if he is your friend."

They argued more while the medic continued to load Reuben in the ambulance.

"I get it. You wouldn't care if we drove this guy around for a while or got in a traffic jam, but that's not how we do it here. New York or Chicago maybe, but not in Houston."

One of the SWAT guys from the roof, Donovan, joined the conversation. "Let the man do his job. The medic is right. Another one will be here for our guy soon enough."

That might have been the end of arguing with paramedics, but once the next ambulance arrived, while they were loading Griff on board...

"Where are you taking him?"

"Memorial Hermann Southwest."

"No, no, no, no. He goes downtown."

"And why is that?"

"It's a level one trauma center."

"He doesn't need a level one. Southwest will be fine."

"He's one of ours. Shot in the line of duty. He deserves the best."

"I understand, but Downtown can barely handle all the level ones that come in. We have protocols. If it's not a level one, it goes to a level two center. That's the whole reason they made Southwest a level two."

The door closed, the lights started up, and the ambulance disappeared down the street.

They secured the scene, and once the crime lab techs had taken over, sent everyone involved to the Southeastern Sub Station for a long debriefing.

***

Later that night, the sniper opened his gun safe, just like he did every evening. He pulled out the two burner phones and turned them on. He put one pistol away and withdrew another one, just like he did every evening and morning five days a week. But today was different. One burner beeped. A text message sent earlier in the day had just arrived.

"What happened? Fix it," it read.

A few miles away, another burner beeped. "See me."

3

A sterile white hallway was awash with a sea of blue uniforms who provided a thundering whisper like the surf on Galveston's beaches. Cops, constantly coming and going, gave this fabric, human sea its motion while other officers stood guard at the doors like blue bollards at a dock.

The staff, clad in their teal-colored scrubs, had given up trying to keep the noise level down.

Inside ICU Room #3 the patient lie in a state of dreamless nothingness as the nurse checked his ID on the wrist ban against the electronic chart displayed on the monitor. She neatly printed his name on the fresh plastic bag of Ringer's lactate already hanging on the IV pole. In a rhythm perfected from countless changes like this one, she stemmed the flow of his old IV with the blue plastic roller clamp on the main line. Effortlessly, she removed the seal from the port of the fresh bag. In one seamless move, she removed the old IV bag from the pole and quickly, smoothly removed the spike from the old bag and slid it into the fresh bag's port.

With no air in the tubing and the drip chamber half full, she returned the controlled flow by adjusting the roller clamp.

She updated the patient record with a few key clicks and left with the old IV bag for disposal. The entire process took less than 3 minutes.

A detective in plain clothes, badge hanging around his neck from a cheap silver-colored chain, approached the guard posted at the ICU room door. "Is he still unconscious? I want to talk to him."

"Nah. He is still out of it."

"Humph. Has the Chief been by yet? He usually stops in for a visit on cops shot in the line of duty."

"Nah. I don't think so. At least he hasn't been here since I've been here."

A shrill beeping that resonated from both the room and the nearby nurses' station interrupted their meaningless conversation. Nurse Herrero shot from the nurses' station, bumping into the standing cops along her way, and slewed past the guard and detective. Both the guard and detective turned inward to see what was going on.

It had been less than 3 minutes since Nurse Herrero had changed the IV and her patient had gone from stable to being in trouble. She shook the patient and called his name while examining the monitors that had alarmed. In a calm voice, she called out, "Code Blue" and began chest compressions.

The crowd of police officers had knotted together outside room 3, making it difficult for the Code Nurse to gain access. "Make a hole!" she called out as she strode toward the door. The blue sea parted like the waves for Moses. Another nurse followed in her wake. "I'm the code nurse," she stated to no one in particular, establishing her authority for taking control of the situation.

Assessing the monitors, she silenced the alarm and directed the third nurse to prepare to ventilate. A male nurse made his way into the room. "Let's get the gel pads on." The male nurse peeled back the paper from the adhesive pads and attached both to the nearby defibrillator paddles. Meanwhile, the third nurse started bagging the man with a manual resuscitator.

The Code Nurse went to a nearby cabinet and pulled out a syringe of epinephrine and slipped it into the pocket of her scrubs.

Less than 3 minutes later, a tall dark-haired man in a white lab coat pressed through the doorway and announced, "I am Dr. Samuel. I'll be your Code Doctor. Who is the Code Nurse?" The Code Nurse raised her hand and stated, "I am." Dr. Samuel continued, "OK. Why don't you rotate compressions and bagging?"

The male nurse spoke, "One, two, three." On the count of three, he seamlessly started doing the chest compressions from his side of the bed. Nurse Herrero, now relieved of doing compressions, reached across the patient's face, put her hand on the resuscitator and swiveled it to her side of the bed, and continued squeezing.

"Do we know what happened here?" The doctor asked.

Nurse Herrero spoke first. "He is recovering from surgery after receiving a gunshot wound. He was stable about 10 minutes ago when I swapped out his IV."

Dr. to Code Nurse: "Charge to 200!" as he took the defibrillator paddles in his hands. "Clear!" Everyone's hands retracted. The Dr. pressed the paddles into the chest and, whomp, the lifeless form jerked. Hands moved back in.

As the crowd of police officers knotted together outside room 3, watching the action inside, Police Chief McCormick stepped out of the elevator and slid up behind them to see what was going on. The body in room 3 jerked again. Normally the cops would have snapped to attention, but they were so focused on the drama unfolding inside the room that they never noticed the Chief's arrival.

The body jerked again. Chief McCormick slid past the knot of men and moved into the next room unnoticed.

"Time of Death: 19:53."

4

"Hello, Chief. Wasn't sure I'd see you here." It was Ivy Iverson, Special Agent FBI, Houston field office.

"I'm the one that is surprised. I didn't think your office had an interest in Benni Sokol."

"It's not that we aren't interested. Organized crime does fall under the purview of the FBI." Trying belatedly to stake some kind of claim, she tried to make it sound important.

McCormick wasn't amused. "Then where have you been the last two years?"

"Oh, Chief," She started back peddling. "You know, they have stretched us thin for the last several years. Our directives have us focused on the border and the occasional terrorist threat. Honestly, that's why anyone lower than Benni's boss, Poliakoff, just doesn't warrant the manpower it deserves."

"Which is exactly why the HPD has been pursuing the case. Benni isn't the biggest fish in town. Poliakoff isn't even a deal compared to the other mobsters in Houston."

"And I appreciate your team's efforts, as well as keeping me in the loop as things developed."

Her it comes, McCormick thought. "And..."

"Well, now that you've got Benni...the agency was thinking...if we could get him to turn on Poliakoff...well, that might be interesting to us. Poliakoff that is."

In his younger days, McCormick would have exploded, but you didn't get to be Chief of Police without being able to control your passions and play the game. Besides,

McCormick held all the cards, and he knew it. "The DA would never go for that."

McCormick continued, "We've got one man dead..."

Iverson interrupted, "A man we would have liked to question."

McCormick gave her a hard look. "Like we wouldn't?" A pause. "As I was saying," His clue for her not to interrupt. "We have a man dead and two in ICU recovering from surgery."

"Perhaps if our team had done the takedown..." She knew it was a mistake as soon as the words left her sultry lips.

McCormick's forehead wrinkled, his eyes squinted. He held back his scathing rebuke. It was BS, and they both knew it.

Iverson shifted in her chair. Hospital chairs weren't all that comfortable to begin with.

"I've got a man right here who took a bullet bringing Benni in." McCormick jerked his head to the side.

Iverson decided it was time to change the direction of the conversation. "Yea, so how did that happen?" Oops, she didn't want that to sound like it was the department's fault he got shot. "I mean, who shot him? Which one of Benni's bodyguards?"

"That is still under investigation." It wasn't. What else could he say?

Detective Kennedy Kuchenmeister popped in the door. "Sorry to interrupt, Chief." She waited for McCormick to acknowledge her presence. "He just died."

"Humph."

Iverson, still intent on sticking her foot in her mouth,

said, "Well, that's two that we don't get to interview."

McCormick's face contorted. Iverson knew it was time for her to leave. Even if she had played it right, she didn't expect HPD and the DA's office to go for it, but it was still worth a try. Unfortunately, she probably burned what little good will she may have had with the Chief.

Det. Kuchenmeister did not know who the impertinent woman was, but stood silently as Iverson stood and left.

"Thank you," McCormick was almost always polite, at least in a public setting. "And you are?"

"Detective Kuchenmeister. From the Southwest Substation."

"Kuchenmeister?"

"Yes sir. But they call me Krunch."

"You like it?"

"I've been called much worse, so yes."

"So, tell me, Krunch, what happened next door?"

She rehearsed what she knew ending with, "The docs figured it was just one of those things. An adverse reaction to a drug or the surgery, I guess." She twisted her mouth to the side a little.

McCormick recognized that look. "And...what do you think?"

"I" She wasn't sure she should speak, it being the Chief and all. "I don't know. It just seems a little...off somehow."

"How's that?"

"I don't know, sir. One minute he seemed fine, then he went into cardiac arrest, then he was dead despite the medical response. At least that's what I've heard. It just doesn't...feel right." She gave the slightest little shrug.

"In this business, you should always trust your gut. Cops without good instincts don't last long."

McCormick thought for a moment. "Get that doctor in here. I want to talk to him. Oh, and pull the guard detail from that room and double it on this room."

Krunch went to the nurse's station and requested the doctor. She went to the uniform that she thought had been the guard outside room 3. She had no authority to assign anyone, but the Chief of Police had asked her to do something, and she wasn't about to say no.

"Um, you the one who was on the door?" she nodded toward room 3.

The uniformed cop smiled. Krunch had that effect on men. "Yes, ma'am. What can I do for you?"

"I'm Det. Kuchenmeister." She blew out a little air. "I was just talking with the Chief. He's right there in room four." She nodded in that direction. "He would like you re-assigned to join the existing guard on that room. Room 4."

"The Chief asked?" He looked impressed that she was on speaking terms with the Chief. "I'll go stand there, but if it's OK, I'll have to clear it with my supervisor when he comes by."

"Of course, of course. Thank you so much."

At about that time, the doctor wheeled into room 4. Krunch followed.

"What happened to the man next door?" McCormick asked.

"Sometimes these things just happen."

"But he made it through surgery OK and was supposed to recover?"

"That is correct. Unfortunately, there is always a slight

risk, even with planned surgery. In a trauma case like this, higher." The doctor showed no emotion. "Statistically, two to four percent of patients with non-cardiac surgeries die of cardiac events post-surgery. The number is only an estimate. Some think that it may be higher."

"Humph." The chief rubbed the bridge of his nose between his fingers. "I want an autopsy done. Right away."

"Of course. I'll put a rush on it."

***

The Houston Police Department wasn't the only one affected by the takedown of Benni Sokol. Manny Poliakoff had his number two man taken into custody, for what he didn't yet know, and lost two of their men. It wouldn't have an immediate impact on the business, but there was risk none the less.

Manny was the great-grandson of a Russian-Jewish immigrant, Solomon Poliakoff. Although Sol had lived in Texas all of his life, Arnold Rothstein, the leader of New York's Jewish mob, affectionately known as the Kosher Nostra, greatly influenced him. Rothstein transformed organized crime into a business. He was even accused of fixing the outcome of the 1919 World Series, resulting in the appointment of the first commissioner of baseball. Although the Kosher Nostra eventually blended into the Italian crime syndicate, Manny thought of himself as the modern-day Kosher Nostra with Rothstein as his Moses.

That night, Poliakoff was holding court in his stately Avalon Place home. After making his guest wait in the elegant oval-shaped foyer, with its hardwood floor and Persian rug, Poliakoff descended the curved stairway and led his guest into an adjoining office.

"Thanks for meeting with me at this late hour. I know it's been a long day for you." Poliakoff said. He pointed to an overstuffed white and mahogany guest chair.

There had been no chair in the foyer. Poliakoff liked to keep his guests standing while they waited for his entrance. The guest sat across from him, nodding his head respectfully. He really didn't have a choice.

"Look, I'm a businessman." Poliakoff continued. "There used to be five businesses that you could get rich from. The internet ruined the pornography business, so now it's down to politics, gambling, strip clubs, and drugs. Politics is far too corrupt for me, and the street gangs and cartels are making the drug business more...challenging."

"Benni handled the strip clubs and some of the gambling. He doesn't believe in the drugs and violence that come with them. That's fine 'cause I got other guys who take care of that end of the operation. But this business with Benni has suddenly gotten very messy."

"It was only a couple of days ago that one of your associates informed me that one of Benni's associates was an undercover cop." One of Poliakoff's confidential informants had delivered the news. That informant was easier than most because of his weaknesses.

Criminals have CIs just like the police do. They use, abuse, and groom them the same way, too. First, they look the other way for a little payoff. Soon a bigger payoff for a tip, a warning in advance of something happening. It's a slippery slope and once you've committed the sin, you can't go back because your deeds will be revealed.

Poliakoff liked to think of these men as confidential informants, not snitches. Of course, that is what his guest was, but criminals, or businessmen as Poliakoff thought of himself, didn't like snitches. They killed them. But he loved these men of low moral character on his payroll. They were worth every penny. He wished he could have more of them. There were certainly enough, but truth be told, no one could afford all of them.

"If things had gone as planned, I wouldn't be too worried about Benni. But your man let me down." Poliakoff was on a roll now. "We have skilled attorneys, and Benni is not a stupid man, so I'm sure that there is nothing illegal that could be directly traced back to him. But a cop on the witness stand would increase my risk. You led me to believe that we can't persuade Detective Hunter to forget certain things..."

"That's correct. Hunter is a real boy scout."

Poliakoff appreciated loyalty and honor, just not when it was manifested in a cop. "I want to believe all my men are loyal to me. But, I also have to assume that Benni may try to make a better deal for himself. Most men in my business keep some insurance. Records that could prove embarrassing to their bosses or other men in the industry. It's unpreventable, really, but it serves to make everyone a little more reliable, ah, honest."

His guest nodded in understanding.

"I have my men looking in our locations for whatever insurance Benni may have, but there are places where we can't go directly." In fact, Poliakoff knew the outcome of the takedown long before 1200 Travis knew, and had dispatched men to search the dead men's homes. He also had Mrs. Sokol swept up and moved to a secluded location both to protect her from police and the media, but also so they could search Benni's home unmolested.

"I need you to locate the insurance from locations that you have better access to and bring it to me. I need it to make certain that I remain safe. And you need me to remain safe so that you remain safe."

"I understand."

"Benni is like family to me. I don't want to see anything happen to him...but if we can't locate his insurance, then he may have to carry his secrets to his grave." Benni was like family. Their great-grandfathers had come over on the same boat.

"I'll take care of it. One way or the other."

"Good. I knew I could count on you. Oh, one more thing, if you find it, don't make any copies. It would be bad for your wife's health."

5

Morning beams of sunlight crept through the windows, illuminating particles in the air drifting throughout the room like fairies on the wing. So much for the room being sterile.

On the other side of the sliding glass door, the sounds of the morning shift launching into the day's activities brought a steady, distant rumble of blended voices and footsteps.

I became aware of the rumble, sounding even more distant than it was, and the sensation of light began to burn through the dark fog that had enveloped me in Goldberg's parking lot. I began to differentiate another set of voices distinct from the rumble. Closer. Finally, a smell. What is that smell? Oh, the smell of a hospital. Huh. I must not be dead yet. And with that, I cracked open my eyes.

Seated next to me was Krunch. Highlights in her strawberry blond hair glimmered in the light like dew on the autumn's morning grass. She was only half looking in my direction and in mid-sentence, so someone else had to be in the room.

I turned my head. Well, at least tried to turn it to see who she was talking to. As my head lolled to the side, the room grew silent and Krunch's head snapped in my direction.

"Well, look who's back from the dead."

The voice was that of my handler, Teddy. He obviously must be in the room, too. I tried to reply, but I think I drooled instead. But at least my eyes had opened more. I found the strength to pull my head back upright.

"You weren't supposed to get shot," Krunch said.

"With keen observations like that, you'll always be a rookie detective." My voice sounded dry and raspy.

A nurse magically appeared by my side and gave me a sip of water. Someone must have let her know I was awake. She typed something into the computer station near my bed. "I'll let the doctor know you are awake. Be right back."

As I watched her leave through the door, I saw the uniformed guard posted outside. "What's with the guard?"

"They have posted one around the clock since you came in. We assume that your cover has been blown and want to make sure that Benni's boss, Poliakoff, doesn't come after you." Teddy's normally friendly faced turned serious. "And after Reuben Heinz's death, we aren't taking any chances."

"What happened to Reuben?"

At that moment, Herrero returned and shoved a digital thermometer into my mouth. Kind of like how the waitress always waits until you have a mouth full of food to ask how everything is.

"Dunno. We shot him at the scene, but he made it here and out of surgery. He was in the next room expected to recover, then the next thing, he was dead." Teddy continued recounting the previous night's drama while I enjoyed the taste of the plastic and metal probe.

Krunch took over the narration. "You also had VIP visitors last night. Our Commander and his Assistant Chief hung around until you were out of danger. And Chief McCormick dropped in to check on you." That was pretty customary. "You were out of it, but he was sitting here in your room, having a chat with Special Agent Iverson."

Herrero yanked the thermometer out when it beeped, make a notation on the keyboard, swiveled, and disappeared through the door.

"What did Iverson want?" It was nice to hear that she stopped by.

"I'm not sure. I interrupted to tell the Chief about Reuben's demise. She made a remark about not being able to interview the dead guys and left. Looked like the Chief wasn't happy with her."

Teddy chimed back in. "FBI is probably trying to horn in on the case."

"In her defense, they weren't completely uninvolved. I know that there was an understanding at the beginning, and I met with Iverson several times while undercover." I had an interest in Ivy, but wasn't sure that it was mutual.

"What happened at Goldberg's? I mostly remember getting shot and my face slamming into a nasty cigarette butt."

After Krunch had excitedly recounted the tale, Teddy said, "How are you doing? Other than the gunshot, I mean."

"Fine. I'll be OK." Wasn't that the de facto answer of all cops, firefighters, and soldiers?

"Yeah, yeah. We're worried about you. It's almost unheard of to be undercover for over a year. Six months is too long."

"I know, but it was the only way to get close enough to Benni. Gain his trust and work your way up."

"And you put your life on hold that whole time," Teddy said. "You're old life is gone. You can't just pick back up where you left off."

"True." One of the many hurricanes that hit Texas in

recent years occurred while I was under. The storm had damaged the house I was renovating from the previous hurricane. I lost friends in the storm. And my father had died. It was at a critical point a year in, and I couldn't risk going to the funeral. I knew my dad would understand, and would probably have wanted it that way, but it was beyond my sister's comprehension.

"Your undercover work is done, and you can't go back to your alternate life, either."

"You think Poliakoff knows?"

"Doesn't matter. We can't take that chance. Besides, once they announce you as a witness, you'll be outed, anyway." Teddy said. "Thinking like that shows you are still in that life."

"So, what's next?"

"Nothing for the next couple of days. You're stuck here. But maybe that's not so bad. It will give you time to wrap your brain around the change."

I was ready to change the subject. "Hey Krunch, could you swing by my apartment and pick up some clothes and personal effects for me?"

Teddy wasn't finished yet. "Look, you know how many guys come out from undercover and end up getting busted off the force? It's far too many."

"I knew that going in. But we both know that most of those guys are on narcotics cases. They do drugs to get inside. They get addicted and then, when the case is over, can't get back off."

The badge can't protect you from addiction.

I continued, "Benni's part of the organization doesn't deal drugs, so I didn't have to get involved in that. That's why I was willing to take the assignment. I've never had a problem with gambling and the house it too smart to play its own game. My biggest risk is hanging around ti..." I glanced at Krunch. "Um, bars too much."

Nurse Herrero reappeared and wrapped a blood pressure cuff around my arm and started pumping it up.

"Even if all that is true, being undercover makes you paranoid."

"You think I'm paranoid?" I said it in a loud, over-emphatic voice. A joke.

Herrero didn't see any humor in it.

"Funny. But it's true. You have to be paranoid to survive. While you are creating a new life for yourself, you are going to be looking over your shoulder all the time. That alone can lead to problems."

The air hissed out of the cuff. After another annotation, Herrero started messing with my IV bag. I turned to her as she was taking the old IV bag down and said: "Can I get this thing out of my nose?"

Herrero shrugged. "You can ask the doctor about that when you see him." And with that, she whisked out of the room as quickly as she had arrived.

Krunch changed the subject. "Did you know that you probably saved Nick Lawry's life?"

"What. No. How?"

She gave the details about me taking out Jonah. Krunch finished with a flourish.

"Hey, I just realized, if you ever make it to Captain, then you'd be Captain Krunch." I was quite pleased with myself for this quip. It was not like me.

"No. If I made captain, people would have to call me

by my real name; Captain Kuchenmeister."

"Yeah, except that no one could pronounce it," I smirked. I was feeling much better now.

Krunch made a pouty face. I was sure that she only used that face to manipulate men, but it was cute nonetheless.

Teddy was speaking now, but I was having a hard time following what he was saying. A blizzard of sparkling stars filled the room and the sounds and smells that had only recently filled my senses were now being smothered out by a blanket of snow. There was a shrill beeping somewhere off in the distance, then nothing.

I saw Herrero burst into the room, but it was hard for me to process. I was looking down. And I was still in bed. How could that be? Oh. Herrero was shouting at me and shaking me.

In a calm voice, she called out "Code Blue" to no one in particular and began chest compressions. "You need to clear the room."

Teddy left, but Krunch stayed behind, tucked into a corner of the room.

A minute later, two nurses entered the room. One of them said something about being the code nurse. Was there a code to be solved? Herrero was practically jumping on my chest. The others were busy grabbing supplies.

After that, a guy who looked to be a doctor strode purposefully into the room. Herrero was talking very animatedly to him. Then Krunch was over there yelling at the doctor. Someone picked up the phone.

The doctor turned and squeezed the IV bag. Herrero yanked the IV right out of my arm. I couldn't help but think,

"That must have hurt." Suddenly, the nurse who appeared to be in charge went to a cabinet and pulled out a syringe. As the nurse plunged the syringe into the other me, everything went dark.

In the darkness, I saw the tip of a needle. It plunged into an IV bag. I could see a clear liquid being squirted into the bag. Like watching a movie where the camera pulls back, I saw more of the scene. Now I could see the hand attached to the syringe that the needle protruded from. And now a sleeve. A blue sleeve. Abruptly, the vision ended.

I sucked in an enormous gulp of air. My body convulsed. My eyes flew open and instead of looking down at Herrero's head, I was looking into her black eyes. I was no longer at peace. In fact, a wave of indescribable pain washed over my entire being.

Then everything went black. Again.

6

I became aware of a familiar distant rumble. There was a sensation of light burning through a dark fog. I differentiated another set of voices distinct from the rumble. What is that smell? Oh, the smell of a hospital. No, this can't be happening. It's like a nightmare Groundhog Day. I was almost afraid to crack my eyes open, but I had to look, to be sure. The room was backward from what I remembered it being.

"You gave us quite a fright," Krunch said. Her indigo eyes were focused completely on me.

"I had the weirdest dream." My throat was dry, and my voice was raspy.

A hand appeared with a welcome glass of water. Well, as welcome as a plastic hospital glass can be. Attached to the hand was Det. Nick Lawry.

"What was this dream?" Nick had this unmistakable Texas drawl.

"Someone tried to kill me."

"Yea, someone tried to kill you alright!" Nick said.

"No. I don't mean getting shot in the parking lot."

Nick replied. "That's not what we're talking about, either."

A tall, heavyset nurse materialized. Her hospital ID tag said, Packer. "Are you in any pain?"

"No. Should I be?"

"Not really, but we've had to dial back the morphine because of last night's incident. I'll let the doctor know you are awake."

"What incident?" She just turned and walked out without answering.

"Someone poisoned your IV with a large overdose of drugs." It was Teddy. "Whoever it was, did the same thing to Reuben Heinz' IV, only they succeeded in murdering him."

"What?"

"Krunch saved your life," Teddy said as Krunch blushed.

I looked from Teddy to Krunch, then back to Nick. "How?" I turned back to Krunch. "Did you give me mouth-to-mouth?"

"In your dreams, cowboy. That's never going to happen."

"She was the first to see the similarity between your rapid deterioration and the way Reuben crashed," Teddy said. "She wouldn't leave the room and insisted they call downstairs to see if they had determined Reuben's cause of death. While a nurse did that, Krunch pointed out that both events had occurred shortly after an IV change. That made the doctor squeeze your IV bag and sure enough, liquid spurted out a pinhole at the top. By then, the pathologist told them that Reuben had died of a massive overdose."

"They gave you Narcan."

I couldn't help but turn and look at the IV bag hanging next to me. Suddenly, that innocuous plastic line dangling from it and into my arm looked like a poisonous viper hanging from a limb. "Get this thing off me!" Everything that I had been thinking and wanting to say had disappeared. All that I could think about was getting out of there.

Teddy said, "We've doubled the guard and screened

everyone who comes in here now, but they want to keep you for at least another day for observation."

Nick spoke again. "Yeah, your old room is being treated as a crime scene. The forensics team went over it yesterday, but they don't think they'll be able to pull anything useful from it. The hospital is not too happy that we haven't released it yet, but the boys want to be sure before it gets scrubbed down. By the time we realized Reuben had been murdered, the hospital staff had already cleaned and disinfected his room and the IV materials destroyed."

Teddy chimed in. "Yeah, we would not make that mistake again."

My head was spinning. As I was getting ready to speak, a doctor entered the room. He had a purple stethoscope draped around his neck. His white coat had Samuel embroidered on it. Was that his first name or his last name?

"We are glad to see you awake, Mr. Hunter. It was touch and go there for a while. How do you feel?"

"Like I want to get out of here."

Samuel was shining a bright light into my eyes at this point. "Oh, I understand, but that's not a good idea right now. Your body has been through a lot over the last two days."

"Honestly, I think I'd rather take my chances."

Teddy took the doctor's side. "You might as well stay here. You know you can't come back to work until IA clears you. You can't go back to your undercover pad, and you no longer have a home to go to."

He was right about the rundown apartment I called home for the last fifteen months while undercover. And a hurricane had severely damaged my actual home a year ago. "Wait. Until IA clears me of what?"

"That triple tap you put on the bodyguard," Teddy replied.

"Yeah, that probably saved my life," Nick drawled.

I really didn't remember shooting Jonah. But then I really remembered little about the shootout at all. "Be that as it may, I'm still leaving here today."

"That would be against medical advice, Mr. Hunter."

"Fine Doc. Just get me the papers to sign."

"As soon as we run a couple of tests. Someone will be here in a couple of minutes to draw some blood." And with that, the doctor turned and left the room.

"That still doesn't answer where you are going to stay?" Krunch said.

I offered a weak smile and stared right at her.

"Don't lift those eyebrows at me," Krunch said. "I won't play a part in corrupting you."

I turned my head toward Teddy and Nick, but they were both already shaking their heads.

With Reuben murdered here, and an attempt on my life here, it just didn't seem like a good idea to continue to stay at the hospital like a sitting duck.

I turned my head back to look at Krunch. She said "We're not surprised. It is what we would do too. I brought you some clothes. Paramedics cut your old shirt off you and the slacks were too bloody to wear."

"Thanks for having my back. What about my belt?"

"You mean this?" Krunch reached into the paper sack at her feet that I assumed my clothes were in and pulled out my silver cowboy belt buckle. "The leather was pretty bloodstained, but this will clean up OK."

I shot her an appreciative smile.

"But you're still not staying at my place." As Krunch studied the belt buckle, she exclaimed, "Hey, we can call you the Kosher Cowboy!"

"No. That's not funny. You guys know I'm not Jewish. Besides, a name like that can stick. I mean, think about poor detective Cox." Most cops who were either good or terrible at their job ended up with nicknames. Or sometimes, it was just because of their name. Ed Cox had been the brunt of quite a few nicknames, none of them flattering. No one called him by his real name anymore.

"We figured maybe you converted sometime over the last two years," said Nick. "You know, to gain Benni's trust."

Krunch put on her pouty face. "And you didn't invite me to the circumcision."

Everyone else laughed, but I was speechless.

The phlebotomist rolled her little cart through the doorway and took a position near my side. The blood sample was taken. Then, without a word, she put the vials in a tray and trundled out the door.

I pulled the cannula out of my nose and lifted the tubing over my head. A sharp pain shot through my left shoulder as I sat up. I felt a little woozy, but I didn't want to let my visitors know I wasn't anything but one hundred percent. I just sat with my legs dangling off of the bed while the wave of pain and insecurity washed over me.

The trio smirked in unison. I wasn't fooling anyone.

I pulled at the little pads dangling from electronic wires attached to my chest. They pulled out some of my chest hairs. As soon as they broke free, a shrill beeping screamed from the machine the wires that were attached to. A similar alarm sounded from out in the hallway. One of the uniformed guards swung into the room, closely followed by a nurse with no name.

I looked at them sheepishly. Teddy, Nick, and Krunch let out a laugh. The uniform looked relieved.

Nurse Packer was next through the door. She stated, "You're not ready to go yet."

"Oh, I am more than ready."

"Not until I remove your catheter."

All eyes moved down to my crotch.

Without asking anyone to leave, Packer just flipped the sheet back. I chanced a furtive glance at Krunch. She hadn't turned away. No one had.

"Oh, I see. Circumcision wasn't necessary," Krunch said.

Packer removed the tube and clamped it off. She didn't bother to replace the sheet. What was the point in that, anyway? She removed the IV needle from my arm and shoved a bandage on it. "You'll get a little farther without that." Then she pivoted on her heels and left.

Krunch had a bemused expression on her face. She tossed the bag of clothes my way. No one made a move to give me any privacy. Realizing that I had been laid bare, quite literally, I just stood and started to get dressed. When I bent over, I thought I was going to black out but held on to consciousness until I could sit back on the bed.

"What's with her?" I asked no one in particular.

"Your other nurse got hauled down to the station for questioning after two people whom she changed IVs on were poisoned," Krunch said. "She is the replacement, and I gather everyone who has access to this room got looked at pretty carefully. I don't think that she is too happy to be here."

Getting dressed was slow. When I finished dressing, Teddy applauded mockingly.

The doctor arrived and tried to talk me out of leaving, but even he realized it was a lost cause. Packer arrived with a clipboard full of papers to sign, and another stack of papers for me to take home.

A volunteer arrived with a wheelchair. "I don't need that." But I knew that I really did. I didn't want to collapse on the way out to the car. The doctor said it was hospital policy then and Packer left.

I slid gratefully into the wheelchair. As we left the room, one of the uniforms took the lead to the elevator. The rest of my entourage followed behind.

"I'll get the car," Krunch said as we exited the crowded stainless steel elevator. Nobody knew what to say as we waited in the lobby. When Krunch pulled up out front, we crossed the lobby to the exit doors. The uniforms stood, not knowing exactly what to do next.

And then I was wheeled out into the hot, humid Texas sun. The scent of Houston air smelled much better than I ever remember it smelling.

7

We bumped along in the department-issued car.

I felt broke and naked. "What happened to my wallet and gun?"

Nick replied. "They are in evidence."

"And my car?"

"In the impound yard."

"Well, that's just peachy. At least I should be able to get a department issue."

Teddy chimed in. "No such luck. The department will not issue you a gun or car until IA clears you for duty."

A convict knows the day they will release him. He has a lot of time to contemplate what he will do and where he will go on that anticipated day. Here I was, a sworn law officer, at a disadvantage to a common criminal. I hadn't had the luxury of knowing when I would be out from under cover. I hadn't allowed myself to think ahead to this day. I'd been under so long that I'd nearly forgotten my life before going under.

Maybe I was rash for leaving the hospital without a plan. Krunch. Teddy. Nick. They were all correct.

"Can we make a quick detour by my apartment? I can grab some cash and collect a few things."

Krunch nodded and flipped on the blinker.

"Where are they holding Benni?"

Nick said, "I'm not sure. They didn't take him to county for fear that one of Poliakoff's henchmen would have him shived."

We pulled up in front of the dump that had been my

home for the last two years. The tired brownstone probably didn't look all that nice when it was new. Rusty fire escapes scarred its front like wrinkles on a sea Capitan in a nursing home. White window air conditioners randomly appeared like pimples on a teenager's face. Who knows how much misery this facade had hidden over the decades?

The last insult to the brick tenement was a white limestone facade that jutted out from the original building. Added in the seventies, it housed a small rental office. Someone must have thought that the stark white cube with its stainless steel lettering would add a touch of class, as if the viewer couldn't see the drab brick hulk behind it.

Krunch circled the block to ensure that no one was watching the building. We pulled up in the loading zone in front, and Teddy and I got out. Krunch and Nick stayed behind in the idling car to keep an eye out, just in case.

Once inside, Nick and I crossed the small, dank lobby and took the stairs to the second floor. Left down the hall, third door on the left. I turned the key Krunch had returned to me and swung wide the wooden door.

I stopped as quickly and looked at Nick. Exchanging glances, Nick said, "We shouldn't go in. We need to consider it a crime scene."

Someone had trashed the apartment, obviously looking for something.

"It's my place. My fingerprints and DNA are going to be all over the place. Anyway, I have to get some cash. Unless you are going to give me some."

Nick jerked his head to the side, both showing that I could go inside and that he would not give me money. "Make it fast and try not to disturb the scene. Stay where I can see you." He pulled out his weapon.

I picked my way to the cramped kitchen. Next to the outdated refrigerator, on the Formica counter, sat the cookie jar, undisturbed. As I reached for the lid, I stopped, grabbed a paper towel off the roll hanging under the cabinet nearby, and lifted the lid using the towel.

Like a cat teasing a fish out of a fishbowl, my hand circled the interior of the cookie jar. I was half surprised to feel the loose bills. With the cash stuffed into my pocket, along with the paper towel, I walked toward the door next to where Nick was waiting in the hall and picked up a Mason jar with change in it, and started to leave. I stopped and turned back toward the open cabinets in the kitchen. Taking inventory, I reentered the room and snatched a nearly full bottle of Yukon Jack from the shelf. With that accomplished, I exited the apartment. We locked the door and headed down to our waiting comrades.

As we exited the building, Nick pulled out his phone and called it in. We entered the car.

Nick said, "We should wait until they arrive." Teddy and Krunch turned and stared at us with "What?" written all over their faces.

"No. Who knows how long that would be and the arrival of police would only draw attention and I don't want to be seen with cops yet."

"Thanks," Krunch said. "What's this all about?"

"How was my place when you got my clothes earlier?"

Krunch just stared at me and jiggled her head a little from side to side.

Nick said, "Someone tossed it. We assume it wasn't like that when you were here."

"Well, of course not! I certainly would have said something if it was. What were they after?"

That was a good question. I had nothing of value in the apartment and didn't keep any records, notes, or evidence there. At least not any longer than it took for me to get it to Teddy.

When we got to the station house, I went straight to evidence. It took longer than normal since everyone who I passed wanted to shake my hand and welcome me back. Like that. Even people that I had never met before. Word had circulated and a cop shot in the line of duty had a bit of celebrity status.

At the window to the evidence cage sat Amber "Bleacher" White. I knew her from before my undercover sting, but I introduced myself anyway.

"Hey, Griff. Glad to see you are OK. Didn't expect to see you this soon."

"Bleacher. Glad to see you too, or anybody for that matter. I have a problem. Maybe you can help me with."

She blinked.

"I just got out of the hospital. My apartment got tossed and I don't have ID, credit cards, or a weapon. Nothing. Rumor has it that you have them."

"Normally, I wouldn't consider a request directly." She paused. "But let me make a call."

Even though there was a phone right next to her, she disappeared around a corner for a minute. Upon returning, she said, "They have authorized me to give you back your wallet, but nothing else."

I tried to look crestfallen. "Well, can I at least look at what else of mine is in there?"

"No." With that, she turned away again and disappeared to retrieve my wallet.

"Hope you get cleared soon." She said as she slid the wallet through, along with the clipboard for me to sign.

I sighed, signed, and said, "Me too. See you around."

I took inventory of my wallet as I walked down the hall. "Great. That's just great." It didn't occur to me that the contents in my wallet were all for my undercover persona. I was still Palmer Woods, AKA Woody. "I can't live on this."

They wouldn't issue me a vehicle until they cleared me for duty, either. This was getting to be a real pain. As much as the one on my left shoulder. My meds were wearing off.

Krunch was nice enough to drive me to the impound yard with a stop at the pharmacy along the way. At the pharmacy counter, I requested my prescriptions. "The hospital phoned them over and I can give you the antibiotics, but you have to have a paper prescription for the oxy."

I pulled the small note with its anti-forgery strip on it and passed it to the clerk. She reached around behind her and pulled three white bags from a bin labeled "H" behind her. "I'll need to see your ID and insurance card, Mr. Hunter."

I pulled out my wallet and hesitated. No insurance card for sure. I passed over Palmer Woods' driver's license.

"Without insurance, this will come to $217.48. Um. This isn't for you." She withdrew the white envelopes.

"Look. I really am a Hunter. You see..."

The clerk was stone-faced.

Krunch interrupted. "Mr. Hunter is in too much pain

to come in. He sent us to get his meds."

"He's not getting them." The clerk was referring to me.

Krunch pulled out her badge and her driver's license.

"But you can have them." How are we going to pay?

My credit card was still on the counter, but apparently, that wasn't being considered as an option. I reached into my pocket to see how much cash I actually had, but Krunch pulled out her credit card, smiled at the clerk, and shot me a look.

"Sign here, here, and here. Have a nice day and thank you for choosing us."

"Thanks, Krunch."

"Oh, you will pay me back. And you owe me one of interest."

My saga continued as we went to the impound yard. Almost surprisingly, they handed me the keys without a hitch. As I signed out the car, Krunch said, "You're on your own from here, Cowboy."

The day was fading, and I wanted to go to the bank before it closed. I scratched that idea as I reflected on the pharmacy incident. I didn't have my old checkbook or debit card, couldn't remember my bank account number to write a counter check. Who memorizes their account number, anyway? I could probably talk to a clerk, but without an ID that matched, I would not get very far.

Still, without a plan, I wheeled onto I-45 South and drove toward Galveston. The Oleander City seemed to be the place I always returned to when there was no place else to go. I was getting tired after having taken the oxy earlier and stopped at Webster. It would be closer for me to get back to the office, anyway.

I pulled into the Best Western one exit down from Walmart. I went to the desk and registered as Palmer Woods. Much to my amazement, my department-issued credit card in the same name went through. Apparently, they hadn't cut it off yet. The snail's pace of the bureaucracy benefited me for once. "On second thought, why don't you put me down for a week?" Who knew how long it would be before they cleared me to return? The less the department could do was put me up while they twiddled their thumbs.

I dragged down the hallway to my room. No luggage, just little white pharmacy bags. I held the card next to the door and saw the LED turn green. A faint whirring sound and I was in the room. I turned left immediately inside the door, entered the bathroom, filled a plastic cup with water, and took an antibiotic.

I returned to the main room and flopped, face first, down on the nearest queen bed. And drifted off into a drug-induced sleep.

I dreamed of Galveston.

My great-great-grandfather, Leo Hunter, came to Galveston after the Great Storm of 1900. Prior to that time, Galveston was a booming metropolis. As the trade center of Texas, it was one of the busiest ports in the nation. During this golden era, the city was home to several firsts in Texas: first post office, first naval base, first gas lights, first opera house, first telephone, first electric lights, and the first medical college.

The Great Storm changed all of that forever. That hurricane still holds the dubious record for the deadliest natural disaster in U.S. history. The city was inundated, every house in the city was damaged, and it killed eight thousand people. Maybe thousands more. The devastation caused investors to turn to Houston instead. Galveston built a seawall and raised the grade of the city behind it, but the city never recovered.

Between 1907 and 1914, the Galveston Plan brought ten thousand oppressed Russian Jewish immigrants through the port. Ironically, Benni's ancestors were among those immigrants.

During these years, Leo took advantage of the depressed economy to invest. His investment paid off during the roaring twenties when Galveston again prospered. It became a trade center of a different sort. Tourists traded dollars for prostitutes, illegal alcohol, and gambling. The community made little to no effort to hide the illegal activities. Everyone from legitimate businessmen to organized criminals prospered.

It was during this "open era" that my grandfather was born. His name was also Griffin Hunter, but the name skipped a generation, so it spared me from being named Griffin Hunter the third.

When I was born, my grandfather became known as Great Griffin.

Great Griffin was a Texas Ranger. He helped in the 1957 massive campaign of raids that closed Galveston's casinos and prostitution.

Las Vegas had been eating away at Galveston's sin trades, but the raids were the final blow. The local economy was again ruined and the Hunter Family could again capitalize on the city's depressed economy with land and home purchases in the sixties and the eighties.

Nature wasn't done with Galveston. Hurricane Ike

trashed the economy again, enabling me to buy a storm-damaged home on manmade Tiki Island.

8

The blazing sun reflected off of the crystal clear blue water. Rippling caustics off of the waves danced in their endless blue and white ripples. It was warm, as any good day on the Texas coast should be.

I could almost hear the muffled sounds of children splashing about in the water. A smile danced across my face as I remembered good times as a boy playing in the surf on the beaches of Galveston Island.

The sun became brighter, the sounds of the children louder, and the heat warmer.

A sudden pounding of a key against a door. "Housekeeping."

I cracked my eye open. Instead of the blanket of sand I expected to see, I only saw a muted orange bedspread.

"Housekeeping!" The soft electronic whir of the door unlocking followed by the door opening.

I rolled around toward the foot of the bed when I spotted a stout Hispanic woman in a uniform. "Oh, excuse me, senor," she said in a heavy Mexican accent. "I will come back later." And then she was gone.

The bright light streaming through the sliding glass window danced off of the white ceiling and stung my eyes. I had forgotten to close the blackout curtains. It was stuffy, dank, and uncomfortably warm. I had forgotten to turn on the air conditioner. In fact, I didn't even remember laying down on top of the bed.

As I rose from the bed, my shoulder told me that my pain meds had worn off during the night. I trudged over to the thermostat by the sliding glass door. Through the gossamer curtains, I couldn't help but see the pool directly outside, though it hurt my eyes to look directly at it. As the air conditioner kicked on, its steady hum helped to drown out some of the merry noise coming from the pool area.

In the bathroom, I didn't like what I saw looking back at me in the mirror. I splashed some water on my face and looked at the slender amber bottles of pills on the counter. After filling a paper cup and taking the antibiotic, I reached for the oxy but decided that maybe I should wait until I ran a couple of errands first. After taking care of my other business, I headed out the door.

The heat reflected off the recently resurfaced parking lot. A blast of even hotter air shot out of the car as I opened the door. I knew better than to hop in until a moment had passed.

Once out of the parking lot, I passed a Barnes & Noble, took the I-45 on-ramp, and headed one exit north. I took the El Dorado off-ramp, crossed under the highway, and turned right into the Super Walmart parking lot. The outside looked like every other Super Walmart that I had seen. The inside looked like every other Super Walmart I'd seen except that this one was laid out backward. Who knows why?

First stop, a pair of sunglasses. I didn't know what happened to my Ray-Bans, nor did I care. I needed it all. Socks, underwear, pants, shirts. After grabbing a couple of jeans in my size, I picked out a few western shirts, a size larger than I required. The shirts with snaps on the front, not buttons. I preferred the snap style because it let me have easy access to a shoulder holster concealed under my shirt.

As I looked at the shoes, I wondered what had happened to the Gucci loafers that I had been wearing the day of the takedown. I held off on any shoes so I could pick up something better. Something appropriate for spending hours on my feet.

I started to the front, but then remembered I needed something more. In the back of the store, in electronics, I found what I needed. A burner phone. I'd have to get a new personal phone under my real name soon enough, but this gave me something that I could use to communicate with today.

Back up front, I stopped by the health and beauty section to pick up the essentials. Toothbrush, a tube of Crest, a comb, a stick of Black Jack Pit Boss antiperspirant, and a large bottle of Equate naproxen sodium, Walmart's generic for Aleve. A razor and some shaving cream were next. Shampoo and soap could wait until I got settled in some place more permanent since the hotel provided those.

I looked at some hats, but decided I'd hold off until I could shop for a Stetson.

At check out, I used the department-issued card with Palmer Woods' name on it and took the maximum allowable cash back. It still worked. The card wouldn't let me use it at an ATM to withdraw cash, but apparently, someone didn't consider cash back as a loophole.

Back in the car, I considered my options. There was much to be done, but I hurt and was exhausted. I hadn't felt this way in the hospital, but then again, they had better drugs. In the end, I took the four-minute drive back to the hotel for another dose of drugs, a hot shower, and a nap.

I'd only been gone a short while, but housekeeping had

already vacated the hallway. I held up the plastic key. The LED turned green, and the whir unlocked the door.

Pushing past the door, a glint of light caught my eye, reflecting in the mirrored closet door. The blade of a knife just around the corner on the opposite side between the bed and the wall. I turned just as a big, muscular guy rushed at me. I raised the shopping bags in my hands as he thrust out the knife. He slammed me up against the closet door as he barreled out the door and into the hallway.

At first, I thought he had stabbed me. Pain radiated from my left shoulder. Dropping my bags, I reached up and felt blood oozing out from under my bandages. I had probably torn a stitch. I looked down at my bags. There was a hole in one of them. Levi Strauss had just saved my life.

Not eager to take on a knife-wielding assailant unarmed, I moved to the door and took a furtive look. No one was in the hall. The guy was gone.

Closing and locking the door, I turned back and made my way into the bathroom. I removed my shirt and assessed the damage. Nothing that couldn't be fixed at a doc in the box. I hurt more than ever now and went to take an oxy. The bottle was gone. I was instantly angrier that he had stolen my pain killers than I was that he tried to stab me.

Sitting on the edge of the bed, I dialed 911. "What's your emergency?"

"I'm a Houston detective. Someone just tried to stab me."

"No, I don't need paramedics. Yes, he's gone now."

"Uh-huh. The Best Western." But she already knew that. "OK. Thanks. I'll be waiting."

Webster PD sent a patrol officer to investigate. Hotel

burglary warranted little else. I rehearsed the attack, the missing prescriptions, and the cut bag full of jeans.

"Can you describe the man?" The cop asked.

"Umm. The room was 'kinda dark. I hadn't been able to turn on the lights yet. I just glimpsed the blade. He was black. Kind of bulky. He had an Afro."

"Like from the seventies?"

"Yes, and no. Not that big, maybe like only four inches." I held my hands on either side of my head, trying to show how far the hair stuck out.

"Did you see his face?"

"Honestly, I was looking at the blade coming at me, not the guy's face."

"What *can* you tell me?"

"For a cop, I guess I make a lousy witness."

"As a cop, you should know that every witness is a lousy witness." Of course, he was right.

"He was just about my height. The knife was kinda' special though."

"How so?"

"I am not exactly sure. It was military, I think. Like something a special forces guy would have."

"Well, we don't have that much to go on. We'll let you know if something turns up. But I have to be straight with you, I doubt that it will. This guy probably breaks into rooms looking for valuables or drugs and slips away. The only reason you even bumped into him at all is that you returned to your room so soon after you left." The cop closed his notebook and turned to leave.

One clinic nearest to the hotel was Memorial Hermann Urgent Care. Right across the street from the Barnes &

Noble I passed yesterday. Maybe I'd have to pick up a good book to read while I was resting. John Sandford. Something like that.

I thought it would be easy since my surgery was in the Memorial Hermann system. They pulled up my record based on my name and birthday just fine, but when they asked for some ID, it all came apart. This was getting really tiresome. I was going to get my ID back, and it was going to be today.

When I realized I would get nowhere with the clinic staff, I called Krunch on my burner phone. She answered on the second ring. "What now? Did someone plant a bomb in your car, too?"

"That's not funny. Look, I need you to do a favor. I'm at Memorial Hermann Urgent Care..." I looked up at the sign "Clear Lake. I'm still having my identity crisis and can't get my stitches fixed here. Please call someone at Hermann Southwest and have them call down here and convince them that Palmer Woods is Mr. Hunter. Thanks. Yes, now that is two that I owe you."

Deciding that this would probably take a few minutes, I took the frontage road up to El Dorado and crossed under to the Walmart. It didn't take long to grab another couple of pairs of Levi's and hop back into the truck. On my way back to the clinic, I realized how much the sunglasses helped.

They greeted me with a warm, welcoming "Hello Mr. Hunter. We are glad you are back." when I walked through the door of the clinic. Apparently, Krunch's effort had put the boot down. "Come right on back."

A short little man with a white coat and a heavy Indian

accent cleaned up my wound and put in another couple of stitches. As he was putting a fresh dressing over the wound, I said: "I'll also need a new prescription for OxyContin too."

He glanced up at me, paused, then looked at his tablet sitting nearby. "It looks like they gave you some yesterday. As you know, the government has cracked down on our prescribing this, and with your prescription not due for a refill, I won't be able to grant your request."

I was ready for this one. I pulled out the police report and handed it to him. "They were stolen earlier today." I pointed to the wound. "When this got re-injured."

The doctor scanned the report. "It looks like it won't be a problem then. You can pick up the script on your way out."

Back in the parking lot, I thought about going back to Walmart to get the prescription filled, but three times in one day seemed like too many visits. Given the effect that the oxy had on me, it probably wasn't best that I drive under the influence, anyway.

Pulling out of the Clinic I crossed over I-45 and turned left onto the on-ramp. The big green freeway sign read "Galveston."

Home was only 30 minutes away.

9

The drive on the Gulf Freeway is usually boring, at least until you got to the massive interchange where TX3, TX146, TX197, and TX 6 all connect with I-45.

I shoved a Big Bad Voodoo Daddy CD into the player to pass the time. I skipped tracks to their rendition of Cab Calloway's "*Tarzan of Harlem*." Possibly one of the top three swing songs of all time. I hoped it would get me out of the funk that had settled over me.

It did. By the time I reached the Gulf Greyhound Park, I was feeling better and the collection of roadside business had given way to flatland and an ugly series of high-tension towers paralleling the east side of the highway.

Two miles out from Virginia Point, I contemplated taking the ramp and cruising Tiki Island where my damaged home was. I realized that without my keys, it would be a pointless exercise. The day was growing old anyway and once the sunset, there would be nothing to see there.

Even though the windows were closed, the sea air had infiltrated the cab. It smelled so familiar and comforting. As I crossed the hump in the middle of the Galveston Causeway, I realized I didn't know where I was going next.

Three miles later, at Burger King, where I-45 unceremoniously became Broadway Avenue J, I knew my first stop. I cruised on down to Kempner Street and hung a left.

Cleverly named Galveston Storage was an old whitewashed brick building with high arching windows on the third and fourth floors. The side of the building still bore vestiges of previous tenants. E. Dulitz Furniture, a faded

Wrigley's gum sign painted on the bricks that covered a quarter of the building, and a freshly re-painted red and green Coca-Cola sign. Five Cents.

Although I liked the look and feel of the facade, I ultimately had chosen the place because it was Galveston's only above-ground, climate-controlled storage facility. Being above ground is important when the elevation is seven feet above sea level in an area with a history of deadly hurricanes. The interior was a different story. Clean, well-lit hallways were lined with white corrugated steel walls and the typical roll-up doors. Smaller units were on the upper floors, which suited me fine.

I entered my access code. After exiting the elevator and locating my unit, I spun the combination lock, and on the second try; it opened. A stack of boxes reaching the ceiling greeted me just a foot inside the door. I had taped up the empty boxes and stacked them there to make the unit less interesting if anyone walked by or broke in. I pulled a couple of stacks out into the hallway and entered the cramped space behind. The Liberty safe stood dusty and undisturbed. I spun the combination carefully and opened the safe by turning the three-handled locking mechanism. Inside the heavy door was what I needed to regain my old identity.

I scanned the contents of my old leather wallet. Driver's License, Debit Card, shield in its leather holder, insurance cards, a ring of keys, etc. I pulled out my passport, but then put it back. In an envelope near the back was some emergency money, one thousand dollars in assorted bills. Finally, I pulled out my Sig Sauer P238 and a larger Sig P220 Hunter. The hunter was two and a half pounds unloaded and felt strong and hefty in my hands. After pulling 2 boxes of ammo for each caliber, I swung the door shut, turned the mechanism, and spun the combination dial.

A generic black gym bag lay on top of the safe. Since you aren't supposed to store firearms and ammo in a storage unit, I tucked my weapons and ammo into the bag. I pushed the stacks of empty boxes back into the unit, rolled down the door, replaced the lock, and took the stairs back down to the street.

I would have gone to the bank, but it was now past closing. Instead, I went into Walgreens and waited to have my prescription refilled. With that done, I drove on down to Seawall Boulevard and the tourist hotels. I was headed toward the Hilton, but when I passed the historic Hotel Galvez, I made a U-turn and headed back.

I had never been in the Galvez, but I decided I had seen it all of my life and now that I was a tourist in my hometown, it was a fitting time to venture in. Its stately white facade and the red-tiled roof looked larger than life as I pulled up the driveway. My humble truck felt out of place among the luxury cars stacked up by the valet desk. The bellman cast a wary eye at my gym bag and Walmart bags. "I won't be needing any help with my luggage today." That was an understatement.

Past the cream-colored enclosed arched portico, the cavernous lobby was every bit as stately as the outside. The clerk at the counter asked, "Reservation?"

"No, it was a spur of the moment. Do you have something facing the gulf?"

"How long will you be with us?"

Again, I hadn't thought that far ahead. "How about two nights?"

"We can accommodate that." She quoted me at the rate. "May I see a credit card and ID?"

I slid them across to her.

"Um, Mr. Hunter. This card is expired."

Of course it was. "Oh. I'll be happy to pay with cash in advance." I knew this would not turn into a problem since it was the off-season.

"We normally require a credit card for incidentals."

While I hated cops who flashed a badge for favors, I pulled my gold-colored shield out and gave her a puppy dog look.

"Of course. No problem, Mr. Hunter." How I had longed for those words. I was going to like it here. She typed on the keyboard. "I see you're a local. Tiki Island. What prompted you to stay with us?"

"My home needs some renovations." An understatement, but still true.

She slid my things back across the counter. "Have a pleasant stay and let us know if there is anything that we can do for you." She smiled.

Upon reaching my room, I turned into the bathroom and filled the crystal glass with water, and chugged down an oxy. Then I headed down to the formal dining room.

And formal it was. Alone at a large table adorned with a silk tablecloth under a high chandelier, it dawned on me that maybe I should have gone to the bar for something to eat. The fish from Galveston's Pier 19 was caught today, cleaned today, and simply grilled. Accompanied by Lump crab in white wine cream, it was the best seafood I had eaten in a long time.

Before finishing my meal, I realized that I should have

eaten before I took the oxy. Taking opioids on an empty stomach leads to nausea. I walked slowly and carefully to the elevators, up, out, and to my room. My meal was delicious going down. I didn't want to experience it going in the other direction, though.

After walking over to the window, I closed the curtains and set the thermostat for sixty-eight. I pulled back the covers and crawled into the king-size bed.

Then I turned out the light.

***

Today was going to be a productive day. I felt better, my shoulder hurt less. I took an antibiotic and slid the bottle of oxy into my pocket.

Downstairs, I had a ham and cheese omelet with two slices of bacon and some orange juice. I used the knife to cut an oxy in half. I took one half and dropped the other half back into the bottle, which then went back into my pocket. Robin Williams' voice from "*Aladdin*" echoed in my head. "He can be taught."

From the Galvez, I headed to the bank. I spoke with the manager about needing a replacement debit card right away.

"We prefer these to be issued by our supplier." He had known my family for years. "We don't let customers know, but I can issue you a temporary card on-site. It will only be good for 30 days, and won't have a PIN number with it, so you can't use it at an ATM."

"That will be fine. Thank you. You do not know how much that will help me out."

"Is your Tiki Island address still a good one?"

"Umm, not really." Again, I was caught without a plan. "I'm kind of between addresses at the moment."

I was thinking about sending it to the department when he said: "How about Hannah's address then?"

That was a slap in the face. Hannah was my younger sister. I had never once considered that as an option. "Umm." Without a better suggestion, I finally said, "Sure. That will be fine."

From the bank, I passed the Calvary Catholic Cemetery and swung into the phone store. It took way longer than I cared for, but I eventually left with the latest Android marvel and a two-year contract.

Next, I headed north back over the causeway and immediately exited on the other side. I couldn't cross I-45 right there and had to travel north a bit on Virginia Point Road until it looped under the freeway. I was now heading back south past Tiki Tom's RV Park and Fat Boys Bait and Tackle. Turning right on Tiki Drive, I crossed the short bridge onto Tiki Island. Then left on Molokai Drive and into my driveway.

The house didn't look that bad from the driveway. If it did, they would have been after me to fix it a long time ago. The hurricane had spared Tiki Island from the worst, and many homes had escaped damage altogether. In my case, I had suffered minor roof damage as well as the garage doors being blown in. I didn't have structural damage, but the sliding glass patio door had been shattered by flying debris and water had gotten in. A lot of water. I had gotten a contractor to come in to replace the patio and garage door and replace the missing shingles on the roof. But that was it. I had to call in some favors to get that much done. There simply weren't enough workmen available in the region to do all the work that was needed. Since I was undercover, I could not do the rest myself.

Opening the door, the heat and smell rushed into my face like an eruption from a flatulent demon. I walked directly to the patio door and slid it open as well. The humidity inside the house was even higher than the humidity outside. The electricity had been off since the hurricane and wouldn't be back on again until I had a thorough inspection. I took a tour of the house. The carpets and all the woodwork would have to be replaced. There were brown stains on the drywall near the floor in places and similar stains on the ceiling where water had dripped through from the roof. That also meant that the insulation in the attic would have to go.

I briefly thought about starting the project while I was on administrative leave, but then decided that my shoulder wouldn't appreciate me pulling up carpet and such. While I was in town, maybe I could locate someone to haul out all the debris. At least it would be a start. I headed back out and locked the door behind me. The salty sea air was welcome and cleansed my nostrils.

On my way back, I stopped at the Tiki Food Mart, a convenience store and gas station. I filled up and went inside.

"Look what the tide brought in." It was the owner. "Haven't seen you in a while."

"Yea, I've been stuck on a case up in town. Hey, do you know of someone that I could get to come into my place and pull out the carpet and the insulation in the attic?"

That was my real reason for coming inside the store, not to catch up on old times.

"I think so. All the bad workers are gone after the hurricane repairs died down. Can I call you when I got someone? I figured you were here about the remains."

"Umm, what remains?"

"Human remains. They washed up on Tiki. The locals didn't seem to do anything about it, so I figured maybe you were here to have a look."

"Huh. I hadn't heard." Maybe it will be an interesting inquiry while in town. After grabbing a deli sandwich and a drink to go, I gave him my number. "I may not be here to let him in, so can I leave this with you?" and left him a key to the place. Time to take the other half of the oxy.

I had planned on dropping by Hannah's to let her know that I would have some mail coming, but seeing and smelling my house had been enough of a downer for one day.

Jumping back on the freeway, I crossed the causeway back to Galveston. Once on the island, I went south this time and drove down to Galveston Island State Park. I passed the rustic brown sign with yellow lettering warning of alligators in the park. A Reddish Egret took wing as I walked across the dunes, past the prairie grass, and plopped down in the sun-bleached white sand.

My head was clearing up, and this was a good place to think.

I had been shot, but nobody knew by who.

They had murdered Reuben while under guard in a hospital, but nobody knew by who.

Someone tried to murder me while under guard in a

hospital, but nobody knew who.

Someone searched my apartment. Why?

Someone got into my motel room and attempted to stab me. Who and why?

All of this in less than a week.

I thought about the incident at the motel. The Webster cops assumed it was just a common thief looking for anything he could find, and he succeeded with my oxy. I had merely interrupted him. They wrote it off as a coincidence. Cops don't believe in coincidence, but it did seem random. If it was part of the previous attempts in my life, how did the attacker know where I was staying? I was supposed to be in the hospital, or at my Meyerland apartment.

My apartment. Maybe there was a connection there. Suppose whoever tossed my apartment didn't find what they were looking for? I did not know if they did or didn't because I couldn't imagine that there was anything there of interest. If they didn't find it, then perhaps I was tailed to the motel, and he waited until I left to search it for whatever he was looking for. That seemed to fit. It went from being a random event to part of the pattern. It wasn't a good pattern.

Deciding it was time to get out of the sun, I looked around for a tail. I would be more careful now. I got into my truck and headed back to the Galvez. On the way back, I kept a close lookout for cars following me. This was easy since Termini San Luis Pass Road was divided, flat, and reasonably deserted. Paranoia was starting to set in. I didn't like the feeling. But as they say, it isn't paranoia if they are out to get you. I just didn't know who. I didn't like that either.

Back at the Galvez, I had a quick meal in the bar, cut another oxy in half, chugged it down, grabbed a complimentary USA Today, and headed up to my room. I would have liked to have had a notebook to keep notes and observations in, but I had decided that I was better off in the Galvez than being out and about and that at least their security cameras would capture an assailant if there were another attack. So I grabbed the little notepad and cheap pen from next to the room phone and jotted down my reflections from the beach.

I called Krunch. "Has anything new turned up since I left?"

"Not that I know of. You know I am not part of that investigation. You should ask Nick."

"I know, but I figure Nick is busy, and if something important turned up, you would have heard about it, anyway."

Her voice changed pitch. "Are you saying that I'm not busy?"

I lied. "Of course not Krunch. It's just that as a rookie detective, you are not as likely to be as busy." I emphasized the "as." I gave her my new number and asked, "Can you send me everything they have on Reuben's murder? Uh-huh. Reuben Heinz. Right, like the catsup."

I could hear her clicking on the keyboard. "One last thing. Would you give the new number to Teddy and Nick? No, you are not my personal assistant. Just the rookie." She hung up without saying goodbye.

I made a list of things to do tomorrow, took a long hot shower, checked carefully before coming out of the bathroom, and pulled the blackout curtains. I ate the little mints that had been left on the bed when housekeeping had turned it down. Then I took the USA Today, crumpled it up page by page, and spread the crumpled pile between the door and the foot of my bed. Then I turned off the light on the nightstand.

I lay awake in the dark.

10

The ridiculous default ring of my new phone woke me up. I was going to have to change that. Who would call me at this hour? I glanced at the clock. 10:15 a.m. Apparently, my body needed rest to heal. Turned out it was Nick calling to tell me they had cleared me for "light duty" starting on Monday. Light duty was code for sitting at a desk and shuffling papers. Nevertheless, I was overjoyed.

I was due to check out today, so that worked out. And I did. Check out. I had planned to drop by Hannah's today, but now I had a good excuse to leave Galveston. I also skipped going by the house or the Tiki Mart. The latter I could do by phone, anyway.

As I headed across the causeway, I put another BBVD disc in and started my hours' drive up I-45 to Houston. As I drove, I checked my mirrors for a tail and it occurred to me that maybe I was ready for a new car.

Taking the interchange, I headed west on I-610 toward Bellaire. Twenty minutes later, I pulled into the parking lot of the Bridal Mall building.

I hadn't been in the Spy Emporium before. Any surveillance equipment I needed was always provided by the department. Businesses like this usually catered to amateur detectives or the paranoid. I wasn't the former, but had become the latter. I didn't want to explain to anyone at work why I felt I needed equipment and expose my inner insecurities.

I selected an alarm clock with a hidden night vision camera/recorder inside and a motion sensor that barked like a dog if movement triggered it. I wanted another camera that I could set out in the living room, like a nanny cam, but thought the same clock might look odd. The salesman steered me to a clever but expensive electrical wall socket with a camera hidden in the ground hole. You removed a regular plug and replaced it with the spy socket and no one would ever see it. I thought about anti-surveillance equipment so that I could sweep my new apartment, the one that I had to find today, but realized I was being overly paranoid. Now that I had my debit card, I didn't need to use the department's card. I hadn't been comfortable using the department card before, but I didn't have any choice, did I?

By that evening, I had secured an apartment in Northshore. I don't know what shore it was supposed to be next to, but it was just north of I-10 on the east side of Houston. It represented an ugly cross-town commute for me, but I didn't want to be too near my previous stomping ground. I headed across Green's Bayou to a Walmart Supercenter and filled a cart with the first wave of purchases needed to make an empty apartment livable.

Returning to my apartment, I unrolled the 4-inch memory foam mattress on the floor, put linens on it, and the new pillow. I strategically positioned the motion sensor so that it would cover the front and patio doors. The alarm clock went into the bedroom on the empty box my new dishware came in that served as a nightstand. I wanted to install the outlet cam, but I would need to shut off the circuit breaker to do that and it was too dark to do it without a flashlight. I noted on my phone app that I would have to pick up a quality flashlight and a couple of screwdrivers on tomorrow's shopping trip.

No one knew where I was that night, so I slept better.

***

By the end of the weekend and after a couple more trips to Walmart and one across town to Ikea, the apartment was livable. At least for now. I was feeling better physically and mentally.

While many of Houston's detectives worked at 1200 Travis, the building was far too overcrowded. The department's new concrete and glass Southwest Substation had only opened at the end of 2017, and it was here that Teddy, Nick, and Krunch worked.

The drive around I-610 took a full hour, much longer than I had expected. Fortunately, no one seemed to care that I was late. Everyone stopped by to welcome me back, see how I was healing, etc.

The first day back was like the first day of a new job. Nothing of importance happened. I had to get a place to sit, get new network credentials, update my HR records online with my new phone number and address, schedule some time with the department shrink, and turn in my undercover identification and credit card.

By the afternoon, I had run out of things to do. Teddy had told me that the crime scene crew had released my old apartment while I was in Galveston, so I risked a stop there to collect a few things that I could use at my new place.

It was just as big a mess as it was the last time I saw it. In the end, there wasn't that much there that I wanted, anyway. I looked for any clues, but I knew I would not find anything that the team hadn't found. I'd look at their report tomorrow.

Back at the Northshore apartment, I made a bachelor's dinner and realized I had little to do there. Nothing to read and I hadn't thought about having the cable turned on yet. Instead of sitting there bored, I headed out to find a good novel, only to discover that the area didn't have any decent bookstores. Wondering why that was, I did the only reasonable thing left to do: find a bar and drink.

***

Peanuts, beer, and stale smoke. Even though the city had outlawed smoking in bars in 2007, the place still smelled. I suspect they burn tobacco in the place when it is closed just to keep that nasty smell and thus drive away a trendier clientele.

A red neon Pabst beer sign with a blue neon border hung slightly askew as the main centerpiece behind the tired bar. Next to that, they taped a faded handwritten note that stated "cash only" onto the wall. And next to that was the barkeep. His faded gray shirt made him look faded too in the dim light. The black creeper mustache and goatee didn't really help, either. "Done?"

I guess I had been staring into the mostly empty pitcher in front of me for too long. "No, I'll finish this off." I tipped the pitcher and refilled my thirsty glass as he walked away.

I called this place the No Name bar. Not because it didn't have a name, but because the old sign had blown down during Hurricane Ike and the owner had never bothered to replace it. All that was left was a rusting pole thrusting out of the decaying facade that the sign used to hang from. I didn't come here for the atmosphere if you could call it that. Nor for the good times. Those were rolling somewhere else.

No Name's was simply a place where you could drink occasionally with a couple of buddies, but mostly, I was banished here alone. I couldn't go to the usual cop bars. The department didn't want me to risk being seen in one and identified as a cop. Maybe they were right on that one. I couldn't go to the many bars that the organized criminals in town ran because of the risk of me having been identified as a snitch. After two, maybe three attempts on my life, I needed to be careful until I figured out who was after me. So, in the end, it relegated me to a local neighborhood dive where no one of any importance went.

Finishing the last sip, I scooted my stool back on the wooden floor, tossed some cash on the bar, and headed past the line of tap handles for the door. I pulled on the worn brass handle of the heavy door with its dated window. A square piece of glass, but rotated 45 degrees so that it appeared more like a baseball diamond.

The Houston night air continued to be still sticky and oppressive.

As I turned the corner into the adjoining parking lot, my shoulder brushed against the chipped brick wall. No, I'm ok to drive. As I drifted toward the back of the lot, I was focused on the pockmarked asphalt and grave. Walking between the few other parked cars and the wall, I stared at a pile of nasty cigarette butts in my way where smokers, banned from smoking inside, had obviously found a place blocked from the wind too, to light up.

Passing the rear bumper of a navy blue Suburban, I

turned and stepped toward the door to my truck. The rear door of the SUV opened. The hairs on my neck stood up. I dropped the keys from my hand as it moved for my concealed weapon. Caught off guard, I was way too slow. Someone from behind grabbed my hand while simultaneously relieving me of my pistol.

I tried to turn to face my attacker, but he controlled my movement, pushing my head down and into the open door. As the initial shock faded, a slightly familiar voice said, "It's alright. You are among friends."

As I rolled my head toward the voice, my eyes nearly bulged out as I recognized the face.

"I'm sorry we had to meet like this. Please. Have a seat."

It was Chief McCormick. What could I do? The door closed behind me and we pulled away.

"First, I wanted to thank you again for your service to the department."

This seemed like a funny way to show it. I understood why there would not be an award ceremony at 1200 Travis. But this was still odd.

"You did an excellent job on this assignment. Taking down the number two man in a mob is not a simple job, but Houston will be better off for the actions that you took."

I doubted the Chief knew of all the actions that I took while undercover.

"Any idea who shot you?"

"I wish I did." I didn't dare share any of the thoughts I had on the matter with the Chief of Police.

To my astonishment, he said, "You should consider looking internally for your shooter."

"Our profession, yours and mine, used to be an honorable one. But in recent years, our image has been tarnished in the eye of the public." McCormick's expression turned melancholy. "We've always had a few bad cops, but they weren't as visible to the public as they are now with technology. The problem is that the vast majority of solid cops end up protecting the bad ones by holding to the blue code. In doing so, their own reputation goes down the drain in the public's eye, as we are all painted with the same brush."

"IA."

McCormick cut me off. "IA is ineffective. Yes, they pull in a few cops, especially on minor charges, hoping to head off bigger problems down the road. But the last major bust of an HPD officer was Officer Carranza, in 2013. The same problem hampers IA. No one wants to rat out a fellow officer, even if he is dirty."

"Policing was different back in my day, your dad's day. It was easier to take care of our own rotten apples back then. Now we have guys sitting at desks or collection pensions who should have been kicked off the force years ago."

Not sure where this was going, I said: "but they taught us at the academy."

McCormick cut me off again. "Yes." McCormick sighed. "We are changing the culture. But it is too little too late. It will take two, maybe three, generations of cops to root out the rot. We need another way."

"I retire in a few years. They say a commander is only as good as the men under him. I hate to leave this department with a worse reputation than when I came in. It reflects on the city, the department, and me personally."

Since I was apparently supposed to just listen, I waited for the Chief to resume.

"The dirty cops in the department today are very much like their own mob. Not that there is a single godfather at the head. I don't mean organizationally. I mean, they are corrupt. They take bribes, the commit crimes, they kill."

"We'll never get them with the restrictions placed on us today. What we need, what I need, is someone who is man enough to crush the worst of the worst, the meat eaters, with the same justice that they hand out."

McCormick continued his monologue, but I didn't hear what he was saying. Mind was busy reprocessing what he had just said. It pulled me back into reality when the car stopped. Outside the tinted window I could see the expanse of deserted parking spaces stretched out in front of a Lowes.

As my door magically opened from the outside, Chief McCormick concluded, "Like they always say in the movies, I was never here. This never happened."

With nothing to say, I slid out of the Suburban. Parked next to, and slightly ahead of us idled my truck. A brawny guy in a navy blue blazer took my place in the back seat and the Suburban pulled away.

I stood in the dark.

11

Bright yellow enamel paint. On one end, a tan cone with a blue-gray tip. A silver crown adorned the other end. Jutting up out of the crown was a sickly pink cylinder with slightly beveled edges. The gloss black lettering said "Ticonderoga." What was Ticonderoga anyway, and what did it have to do with the number two pencil I slowly twirled in my hands?

Everything, after they left me standing in the unassuming New Forest Crossing Shopping Center last night, was a nightmarish blur. The drive to the apartment I now called home. The long, sleepless night. Replaying McCormick's words in my mind and trying to figure out what he really meant. And finally, I drive back into the office.

Sitting at my desk, mind numb, playing with a pencil. And to think only a week ago I was enjoying a Reuben (the sandwich, not the bodyguard) at Goldberg's Deli. How had my life gotten so upside down in such a short period? Actually, detectives saw that happen to other people all the time, especially in homicide, where a family's life would be shattered upon hearing of, or worse yet, witnessing a loved one's death.

Snap. A piece of the puzzle had just dropped into place. And I had snapped the Ticonderoga.

Moments after someone had shot me, I instinctively reached for the wound. I recalled being surprised at how small the wound felt. As I had been playing with the Ticonderoga, I realized that it was just about the same diameter as the hole in my body. The bullet had a small diameter; .223 inches, a diameter of a 5.56mm round. The rounds used by our SWAT team.

The detectives on the scene, as well as any of Benni's guys, would have been using handguns, and not .223s. Indeed, the smallest caliber would have been .380 inches or larger. Significantly larger. That could only mean one thing. A member of our own SWAT team had shot me.

Now I had my first string to tug at to unravel this mess. But what to do next? I needed to think about that one. My initial thoughts included going to IA, but would that really work out? I decided I should go talk to Det. Jason "Jax" Jackson. He was the detective assigned to investigate the attempt on my life in the hospital. But I'd have to tread carefully. Feel him out to see what he was thinking about the investigation and whether he would be open to the idea of friendly fire. McCormick's words also haunted the idea. Who could I trust? I needed to think about this.

The rest of my day was clear despite having an appointment with the shrink this morning. I walked over to Krunch. "Can we do lunch today?"

"Sure. I don't see why not. The Roach Coach, or did you have something else in mind?"

"I'd rather go somewhere else. Where we can talk more, umm, privately."

"Oh. Now you've got my attention. What's up?"

I lied. "Nothing. I just want to bounce some ideas off you."

"Fine, but you're buying."

"Seems fair. I'll stop by when I get back from downtown." Before leaving, I made an appointment with Jax for later that afternoon.

I focused my thoughts on what I should do with my

new revelation as I drove to 1200 Travis. I found a place to park and made my way to the shrink's office. She finally emerged from her inner office.

"Come on in Detective Hunter." She said. "May I call you Griff?"

"Of course. Just don't call me late for dinner." Where did that corny line come from? I was more nervous than I realized. The shrink held the key to my being able to return to actual police work. Without her giving the all-clear, I would be stuck at a desk forever, or worse. I knew this both subconsciously and at a very visceral level.

"Thank you for coming in voluntarily." She directed me to a chair. "Most officers won't come in until their commanding officer hounds them to do so. That makes my job that much harder. I've been doing this long enough to know that cops just don't like to talk about their feelings."

"I knew I'd have to come in eventually, and, well, I am doing fine anyway."

We both knew it was a lie, but for different reasons.

"Griff, you were just shot and then poisoned the next day. Very few cops get shot, and even fewer still have a second attempt made on their life. Ever."

Of course, she was right. I didn't know what I was supposed to say. I just shifted in the chair and stared at a yellow Ticonderoga on her desk.

"How does that make you feel?"

A groaning noise escaped my throat. How cliché.

She smiled and sat silently.

Knowing that without her OK, I was doomed to desk purgatory, I knew I had to talk. I sighed. "It has been a jumble of emotions. I want to know what is going on. I want a resolution. Some closure so that things can get back to normal."

"That may take some time. You were deep undercover for so long, it usually takes time, and some officers never make a successful transition back." She seemed sincere, but then she would, wouldn't she? "You have been through serious trauma, both mentally and physically. Brought back to life as I understand it."

We conversed for the next forty minutes. A lot of what we talked about didn't seem to have anything to do with being undercover or the shooting at all.

Near the end, she said, "After two years undercover, you have a lot of vacation time coming."

I did not like where this was going. "To be honest, a vacation would not be very restful. While waiting to be cleared by IA, I took a couple of days in Galveston. It wasn't restful at all. I was constantly on guard, looking over my shoulder, and trying to figure out what was going on. I don't see how I will relax until we know who tried to kill me."

On one hand, I realized that being on vacation would give me time to investigate the four SWAT guys, but at the same time, I wouldn't have a good reason to be hanging around the department or have access to departmental resources.

After a pensive pause, she said, "Then I have a suggestion that I'd like to make. I'd like to recommend you to be loaned out to homicide for a while..."

My heart leaped.

"To the Cold Case Squad."

My heart plummeted.

"It will get you doing actual police work again and you

will make a valuable contribution to the department." She paused. "And working cold cases, you will be able to take a few days off here and there without it impacting your investigation. It would help you get your head back into the game and allow you to burn some of your hard-earned vacation time at your discretion when you felt the need."

That was a perfect solution. I could still be at the department when I wanted to, but still take a day here and there to do my own investigation.

"You know, doc, that sounds like a good plan. I'd like that."

She smiled an unexpected smile. "I'll put it in motion. You should expect to hear something tomorrow. Expect to report here the day after. Cold case is on the second floor."

We both got up. "One more thing," she said. "You'll be limited to four days a week. Just so you know. Check back in a couple of weeks so we can see how it's going."

***

I took Krunch to the Wildcat Golf Club for lunch. I'd never been there before, but it was close to the substation and seemed an unlikely place for any cops to go for lunch. We both ordered the Baja fish tacos.

After some small talk, I said, "I need to talk to someone. Someone I can trust."

The corners of Krunch's lips turned upwards.

"But I need you to keep this to yourself. I'm afraid that if you talk to anyone, you could get hurt."

"Why me?" she asked.

"I've thought about who I could trust. You haven't

been off the beat long enough to get entangled and you are the one who saved my life at the hospital, so it's not likely that you were involved in trying to take it."

Her head tipped to the side thoughtfully.

"I realized something today. An important clue." I paused as the waitress returned and set our plates on the table. After she was gone, I continued, "The bullet was almost assuredly a 5.56."

Her eyebrows lifted and her head popped back upright. She knew the implication. She picked at a French fry and dipped it into the catsup. "How do you know that?" Her lips pursed as I explained.

"I don't know what to do next. Who I can trust."

Krunch chewed thoughtfully. A bit of Tartar sauce clung to her face. It was the first glimpse of something non-cop-like I'd seen in her professional demeanor. It was kind of cute. "You can trust Nick."

"Why do you think that?"

"As I understand it, one of Benni's men was about to shoot Nick," she said. "You saved Nick by shooting the bad guy."

I finished her sentence as the scene jumped back into my memory. "After Jonah toppled over, Nick had his weapon pointed right at my face."

"He could have shot you then and there if he had wanted to, and the investigation would have cleared him." She smiled triumphantly.

"You're right Krunch. I hadn't thought of that."

"That's three you own me."

Krunch was right. I really owed her and now with more

than just my life. "Listen. Keep this all to yourself. Until I figure out who is trying to get me, I don't want you to end up in their crosshairs, too."

***

Back at the Southwest Sub Division, I met with Jax. His office, while somewhat sterile, was so much more comfortable than the shrinks.

"I'll be on the level with you. We've hit a dead end on your case." Jax hailed from Mississippi and he spoke with a southern drawl. "Too many people had handled the IV bag to give us any decent prints, and the ones they pulled were from people that we already knew had handled the bag. Whoever was responsible either had their prints smudged, wore gloves, or was one of the staff that we already knew handled the bag."

"What about a cross-match with the prints on Reuben's bag?" I asked.

"Mr. Heinz's bag had already been destroyed by the time we knew to look at it. No luck there." Jax said. "The Nurse was a nexus though. We dragged her in and grilled her in the box until she was in tears. She seemed sincere, and we didn't think she was responsible, just an unknowing accomplice, if you could call it that. We did a full workup on her just in case, but she came out clean. You're welcome to look at the files."

"None of the hospital staff were around when I was shot." I let that hang in the air.

Jax chose his words carefully. "We're not positive that the two incidences are related. IA's initial investigation was inconclusive on how you got shot. Without more to go on, it's hard to make the link."

"You think it's a coincidence that I get shot one day and then poisoned the very next day?" I sounded incredulous.

"No, I don't believe in coincidence," Jax said. "The working theory is that someone in Benni's organization tried to put you down. When they didn't succeed, they used someone on their payroll in the hospital staff to spike your IV. We just haven't figured out who yet."

"The problem with that scenario is the coincidence of Benni having a sniper there at the same time as the takedown, and no one from the takedown team discovering them." I was trying to lead Jax to his own conclusion.

"What then?" Jax wasn't playing along.

Now I had to choose my words carefully. "Who else, other than Benni's men, had access to the takedown, Reuben's hospital room, and my room?"

Jax frowned. "I don't think you want to go down that rabbit hole. You would need some pretty powerful evidence. Evidence that simply doesn't exist. Even if you had it..." His voice trailed off.

"Yeah." I was defeated but didn't let it show. "What was Benni's motive?"

Jax replied. "He could have had any number of motives, but the first thing that comes to mind is that your cover was blown."

"Who could have leaked that I was a cop?" That statement was as if someone had just dropped a dead cat on the desk between us.

***

I was filled with mixed emotions on the drive home. IA would not do anything. Jax was at a standstill, looking in the wrong direction, and didn't sound like he would consider the other possibility. Not that I blamed him.

Who had a motive? Jax was right about Benni's team being most likely. I didn't have a suitable answer for what SWAT's motive could be.

Who had the opportunity? This was the department all the way, as far as I was concerned.

Who had the means? This was a draw. Benni's team had guns and drugs. So did the cops. But there was one nagging detail. If it was SWAT, then why wasn't I dead? Those guys rarely miss.

I knew one thing for certain. A rifle had shot me. The only rifles on the scene were SWAT's. And I knew another thing: no one was going to look at SWAT or any other cop. McCormick as much as said it was a cop and if there was going to be justice, it was up to me.

I detoured by Office Depot and picked up a three-ring binder, a ream of three-hole punched paper, some divider tabs, a laptop, and a couple of thumb drives. And a box of Ticonderoga number two pencils.

I knew what had to be done, and it was up to me to do it. What would happen when I figured out who was responsible? Who could say? I'd have to cross that bridge when I came to it.

If I wasn't dead first.

12

"In 1965, detectives in the U.S. cleared nearly ninety percent of murder cases. Today, only sixty percent get solved. Over in New Orleans, it is only thirty percent. That leaves a growing number of killers on the streets, and a growing number of victims' families without closure. It erodes confidence in our policing ability. Houston has been putting more focus on correcting this problem since they formed this squad in late 2004. We still have thousands of unsolved murder cases in Houston." Capitan Ramos said. He was a handsome man with black hair and black eyes. "If we don't come up with forensic evidence, witnesses become even more important. The problem is that witnesses are not only afraid to come forward, but have a growing mistrust of the police."

Why was it that many citizens had a growing mistrust of the police? What was it Chief McCormick had said?

"In a lot of neighborhoods, gang members have become their own enforcers." Ramos continued to stress the importance of the job as he walked me to my desk. "And since Katrina, that has gotten dramatically worse."

My "desk" was one of six tables crammed into a small area that probably used to be a single office. Two-faced the wall next to the hallway, while the others formed two rows facing each other. No dividers. There were three ugly gray locking filing cabinets the same height as the tables at the end of each row. Ramos finished his introduction to the squad, asked me if I had questions, then left.

I sat in the only open spot, in an ugly chair that

matched nothing else in the room. The wood grain Formica top reflected the harsh glare of the overhead fluorescent lights. I glanced up at the blank computer screen, then into the face of the detective who was sitting across from me. He smiled a welcoming smile. "First day, huh?"

"Yup."

"Welcome. You're probably the youngest guy we got on the squad. There's more of us scattered around." His name tag said, Quaker. "Most of us are senior detectives. I'm not sure if they put us here because our experience helps us solve tough cases, or if they are putting the old guys in less stressful situations."

I suspected it was a little of both.

Det. Quaker had close-cropped curly black hair, rich ebony skin, and a pleasant smile. His mustache and closely cropped beard were showing signs of gray.

"My friends call me Q. The rest of the guys are out trying to find people to interview."

He picked up a paper coffee cup decorated with artistic renderings of the planets and took a sip. "As you gathered, there are plenty of cases to choose from. Here, you can pull your own files, but there is an unofficial order of precedence. Highest priority is cases that have any current press coverage or involve cops or their families. We don't work those, they get assigned by Ramos. The highest priority cases that we look at are those where a family member checks in regularly to see how we are doing. It not that their lost one is any more important, but..." He shrugged his shoulders. His expression said, "What else can we do?"

"The squeaky wheel."

"Yes." Q continued. "The bottom of the list is apparent gang-on-gang violence. There is a lot of public apathy toward these murders. Not that it makes it any less tragic for the families, but the street code of silence makes it almost impossible to get anyone to talk. There are always suspects, but getting a conviction would be another matter. Still, every case we solve is a win."

After some more chat, I fired up the computer and logged into the system. Staring somewhat blankly, not knowing where to begin, Q spoke again. "We each get one of those lateral file drawers. Yours is that one." He pointed. "There is an assortment of files in there to get you started. We don't have our own coffee. There aren't enough of us to bother trying to keep a pot going. The nearest pot is 2 doors down." Q jerked his head to one side to show the direction. "But they will want you to pitch into their coffee club, and the java isn't that good."

I had never drunk coffee before going undercover. Dr. Pepper game me a much lower dose of caffeine, but the options were limited while hanging out at Benni's clubs, and even more limited at the warehouse. "So then, where did yours come from?" I motioned at his cup.

"Oh. E.T.'s. There is a Starbucks across the street, but on the back side of the block, so you have to come through the garage, through the building, across the street, then around the corner to get there. When you do, there is a long line of cops waiting. E.T.'s is about a block in the other direction from the garage, so on a map, it looks farther, but if you go out the garage entrance, it's not. While a fair number of cops go there, it's not as many. Coffee is cheaper than Starbucks. Some say it's not as good, but I can't tell the difference."

"Thanks. What happened to the guy who was working them?" I asked.

"Retired."

And what an assortment it was. A round white guy with a black mustache in a red, white, and blue cowboy shirt. A young black teenage girl with a wide white smile. A Hispanic man with arched bushy eyebrows and a Stetson. An unidentified Hispanic woman had been found in some shrubbery in 1989. An unmarried couple found dead in a wooded area. The list went on and on. It was a true cross-section of humanity. All murdered. All without justice.

I pulled the files on the unidentified woman and the unmarried couple. The Jane Doe because I realized this woman didn't have a name for over thirty-five years. The couple because it was a double homicide.

I checked out the files and left early. I had something that I wanted to do, so I drove my truck to an inconspicuous spot and waited.

The HPD computer system would not let me, or almost anyone else, access HR files. That is normally a good thing because there is simply too much sensitive information in there. I know I didn't want anyone to know my new apartment's address. Even those who have clearance had better have a legitimate reason to be looking. The system flagged any file that had been accessed and those flags got reviewed weekly by a small panel of senior HR officers to ensure nothing was being accessed improperly or without due cause. Since that wasn't an avenue to explore, I'd have to conduct my own investigation.

After a while, I was rewarded. Enrique was the first SWAT guy to leave. I didn't care which one of the four it was, so I followed. It was a challenge because I couldn't get too far behind and risk losing him, but being in my truck, I didn't want to get made either. I had decided it was better to lose him and fell back farther. It wasn't like I didn't know where to pick him up again another day.

Turned out it wasn't a difficult tail. He ended up on a residential street and pulled into a common brick, middle-class house. I stopped a few houses back, noted the house and how the numbering worked, then made a U-turn so I wouldn't have to drive past.

I struggled back to my apartment in Houston's rush hour traffic. Although Houston is the fourth largest city in the U.S. they considered its traffic being only 11th in the nation, right behind Dallas. That didn't seem to make me feel any better, or traffic go any faster. I couldn't imagine that we only spent half as along in traffic as those in L.A.

Back home, I pulled up a map app and verified the street address of the house that Enrique had gone to. I wished I had taken some pics, so starting tomorrow I would have to pack my camera with me every day. Next, I pulled up Zillow for that address. The purchase history showed the sale date, price, and some other tidbits, including the parcel number. With that information, I went to the Harris county auditor's site and performed a search. Sure enough, the property belonged to Enrique. Easy as that. Enrique was current on his taxes.

Next, I went to Spokeo to create an account. Spokeo aggregates data from multiple sources by deep crawling the web. A stunning amount of information can be found about people, especially if they or other family members are active on social media. Then I realized I didn't want to use my personal debit card to pay for the account. No, that wouldn't be smart. Tomorrow I'd stop at Safeway and purchase a pre-paid visa card that could be used online. And I'd pay for it with cash.

The next day, I did just that. Picked up a five hundred dollar card just to be sure.

***

I parked in the garage and crossed over to the java joint that Q had recommended. E.T.'s was tucked into a small storefront. The sign had a logo that bordered on a copyright infringement and a subtitle that read "Coffee That Is Out of This World."

Inside it was cramped with few tables and a moderate, but moving line. In a bit of irony for a high-tech themed place, they didn't have free internet. Apparently, they didn't want you to loiter in their space.

The open ceiling was painted a dark purple color with random white dots representing stars. The hanging air conditioning ductwork had been painted white. At intervals, there were wide black rings that encircled the white pipe. Running vertically was the inscription "UNITED STATES" in red block letters and in one section an American flag. Overall, it was a pretty good representation of a vintage Saturn rocket for the early days of the space program, and the best camouflage of industrial air conditioning that I'd ever seen. It paid homage to the fact that Houston was home to a large space center thanks to congressional pork from LBJ.

At the front of the line stood a barista underneath a sign that hung from the ceiling by two delicate chains. "We have heard every Uranus joke that you could possibly come up with. Don't bother."

The barista wore a deep purple apron over a white dress shirt and black slacks. The Name tag had the Letters "K C."

When I reached the head of the line, K C simply looked up at me without a word. It seemed implied that I was to give her my order. "Well, Casey, I'll have a regular drip with cream and sugar."

She tapped the register, looked up, and flatly said, "Three twenty-five." Her plain Midwestern face offered no smile, but then again, she didn't appear sad, angry, or bored. Just distant in some way.

As Griff was leaving, he noted the trash receptacle. It was in the shape of a 1950s rocket, complete with fins supporting the base, with the nose cone cut off. A neatly printed sign said, "Help us be tidy and clean. This is not Uranus."

Back at 1200 Travis, I sat at my little table and scoured the files I had checked out.

The first case was of an unidentified dead Hispanic female between the ages of 16 and 22. Her body had been discovered by an employee who saw the victim laying in some shrubbery next to the office building when she arrived at work early in the morning. HPD responded to the 911 call, determined that the woman was, in fact, dead, and called in the detectives.

Jane Doe was five foot four and weighed 160 pounds.

She had long wavy black hair and was wearing a white t-shirt, black "Lee" jeans, black socks, and black "Coasters" brand shoes. She had suffered a gunshot wound to the head.

Detectives found no identification on the victim, and despite attempts to have her identified via her fingerprints, all attempts were met with negative results. This girl had remained unidentified after thirty-five years.

The second case was from 1990. I had pulled it because it was a double homicide.

One evening, a couple left a nightclub in the early evening. The next day, neither had reported to work, so a missing person's report was filed.

The day after that, a patrol officer looked at a car that, based on its location, he assumed to be abandoned. There was fresh blood in the car, so he ran the vehicle's license plate. That query showed it belonged to a missing person. That combined with the blood triggered an investigation by HPD detectives. After looking at the car, they responded with a search of the surrounding area. A 23-year-old female was found nude, hands tied behind her back, with her throat slit in some nearby trees. They found her clothes nearby. They had been cut off her body. The crime scene photos were gruesome.

The next day, her date's body was found a hundred yards away. He was clothed, except for his shoes, had his hands tied behind his back with the same rope, and had his throat slashed as well. They ruled robbery out as a motive since he still had his money and watch.

Investigators chased hundreds of leads and even identified several suspects, but in the end, nothing panned out.

They already posted the case on HPD's Featured Cold Case site along with the phone number to call if anyone had information.

After scheduling a follow-up with the shrink for the week after next, I headed down to the motor pool and checked out a department vehicle. I drove out to the locations listed in the report, not expecting to find anything useful, but looking at the crime scene with fresh eyes was still a good starting point. Of course, everything had changed in 30 years. The case was cold.

***

After that, I drove back and returned to my inconspicuous spot and waited again. Enrique left first again, so I waited for the next SWAT guy to leave. It was Skinner. I tailed him the same, but since I was not in my truck, I kept closer. He pulled off the tollway and into the Westchase Walmart parking lot. Eventually, I guess everyone ends up at Walmart. The enormous parking lot made it easy to sit and wait for his return. After he was inside the store for about two minutes, I drove past and took a couple of pics of his car and license plate, then retreated to a more distant spot.

Skinner popped out with a couple of bags, got into his car, and headed to a nearby home. I'd wait for him to settle in, take a pic of the house and a wider shot of the surrounding homes, and then turn back out the way I came. It was too easy. These guys didn't seem to be too worried about being followed, nor had as high a level of situational awareness as I would have expected.

On the drive back downtown, it occurred to me that

maybe my level of situational awareness wasn't any better and that if someone were tailing me, my following cops home wouldn't look good. Although I had been watching for someone following me since Webster, I realized I needed to up my game.

At home, I followed the same online steps with Enrique. Then set up my Spokeo account and pulled reports for both Enrique and Skinner.

***

Back at 1200 Travis the next day, I pulled at the threads concerning Jane Doe.

The file contained an unusual lifelike police artist sketch of a young Hispanic woman with long, wavy black hair. I sent a request to the coroner's office for the actual photos and the autopsy file, but it would take a while to get those from such an old case.

Given her probable age, it seemed likely that she could have been a runaway, so I searched the NCME database. The National Center for Missing and Exploited Children was formed the year after Jane Doe's death, so they hadn't done a widespread search, and there was no notation in the file that they had done it since.

I left 1200 Travis for the day at lunchtime and, after a quick bite, went to have my stitches removed. I'd already decided that Friday wasn't a good day to follow anyone home, since the SWAT team would probably go to a cop bar for a couple of drinks.

Being early, traffic was light. My phone vibrated in my pocket. I glanced at the incoming message. It was from

Nick. "You've got to be kidding me?" I texted back. "Are you serious?"

I changed my plans.

13

Like perfectly spaced fireflies, they float forward and steadily downward from the night sky, then, a short distance beyond, apparently rising again. From a distance, it is a silent, almost mystical dance. It wasn't that dark yet, but the setting sun provided a glint of reflected light that gave the same effect.

Only as you draw closer does the silent display give way to a less-than-silent spectacle repeated endlessly across the globe. A mystery that remained a miracle to most who didn't understand the physics of it all.

Drawing even nearer, the smell becomes unmistakable; bringing back memories of holidays and travel, two things I used to enjoy. Kerosene Oxide.

I watched the heavenly procession as I headed north on I-69. Then the off-ramp and I was there. Houston's George Bush Intercontinental Airport.

I parked my car about 45 minutes after I had confirmed Jax's messages. On the way, I made numerous calls to make the necessary arrangements. I checked earnestly for a tail. It was important that I was not followed. Probably a matter of life and death, although not my life or death. Halfway to the terminal, I headed back to the car to lock my weapon in the small gun safe attached to the truck under the front seat.

Not that it mattered. I had to get an HPD officer to come to get me through security since I didn't have a boarding pass. Police escort aside, I still had to dump my pockets into a tub for an X-ray, then reach for the sky as I went through the full body scanner. At least I got to jump to the head of the line.

As we made our way through a keypad-locked door, then down a nondescript hallway, I said, "I figured you guys would have an entrance on the other side of the TSA checkpoint."

"We do." Came the reply. "But thanks to your friend, we are following a special security protocol. Everyone goes through TSA as an extra precautionary measure." We went through another keypad-protected doorway and then we were in. HPD's Airport Division.

It was nothing short of pure genius. Benni was being held here. Someplace well-guarded and where no one would look for him. No roommates. No prisoners coming or going who could identify him. No visitors. Nada.

Even though I had called ahead, there was a lot of explanation required, a thorough review of my credentials, and a comparison to my online file. Even a last phone call to some nameless commander for final clearance.

As I waited, I couldn't help but notice the rack of black M-16s that had been fitted with tactical hand guards, flashlights, scopes, etc. The Airport Division was well enough armed and trained to go up against terrorists similarly equipped. During high traffic times, like Christmas and Thanksgiving, they even carried them out in the terminal as a deterrent and visible reminder to the Hans Grubers of the world. Yippee Ki-yay.

Once we got the green light, I explained carefully what I wanted the officers to do. They smiled, nodded, turned me around, and put the cuffs on me. It wasn't a very good feeling. Then an officer led me into their small two-cell holding area.

As they led me past Benni's cell, I saw him glance furtively in my direction, just as anyone would do when someone new arrived. He glanced back down at his shoes without a hint of recognition. They put me into the cell next to Benni's. It was small but unusually clean. I sat out of arm's reach of Benni.

Several minutes passed in silence once the guard had closed the door, leaving us alone.

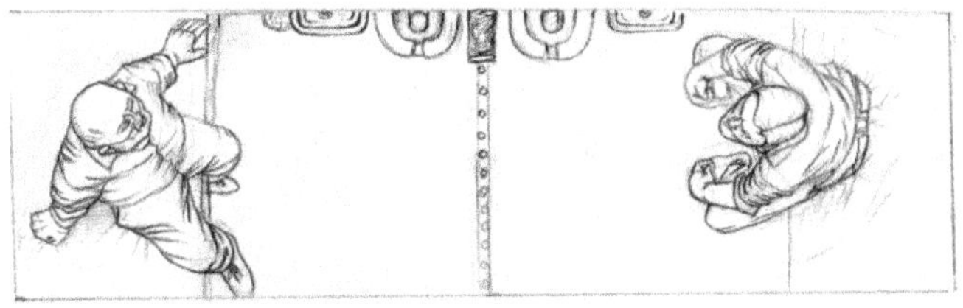

"I was afraid you were dead. Last time I saw you, you were being loaded into an ambulance."

I wasn't sure whether Benni knew I was a cop, so it was best to keep silent and let him tip his hand first.

"Thank you for saving my life. I owe you one." After a bit more silence, Benni asked, "What about the others?"

"Jonah was killed in the parking lot." I decided I shouldn't tell him I was the one that killed Jonah. "They murdered Reuben in his hospital room. The room next to mine."

Benni grunted.

"Here's the thing. After they killed Reuben, someone tried to kill me in the hospital while I was under police guard." I let that hang in the air for a minute. "Who would do that? Any of Poliakoff's people?"

"No. Never." Benni's reply was full of emotion. He didn't know I was a cop.

"There's another thing. My place got ransacked." I almost slipped and added that my hotel room had been broken into too. "Any idea what they would have been looking for?"

Benni grunted again. "My insurance policy, I guess." A broad smile crossed his lips. "If they searched your place, that means that they must have searched my place and not found anything, so they checked to see if you had it. They probably searched the other guys' places as well."

I'd have to follow up on that. "What insurance?"

"In this business, you can't be too careful. I keep some information on Poliakoff and a few other players in town."

I wish that I would have known that beforehand. Both the FBI and the District Attorney wanted Poliakoff, but he was too well insulated to get to. Instead, my mission was to get Benni. If I'd turned up incriminating stuff on Poliakoff, I would have been a genuine hero in the department.

Then an epiphany. It wasn't something that slowly dawned; it was like the proverbial light bulb turning on above my head. My stroke of personal genius. Maybe I *could* get Poliakoff. "Where did you hide it?"

Benni's smile just got wider and his jaw tightened a bit. He would not tell me. I didn't expect him to, but it was worth a shot.

We sat in silence.

"Benni. I'm worried about you going to prison. There's a reason that you are here. So that you won't get murdered before you even get to trial."

Benni waved his arm dismissively.

"No. Seriously. If you go to prison, there will be some serious gangs there. Gangs that you don't, can't control. Black gangs. Hispanic gangs. And I don't see you recruiting a bunch of neo-Nazis to protect you." I thought the latter would drive my point home, but he waved it off again. False bravado or foolish overconfidence in his own power. I didn't know which, but he was overestimating his ability to form and run a family on the inside to protect himself.

"What if?" I waited until I was sure he was listening. "What if, instead of going to prison, you went someplace? Say, maybe a small town in Kansas. Took your wife. Got a menial job, or worked a small farm?"

Benni snorted again. Such a thing was beyond his comprehension. "What are you taking about?"

"Witness Protection." There. I said it out loud.

Benni laughed a jolly old laugh. "That's a good one, my friend. I don't need witness protection for two reasons..." He held up one finger. "I will not be a witness and," he held up a second finger, "I'm not going to prison either. They got nothing on me. They can't make anything stick."

"Benni, a moment ago you said you owed me one. I want to call that in now. Right now."

He lifted his eyebrows such that his already wrinkled forehead wrinkled even more. "Sure. You know I am a man of my word."

A mobster, yes. But a man of his word, nonetheless. At least most times. "The charges are going to stick, and they are going to put you away."

The wrinkles in his forehead were now completely gone and his eyes squinted a bit. "What are you saying?"

The moment of truth had arrived. My entire plan, the one hatched minutes ago, hinged on what happened next. "I'm an undercover cop. I'm the one who will testify against you."

Benni's eyes penetrated mine. Then, unexpectedly, he let out a bigger laugh than he had earlier. It was the biggest laugh I had ever heard escape him. A silly grin returned to his face.

I didn't know what to make of it.

"Ha. Poliakoff put you up to this, didn't he? Send you here to test my loyalty. Well, you can tell Manny I passed the test," he said triumphantly.

Hadn't seen that coming. "The one favor I am asking of you is to hear me out without interruption."

Benni nodded. "Go on."

"I like you in a way." Not really true. "But you need to believe it. Manny didn't send me here, and I am a cop."

Benni still wasn't buying it. "I'll prove it," I yelled for the guard.

He entered, opened my cell door, and took the cuffs off. "You are free to go, detective, whenever you like." Then he smiled a knowing smile and turned away, leaving the doors open behind him.

Benni's eyes bugged out of his fat, round face as he realized the truth of it. Benni practically exploded. He leaped to his feet, grabbed at me through the bars, and began cursing at me like the proverbial drunken sailor. Although I was hopelessly out of his reach, I was showered with the spittle spewing out of Benni's mouth.

I'd never seen Benni like this, and I was glad he was behind bars.

Getting past the initial parade of profanity, Benni said in a dangerous voice, "I trusted you!"

True

"You shacked up with my daughter!"

True

As reality set in, he ran out of steam.

Now it was my turn. "I know how you must feel." Not true, but I'm pretty sure it involved me being sliced up into little pieces while still alive. "I am here and suggesting this out of my concern for you and your wife." Not true. I started to add his daughter, but I was pretty sure that would have triggered another attack.

Defeated, he slumped back down on his cot. His usual cheerful expression returned, but he said nothing. I knew the little gears were turning in Bennis' head. Eventually, I hoped he would see the wisdom of what I had proposed.

My real reason for wanting to turn Benni wasn't for his welfare, it was for my own. As long as Poliakoff was in power, he could reach out and snuff me out. Until that threat was removed, they would destine me to a desk job purgatory. I wouldn't be able to hang out with the cops, have a relationship, and would always have to look over my shoulder. It would be like being undercover in plain sight. I was already looking over my shoulder and I didn't like it. How much worse would it be if word got to Poliakoff that I snitched on Benni?

A half hour went by. I had returned to my open cell and taken up a seat on the cot. Benni wasn't going anywhere. This was the most important thing for my future, so why should I go anywhere?

Finally, "If I turn state's evidence, what will the DA say about your little escapade in the warehouse? Huh?"

Benni was pretty good. I had to give it to him. I wonder if I was in his little insurance book. I pursed my lips. "I'm prepared to take that risk." Who was bluffing who?

"What else is the DA offering?"

He was trying to sweeten the pot and not expecting the next part. "Umm. I haven't actually worked this out with the DA." I quickly added, "Not completely." A lie. "You consider everything I have said and what your future will look like one way or another."

Benni grunted again. "So what happened to my Caddy?"

"It's probably in the impound yard. I saw nothing in the report about it getting shot up." With that, there wasn't too much else to say, so I got up and worked my way out to the car.

The dark, humid night smelled of burned jet fuel.

14

The binder from Office Depot was like the ones I used on the cases at work. It made a clear, stiff, satisfying metallic pop as the rings snapped open. Sliding my fingernail under the sealed cellophane edges of the ream of paper, I pried the end flaps up and withdrew about a hundred sheets. More or less. I wriggled the pre-punched holes in the sheets over the shiny silver points of the rings and snapped the rings closed. The rings aligned perfectly at the point of closure, a sure sign of a new binder.

I inserted dividing tabs about every twenty pages. They would get moved if needed, but for now, four primary sections would be enough; One for each of my suspects. In time, each might warrant his own binder, but without a single page filled in yet, that seemed ambitious.

Like the bar, the binder would have no name. It would be unseemly to have a visitor see a binder labeled "Four Cops Who I'm Investigating for Trying to Kill Me." On further reflection, it wouldn't be good to have anyone find the binder at all. It wasn't a stretch of the imagination to think that whoever it was, would eventually find my apartment and go through it...but this time, I would catch them on camera and I would know who it was. That made me smile.

That thought jogged my mind. Camera. I was going to need a good surveillance camera. Sigh. Mine was in my unit in storage. I dismissed buying a new one. I had been spending money at an alarming rate since I got out of the hospital. Although I had plenty of money in the bank and would not run out soon, I wasn't used to burning through cash. Besides, if I got a new camera, there would be a learning curve for how to use it to the best of its capabilities. No, I would have to make a trip to G Town to retrieve my own.

Perhaps it wasn't a good idea to keep my investigation notes in my apartment at all. I could, and would, keep electronic files on an easy-to-hide micro SD card, but I really liked the tactile pleasures of working with paper. Many detectives did. Except for the new kids. But there was something about leafing through the paper files, and being able to set them next to each other, rearrange them, etc. that seemed to make things pop off the page and into the subconscious mind. Just then, a thought popped out. I could use cryptic summary notes on index cards in the apartment to approximate the effect of hard-copy investigative notes supplemented by my computer files. Was there software that could do that?

They say that every journey begins with a first step. The first step for my journey to find my would-be assassin was returning to Galveston. And so it began.

***

Back on Tiki Island, I pulled into my driveway. On the gulf coast, they built homes on stilts because of the frequent tidal surges from hurricanes. Mine was no different. The garage and open spaces were below. Pressure-treated, painted poles raised the house ten feet above. I got out and opened the garage door, then headed up the stairs, across the front deck, and opened the front door. Something again assaulted my nostrils with a smell not all that uncommon in the south.

A heavy, dank smell. I walked through the house and opened every window. This place needed to air out. With that done, I closed the front door behind me and returned to my truck. I wasn't worried about anyone coming in the open patio door or windows. There wasn't anything of value to steal.

After crossing over the causeway into Galveston, I crossed the bridge over Offatts Bayou, past Darlene's Shrimp Shack, and ducked into Office Depot. It sits next to Calvary Catholic Cemetery, but on the opposite side from the phone store. I grabbed a pack of multi-colored three-by-five cards, a corkboard, a white marker board, a pack of clear push pins, and a pack of multicolored map pins. The ones with the small round heads. On impulse, purchased a jug of chocolate-covered almonds.

From the Cemetery, I crossed back over the bayou, merged onto Broadway Avenue J, took a left at Kempner Street, and returned to Galveston Storage to repeat my ritual. After retrieving my camera equipment and a few other items that might help my apartment seem like home, I stopped for a cold beer.

***

The bar was in a turn-of-the-century red brick building that was originally some kind of market. Square brick pillars divided the front of the structure into thirds. Recessed a couple of inches between the pillars, someone had plastered the brick walls from waist height up and pained them white. Red vertical lettering adorned the white sections advertising various beverages served inside.

There were three sturdy wooden doors; one in each section. The doors were permanently closed on the two outer sections. Above the doors was an old wooden transom with mullions radiating out from the center. The transoms let in light, but not air.

Suspended by red poles sloping down from the upper facade was a white vinyl awning jutting out over the sidewalk. The awning had a small arch over each one of the door sections. Above the awning, old-school neon lettering heralded the bar's name. The first section had the word "The" in smaller letters, the middle section was just a large letter "G", and the last section had the word "Spot."

The G Spot. A double entendre to be sure. With a name like that, it didn't cater to a female clientele, although maybe it should have. At least it wasn't called the Galveston Spot or the Galveston Bar.

Inside it smelled about the same as no name's. Smoke, beer, peanuts. Maybe all bars bought an aerosol spray that smelled like that. Although The G Spot was a dive, it was cleaner and trendier than no name's. Somebody had at least tried. There was a mirrored wall behind the bar with all the liquor bottles on display. The bar top was in decent condition and they had covered the front surface of the bar with shiny metal, probably aluminum. A row of fifties-style swiveling bar stools completed the counter. Silver legs with padded red round tops.

Similarly upholstered booths lined the opposite wall. Small, round cocktail tables and chairs littered the space between. Except for the very center of the room. Squatting there sat a four-foot diameter metallic base, topped with a silver metallic disc, surrounding a chrome pole for strippers to dance on. The thing was, there weren't any strippers, nor indications that they ever had any strippers. Either they planned to have them, but never got around to it, or aspired to have them in the future, but hadn't yet. Or the guy just got a good buy on the pole. Honestly, it looked a bit small. It would be very easy for a dancer to fall off the platform.

"A Lone Star. And a glass."

The barkeep brought it; I poured it. "Some salt too."

He brought the salt, and I sprinkled a bit on top of the brew.

A few locals dotted the booths. There were also a few tourists who had ventured off The Strand. I think they were waiting for the dancer to come out, but they were in for a long wait if they were.

The men's room was adequate, but what stood out was a sharps container bolted to the wall for addicts and diabetics to put their needles in. Never a good sign. It seemed especially so given that Galveston didn't have as big a drug problem as the larger cities in Texas.

Actually, Galveston's drug problem was of a different sort. Every so often, thousands of dollars' worth of cocaine will wash up on the shore. The record was over Two Million dollars' worth in 2010. Usually, the bricks are thrown overboard from a drug runner's boat if the Coast Guard is approaching. Surprisingly, the good citizens of Galveston usually turned the contraband in.

"What's with the Sharps container?" I stuck my thumb in the restroom's direction.

The barkeep made an unhappy face. "We kept finding needles in the trash can. Decided it was safer for everyone if we installed it. Especially for the guys emptying the trash at the end of their shift."

After another Lone Star, a few people drifted in. I drifted out, retreated across the Galveston Causeway, around the loop on Virginia Point Road, and pulled into the Tiki Store. After filling up, I headed in and grabbed a two-liter bottle of Dr. Pepper, some beef jerky, and a roll of paper towels.

"You know, why don't you add a bag of ice to that? Oh, and a pack of Styrofoam cups." On the way out, I grabbed the cups.

Outside, I grabbed a bag of ice from a white cooler with glass doors, got in the truck, and returned to the house where everything was just as I had left it.

The small guest bedroom was where I decided to work. It didn't seem to smell as bad as the rest, probably because the carpet didn't get as wet in that room.

I went back down to the truck and grabbed the office supplies and a hunting knife I kept in the glove box. Back upstairs I cut the carpet at the threshold of the doorway to the bedroom, now office. I pried up one edge and tugged the carpet up and away from the walls. I had to ease off a bit on my left side since it was still tender. After pulling the carpet and confetti-colored padding up, I dragged them into the living room and wondered, "How do I get rid of a chunk of carpet and pad?"

We had a homicide case in which the guy wrapped a dead body in a carpet like a burrito, but I was fresh out of dead bodies. The murderer who had wrapped the body in the carpet just left it in his backyard. That's how he got caught. Apparently, he didn't know how to dispose of carpet either. Fresh out of ideas, I dragged the carpet and pad down to the garage. At least they would be out of the house that way.

I was glad that I had enough foresight to get the ice. It was hot. The Dr. Pepper sizzled and danced over the milky white cubes. I wasn't impressed that I didn't have the foresight to bring a hammer and nails to hang the cork and marker boards. Next time. I also quickly figured out that a table and a chair could be a great asset. For a brilliant detective, I didn't seem to have much foresight these days. I wasn't being vain. All detectives thought of themselves as skilled detectives.

With little else to do, I locked the patio and front doors and slid out the front to my truck. I left the windows open. What was the worst that could happen? Even if it rained hard, what more damage could a bit of rain do that Harvey hadn't already done? I stopped at the Tiki Store to see if Bob had a hammer and a couple of nails that I could borrow. He didn't, so I put on a BBVD disc and headed north.

15

Sunday arrived, and I discovered I had little to do. I thought about the meager results of my investigation into SWAT so far, and nothing popped into focus. I also thought about my conversation with Benni. There was something odd about the conversation, but I couldn't quite put my finger on it. Still, it hovered near the edge of my mind.

Perhaps I should have spent the night at a hotel in Galveston and returned to work on the house. In the end, I decided that I'd drive by the Southwest Station and pick up the few of my things that were there.

I'd taken the Oren Drive exit from the South Freeway and was sitting at the light where FM521 Road angles across. "Hello there." Crossing right in front of me, going north, was none other than Donovan's car. At least it looked like his car. What serendipity. Having nothing better to do, I turned right to tag along for a while. I almost lost him when he turned left onto Clover Lane. I'd been here once before.

Clover Lane was the dead-end entrance to the Wildcat Golf Course. I'd lost sight of him completely. I drove in slowly, scanning for his car so that I wouldn't run up behind or park next to him. That would require some explanation. I turned into the first of three entrances into the long, skinny parking lot. No sign. Slowly cruising through the lot, I traversed the entire length on the back row. As I rounded the turn at the end of the row, I glimpsed his car through the ugly metallic crisscross of a high-tension tower. He was in the bag drop-off area, trunk open, pulling out his gear.

He plays golf on Sundays. It was a tidbit for the file, but probably not that relevant. I decided I should leave the area before he parked his car. Just then, he closed the lid to the trunk. And who did I behold? Skinner and French. The tidbit just got more interesting. Where was Enrique? I didn't see him. I stayed where I was. The front end of a white pickup truck in Texas was so common a sight as to not even register in the conscious mind, and I already knew that Skinner and Enrique didn't seem to be too aware, anyway. The tower would also help to obscure my presence.

Another man that I didn't recognize mingled with Skinner and French. They loaded the bags into two white golf carts. After Donovan returned from parking his car, he joined Skinner in one cart while French and the other man climbed into the other cart. As the cart caravan disappeared behind the clubhouse, I pulled away to find a place to park under one of the few trees on the far end of the back row.

Sitting there, I realized I didn't know what to do next. I hadn't planned this. I didn't know how long it took to play golf, but I was pretty sure it would be awhile. Even if I waited, what did I think I was going to do when they returned? I pulled out and circled the parking lot, locating the three men's cars. Who was the fourth man? Did it even matter? I looped the lot a second time looking for security cameras. There were none, nor were there any light poles to put any on. Apparently, security at a public golf course wasn't a top priority.

Since I had a wait ahead of me, I pulled out of the parking lot and made my way back to the street. I drove the circumference of the golf course to see if there was a good place to park and observe the foursome when they played a hole, any hole. There were none. There was a sufficient amount of treed areas and a lack of parking to make that idea a non-starter.

I cruised past Enrique's house since it was only a few minutes away. As I drove past the single-story brick rambler, there were no signs of life. If the car was there, it was in the garage. I pulled to the curb a couple of houses down and pulled out my phone to search for the nearest thrift store. As I was about to leave, Enrique pulled into his driveway. In my driver's side rear-view mirror, I watched as Enrique, his wife, and two children piled out of the car and headed toward the door. They were all dressed in Sunday church attire. Although killers have been known to go to church, I mentally moved Enrique down my list of suspects.

After picking up an oversized nondescript T-shirt and a baseball cap at Goodwill, I drove to Sonic and got some lunch to go; a bacon cheeseburger toaster, chili cheese fries, and a banana malt. I ate as I drove Oren Drive back to the Golf course.

The parking spot next to Skinner's car was still empty. There hadn't been too many golfers arriving after him. I parked next to his car, opened my glove box and pulled out some nitrile gloves, slipped on the baggy T-shirt, pulled on the cap, looked carefully around, and slid out of my truck. Sheltered between the two vehicles, I had just started to pick the lock to his car door when I realized it was unlocked. Was it always this easy on Sundays? If so, maybe all HPD detectives should start working weekends. Maybe criminals knew the detectives were at home and let their guard down. Not likely.

Nothing of interest in the passenger compartment or glove box.

I checked the time. It had only been an hour. I

suspected I was still good.

Emboldened, I casually walked down the aisle to Donovan's car. The black Camaro SS was locked but was easy to open. Not much to see here either, although it took longer because of the amount of littered coffee cups, food wrappers in bags, and the like. The glove box was locked, but it also gave way to yield its secrets. Besides the usual paperwork, it held a pistol, a spare magazine, and a couple of prescription bottles.

I briefly thought about taking the pistol. IF Donovan was dirty, having one of his weapons with his prints on it could come in handy. But I didn't know if he was dirty or not. If not, then having a firearm go missing could be problematic for him. And it would start him trying to figure out who got into his car. I didn't need that, nor did I want to jam up a good cop, if he was one. Instead, I pulled out my cell and photographed the serial number etched into the frame. Next, I photographed the two pill bottles, making certain I had captured the drug name and prescribing physician. Finally, I opened each bottle individually, dropped out a pill into the palm of my left hand, one facing up, the other down, and photographed them. With that done, I pocketed the two pills and left everything else as I had found it, and walked back to my truck.

I hadn't tried French's truck. I was beginning to feel that I was pushing my luck. He had managed a parking spot directly across from the clubhouse. I was certain that there would be a security camera there, even though it was probably too far away to be a threat. But it had gone too well so far to risk someone spying me from the clubhouse, or coming out the front doors.

Eager to see what I'd learned, I completely forgot about going to the station house and returned to the apartment. I made a few notes on my laptop, then browsed over to the pill identification wizard at Drug.com. The first bottle was labeled atorvastatin. The pills it contained were white, round, and bore the letters "Roche" and a number two inside a small circle. Rohypnol; the famous date rape drug, roofie. Looks like Donovan and his doctor warrant closer investigation. The second bottle was labeled Carbinoxamine. The pill it contained was a triangular white pill with the letter "M" on it. The wizard identified it as Hydromorphone. Uh oh Lucy, somebody has an opioid problem.

Donovan moved up to the top of my list.

16

Monday was appropriately dreary. A gentle rain from a murky gray sky added to the humidity, already oppressive, in the morning hours.

I grabbed a cup at E.T.s. "Morning, Casey." The barista had the same distant feel about her, yet something had changed. "Did you do something different with your hair?"

A flash of...something crossed her face. She said, "Not really, just a trim."

"Well, it looks good then. Regular drip with cream and sugar, please."

I had arrived a few minutes early because I wanted to run Donovan's pistol's serial number. There was nothing wrong with that necessarily, but I didn't need my roomics asking questions either. The task was pretty simple. But it yielded no results. All that meant was that the gun hadn't been reported stolen or had been used in a crime and then purloined out of evidence. I still wanted to know more about it.

Through the online calendar, I could schedule my next appointment with the shrink. I didn't want my roomies to see that either. Two weeks out. That was the soonest open appointment.

A couple of detectives that I didn't know trickled in. An old guy and a younger woman. After a few introductions and pleasantries, I turned back to my monitor.

Dr. Rajiv Patel. There were two of them in Texas, but only one who would have written the Rx for Donovan. No outstanding warrants, no arrest record. Next, I looked him up on HealthGrades. He had emigrated from Hyderabad, India, and had a lot of positive reviews.

Overall, he looked like a legitimate MD. I considered calling over to the drug guys in Vice, but decided that I should hold off on that until I figured out where Donovan was getting his supply. I'd keep the good doctor on the radar for now.

***

Having made no progress on my private investigation or the cold cases, I pulled another file and read.

The phone rang. It was the Cold Case Tip Line. No one else reached to pick it up, so the new guy, me, answered.

"I have some information on an old case." The voice was dry, scratchy, and brittle, with a Hispanic accent. "A friend was raped and murdered years ago." She, at least I think it was a she, hesitated. "I know who the killer was. I should have come forward sooner, but I was too afraid."

"Ok. What was your friend's name?"

"Azúcar Mendez. She died in 1989."

I spelled out the name as I typed it in. "Umm, I don't see anyone by that name."

"Oh, try Mary Mendez."

That yielded a single file from that year. "Ok, hold a minute, and let's see what we got."

Quickly scanning the file, I saw the victim had been an exotic dancer at a local club. She had been raped and strangled to death. I quickly tagged the computer file to get the full hard copy sent up.

"I see the case you are talking about. And what is your

name?"

"I'd rather not say. I thought this could be anonymous."

"Yes, it can be. How did you know Ms. Mendez?"

"We worked together."

"And you say you know who the killer is. How is that?"

"He raped me, and strangled me too, tried to kill me, but I escaped."

"Uh hum, so, who did this to you?"

There was a long pause, then she said, "This was a bad idea."

"Wait! Why didn't you call us sooner?"

"I was too afraid. I still am."

"Afraid? Why?"

"Because of who he is."

"We can protect you. Who was it?"

"No, you can't. Not from him." Then the line went dead.

Well, that wasn't helpful at all. It would be tomorrow before the full file would show up on my desk.

I was so deeply distracted by the call and pondering what I could do about it, I didn't notice Q's arrival.

"What's got your antenna up?" asked Q

"Oh. Good morning. What makes you think my antenna is up?"

"I'm a detective, remember?"

I told him about the call.

Q; "You know how many women are raped, killed, or disappear from strip clubs?"

I had no idea.

"Your perp is probably a serial rapist and probably a

serial killer. He just didn't pop up on that radar because no one could tie a third victim to him, especially at the time."

That seemed to make sense to me. "Then why hasn't there been a DNA hit on our suspect?"

"Could be that he never got caught, but that doesn't seem likely for a serial rapist." Q thought for a moment. "The perp could have died, or they had never found his other victims. Maybe he got more careful after this woman got away."

Q continued, "This connection may be a thing. I'd look at all the other stripper cases from that year, the one before it, and the one after it. If you can make a loose connection, you will have more data points to go on. If you get a rock solid connection that makes it a serial rapist or killer, then more resources will be brought to bear."

"Thanks," I said. "That is good advice."

"I'll give you one more piece of good advice; the city has an..." Q paused to choose the next word carefully, "Interesting relationship with strip clubs and their owners. The corruption isn't as bad as in New Orleans, but still... I'd tread lightly if I were you."

I started digging through the murder cases that involved rape for the three-year period. There were more than I imagined. I had thought about looking through the rape survivors during that same time period, but seeing the number of murder/rapes, there would be way too many to deal with if I didn't find something to pull at.

"Q. What's the deal with the barista at E.T.s?"

"Oh, the quiet one?"

"Yeah, Casey."

"I dunno. She arrived a few weeks ago. Always been

sort of standoffish."

"I bet she would get better tips if she smiled a little and interacted more with the customers. And what's up with Uranus jokes?"

Q let out a baritone chuckle. "Wo ho ho. The owner had this idea. He would put up a daily joke on a chalkboard. Like those clever signs that you sometimes see outside of churches and restaurants. So he started a contest to have the customers submit space-themed jokes so that he had a pool of them to draw from. By the end of the first day, he was flooded with jokes playing off the pronunciation of the planet Uranus. Almost none of the jokes were usable. So, he called an end to the contest and awarded the prize to the guy who submitted the only non-Uranus joke."

By the end of the day, I had scanned most of the rape cases for 1990.

***

Northbound traffic on I-65 was at a standstill. The Texas Highway Patrol had all lanes closed because of a fatal accident and were waiting for a Life Flight helicopter to land on the freeway to pick up a severely injured survivor. Although Houston traffic is considered better than average for a city our size, the death rate among our accidents is higher than average. When Texans do it, they do it big, and car crashes are no different.

I wouldn't be going anywhere soon. I put it in park, shut down the engine, and picked up the phone. "Hey, Iverson. Glad that I caught you."

"How are you doing, Griff?" Her voice had a slight rasp to it. Not entirely displeasing, but it made her sound hard. It gave her an edge.

"Umm, I was wondering if you could trace a serial number of a pistol for me."

"Was the purchase made in the last 24 hours?" She asked.

"No."

"Can't help you. You know, we cannot do that, right?"

"I know that is what everyone is told."

"Well, it's true."

"Umm, you want me to believe that every time a gun is sold through a licensed dealer, they call you for the background check, you take all the information, and then once they have approved the purchase, you don't keep any record of it? Has anyone at the Bureau thought how ridiculous that sounds?"

"Well, yes, but that is how NICS works. It's the law."

It was the law. A compromise between federal background checks and the privacy of legitimate buyers. It was a suitable compromise, but few actually believe that the feds don't keep a list of who bought what.

The helicopter buzzed by heading toward the Red Duke Trauma Institute. Traffic would move again soon.

Iverson said, "You have to go to the dealer who sold the gun, then go through his records to get the buyer's information. You may or may not need a warrant, depending on who the dealer is. BATFE guys almost always need a warrant 'cause no FFL wants them looking through their records. Too easy to get fined for not crossing a T."

"I don't know who the dealer was, *is* the problem."

"In that case, get the dealer from the manufacturer. They know which serial number went to which dealer. There's only one problem..."

"Which is?" I asked.

"That's BATFE's turf. A manufacturer will not give you that. You know any ATF guys?"

"No. Anyone you could refer me to?"

"Let me think about it." She didn't sound hopeful.

I wasn't too hopeful, either. This kind of thing is usually based on a "What have you done for me lately" basis, and I had done nothing for Iverson. "Thanks anyway, Special Agent." The "special" part seemed awkward to say, but the FBI people were pretty sensitive about it. I suppose cops were sensitive about being called by their correct rank, too.

"See you around, Griff. Call me if you got anything useful for me?"

I rolled the problem of tracing Donovan's pistol around in my mind, but realized that I was probably at a dead end. The only other thing would be to borrow the pistol, fire a test round, and get someone in ballistics to see if it matched any slugs in the system from unsolved crimes. That was a long shot. Combined with me not knowing a guy who could do it on the QT, and the firestorm that would rain down on me if it came to light that I was testing another cop's weapon for criminal activity eliminated that as an option.

Once traffic finally broke free, I called the guy in charge at the Airport Division office to let him know I was running late due to traffic, but was on my way. All good with him. He wasn't going anywhere, anyway. I suspected that watching me get spit at and chewed out by Benni was the best entertainment option that they had.

***

Through TSA, escorted through the locked doors, past the rack of M16s, and into the holding area. I sat in the empty cell next to Benni's again hoping it would make him more comfortable, but my door was open, his wasn't, and that said it all. He glared at me. I stayed beyond his reach through the bars.

I had realized what had struck me as odd about our last conversation and I wanted to push a button. But I needed to point the conversation in a different direction so he might not see it coming.

"You talk to the DA?"

"They are working on it." They weren't because they didn't even know about it. "I've been working on some cold cases. Thought you could give me some insight."

"Why is it you think I would help you?"

I ignored the comment. "A couple of decades ago, there was a string of murders. Strippers..."

"They are called exotic dancers."

"Umm, exotic dancers were raped and killed at night on their way home."

"That is hardly newsworthy. Occupational hazard. What is newsworthy is that someone from the department is investigating it."

I raised my eyebrows to give Benni a questioning look.

"Cops think of the dancers as prostitutes. Some are, some aren't. You know that. But cops don't care if some prostitute gets raped. Figure they had it coming."

"But murder is a different thing."

"Maybe, but how much work does a cop put into solving a gang banger's murder? Huh?"

I shrugged.

"Only this case is worse. With the gang banger, the cops, the politicians, they have no vested interest. With a dancer...Well, the relationship between the clubs and the officials has always been a special one, so there is even less interest."

Benni continued, "The girls know they are targets and tend to be careful. Your killer would have to have some way to get them to let their guard down. Now, if the killer had some kind of uniform or other connection to the club or the girls, then he would have an easier time getting to them. All clubs have some kind of security. Both for the money and the girls. It's usually an off-duty cop collecting some cash on the side. The cop walks the girls to their cars. Stuff like that."

That made sense. "What about roofies?"

Benni's face scrunched up. "Come on. You know I only do clean money. Don't traffic drugs." He was shaking his head.

"I know. You're a veritable saint. Strippers, booze, and gambling. No drugs. No violence, well, most of the time."

"You know I only hurt people on the inside who deserve it. I don't rough up the public or extort money from business owners, or run guns. All that nasty business."

It was true. Poliakoff had another lieutenant who ran that side of the business. "I didn't mean to say that you sold roofies in your clubs."

"Oh? Were these poor girls drugged? That would be odd. They only take drinks directly from the bartender, never from a customer. Another occupational hazard, but they know how to avoid it. If someone drugged them, that would implicate the bartender, maybe a waitress, or someone else who they explicitly trusted. Which clubs?"

"They weren't any of your clubs. Besides, I'm not sure someone drugged them. The coroner's reports were filed away, and I must wait for them to come back." I knew the victims hadn't been drugged, but I wanted to keep the next question under the cover of the cold cases since Benni was talking to me in that context. "I was wondering, if it turns out that someone drugged them, where would the killer have gotten the Rophynol?"

"Depends."

"On what?"

"If it was real or counterfeit. If it was counterfeit, then it probably came over the border and was sold through one of the other organizations in town. Could have been bought in a bar, club, or even a street corner. Or they brought it over the border themselves."

"And if it were real?"

"Then it had to be imported from Europe or South America. Safer, more predictable, but pricier."

"How would I tell?"

"In the blood, you might not be able to. If it was impure, or of a nonstandard dose, then likely counterfeit. If you had access to the pill then, easy to tell."

"How so?"

"Because of the misuse of the drug, the manufacturer, Roche, started putting a blue dye in the pill. It made it easier to detect when dissolved in a drink, but only if it was a light-colored drink. A dark drink, or even a dark enough room, and forget it."

"Huh." I'd have to test Donovan's when I got home. "Where would the guy have gotten it if it were real?"

"Only one guy in town imports it." He smiled. "Poliakoff."

The fact that he told me that also told me he was going to flip on his old boss.

I got up to leave. Our conversation had been much more productive than I had expected. Benni was talking. Now was the time. "Oh, one last thing. I got your good news, and your bad news."

"All you've been to me is bad news. Give me some good news."

"Your car. It is in the impound lot. Not a scratch on it. All those bullets flying around and it didn't get hit once."

Benni smiled.

"But, here's the thing. The Feds decided you are an organized crime figure. They are going to confiscate your car under the RICO act. Probably going to auction it off."

"No." He dragged out the o like a haunting ghost.

I stepped out of my cell and headed for the door, pausing in front of Benni's cell. "Yeah. The next auction is coming up in a week. Ha. Maybe Poliakoff will buy it."

A sound rumbled up into Benni's throat. Then, "Would you buy it for me?" He croaked it out.

I looked surprised. I was surprised. I hadn't seen that coming, but it confirmed my suspicion. "Oh, Benni. I don't have that kind of money." A dramatic pause. "I'm kind of a truck guy, anyway. I'd look like a pimp driving around in that thing."

Benni looked hurt by the pimp comment.

I turned and moved toward the exit.

"Wait." Benni motioned for me to come back.

He'd taken the hook. "Yes?"

He lowered his voice. "You know I don't like for innocent people to get hurt?"

"Sure, Benni."

"Poliakoff won't buy the car. But he might follow the poor schlep who buys it, well, to kill him to take the car."

I tried to look puzzled. "I'm not following you, Benni? Why would he do that?"

Benni pressed his face into his hands and sighed.

"What is it, Benni? You can trust me."

"No. I can't. That's the problem."

"Fair enough. But I'm all you got."

The moment of truth had arrived.

Benni was unusually humble. "That insurance I told you about..."

"Yeah."

"It's in the caddy."

I didn't dare speak a word and break the magic. They say that the first one to talk loses.

"It's on an SD card."

"You don't think the crime guys or the Feds found it?"

"No. It's a micro SD. About the size of a dime. Well hidden. But if Poliakoff's guys tossed your place looking for it, they've run out of places to look by now. He'll figure out the car and want to tear it apart next. He can't get to it in impound. But, once it gets sold, he'll do what he needs to..."

"And...Without the card, you're screwed?" I tried to

make it sound like as much of a statement of fact as I could while still couching it as a question. He needed to believe that.

He slumped lower. "I need to get that card."

"Gee, Benni. I don't know if even I can get to it. I'd have to get into impound and get back out with no one realizing that I had gone through your car."

He thought carefully. "Get me that card, and we'll call it even."

That was better than I was expecting. "I can try. But you have to tell me exactly where to look. I won't have much time to go on an Easter egg hunt."

He told me.

17

Although yesterday's showers were gone, the humidity was still oppressive. A reminder that summer would be in full bloom soon.

The file on Mary Mendes had arrived during the wee hours of the morning and sat on my desk. Apparently the product of some graveyard shift drone at an offsite storage location for old files. It surprised me that it had arrived so quickly. It was thin.

Mary's corpse had been discovered in an open field in an area that was being developed at the time. Her body lay face up, a short, tight miniskirt pulled up around her waist, no panties. She still wore her blouse. The crime scene photos showed close-ups of bruising around her neck and a twenty-dollar bill neatly lying next to her lifeless form.

The coroner's report concluded she had been sexually assaulted. Death by asphyxiation caused by manual strangulation. A homicide.

More interesting was an update to the file made years after the initial report. It had a report by one Juana Dulce. Ms. Dolce reported someone had raped her near the same location and that her attacker had tried to strangle her as well. Both of the women had been exotic dancers.

Ms. Dolce had given police a description of her attacker and had sat with a department sketch artist. The man, white, six foot two, one eighty, with brown eyes, and close-cropped hair, could have been any one of a hundred thousand in the metro area. He had a military look about him. If he had been in the military, he would have been even harder to locate.

Dolce hadn't provided a name for her attacker, and her late report didn't move the case forward.

I teased up the phone numbers from the incoming tip line around the time I had gotten the call yesterday and started doing a reverse lookup on them. None were listed to anyone named Dolce. Many were from numbers that weren't associated with anyone's name. Not surprising if you wanted to stay anonymous. However, one number stood out; the Chrysalis Hospice Center. Based on the voice and the reason someone would call after all of these years, it reasoned that it could be someone who was at the end of their life.

***

The hospice center was a low sprawling affair built with brick walls, white window trim, and round white columns. Jutting out from the main entrance was a low peaked roof, also supported by white columns that provided cover from the elements to visitors being dropped off at the door. The architect had probably been going for the look of a mansion, but to Griff, it looked more like a funeral home.

Inside the door was a walnut desk with a receptionist who was on the phone. Hispanic, she was in her late twenties, with a round face, smooth complexion, and straight brown hair. She had started college as a nursing student, but then changed her major and graduated with a degree in hospital administration.

She couldn't get a job in a hospital, so she ended up at the hospice until she could move up the food chain. Ironically, she could have if she had stayed in nursing.

Hanging up the phone, her attention turned to Griff. She immediately smiled. Her best smile.

Griff was handsome. At the center, she rarely encountered people within her age group. The nurses have little to do with the desk admin. Visitors rarely come to visit grandma or even their own parents, because it's not what her age group wants to do. Anyone who visited in that age group was too distraught/distracted. She was once attracted to a young, studly male nurse, but he turned out to be gay. She was immediately interested in Griff.

"How may I help you?"

"I'm here to see Ms. Dolce." Griff didn't know if she was there, but this seemed like the best approach.

"And what is your name?" Not that she needed that to look up a patient. It was for her own information.

"Griff. Griffin Hunter."

As the receptionist clicked on her keyboard, she replied, "What a great name."

"Oh, I'm sorry Mr. Hunter. May I call you Griff? Ms. Dolce won't be taking visitors today. They moved her up to morphine for her pain this morning, and she had a rough time adjusting. You should try back in a couple of days."

Griff turned to leave.

"Mr. Hunter. May I call you Griff?" She paused, then with a bit more perk in her voice said, "If you leave me your number, I can call you when she is feeling better."

"That's ok. Thanks."

They were both crestfallen, but for different reasons. At least he had confirmed where Ms. Dolce was.

***

Six minutes north of 1200 Travis sat the HPD impound yard. It was clearly too small, but the city had grown up around the yard. Bound by railroad tracks to the south, Dart Street to the North, and the Fire Department's Logistic Center and Maintenance Depot on the east, it had no room to expand. The remaining lots were a mixture of old and new buildings, primarily residences. It spoke well to the City that they hadn't declared eminent domain on the surrounding homes and expanded as so many liberal cities had done. The yard itself was an eyesore. Chain-link fence topped with Constantia wire, tired asphalt, and four squat aluminum buildings. And lots of cars. Burned-out hulks of cars stacked at the rear of the lot provided a barrier between the railroad tracks and the lot. I've seen junkyards that looked nicer.

A dirty red pickup was being towed in through the gate on the right side of the yard. I drove through the gate on the left that emptied into a few visitor parking spaces. I parked next to the only two cars in the lot, both white SUVs from the Houston Forensic Science Center marked "*Crime Scene.*"

The office was just a single-car garage bay that had been enclosed. Under the watchful eye of a surveillance camera, I opened the simple, solid white door and stepped inside. At the counter, I smiled and put my shield on the counter. "I was following up on a case and was wondering about a specific car."

"Sure. Which one?"

"A white Cadillac CT-6. Belongs to a Benjamin Sokol."

She stroked a few keys, then looked back at my shield, then back at me. "They shot you next to this car, didn't they? The thing may have saved your life, huh?"

"Uh-huh. Have the lab guys gone through it yet?"

She looked back at the screen. "Yup. Looks like they are all done."

"They find anything?"

"No. Clean as a whistle. They've released it."

"Mind if I go take a look?"

She rummaged through a large drawer below the counter as she said, "No, suit yourself." He handed over the keys. "You need help finding it?"

"No, I assume it is the only one out there. I know what it looks like."

Out the front door, I passed eight covered stalls, then through a side gate that separated the visitors' lot from the yard itself. The car was about six rows back, sitting at the end of its row in some dirt. Since the lab had cleared it, I didn't need to glove up, but I slipped on a pair, anyway. I unlocked the car, opened the rear door, and slid in. I looked around to make sure that no one was looking and slipped the edge of my pocket knife into the specified location. The card was right where Benni said it would be.

After pocketing the card, putting the knife away, and removing the gloves, I wandered back to the office. "Car looks in great condition. You sure that they did a thorough search on it?"

"Yup. They don't tear 'em apart like they used to. After an initial look-see in the usual places, they bring in dogs. In your case, they would have brought in both a money dog and a drug dog. Only if the dogs hit do they bother to rip stuff up, like they do at the border. If they still can't find anything, and the dogs still think something is there, then they might bring a portable X-ray machine. Makes people happier if their cars aren't destroyed when there was nothing there."

It made me happy. "Thanks. You have a good day."

"You too." She said as she logged me out.

There was still plenty of daylight left, so after pulling out of the impound yard, I continued looking into the SWAT team. I'd begun to think of them as the four horsemen of the apocalypse.

***

I drove up to Enrique's neighborhood. Parked down the street and followed his wife to the school, where she picked up the kids and returned home. Nothing to see here. Maybe my apocalypse only had three horsemen. On to French's place.

Riverside Terrace was once an affluent Jewish neighborhood. The first African-American to move into the neighborhood was Jack Caesar in 1952. A bomb was detonated on his porch, but he stayed. Over the following decades, the neighborhood suffered as "white flight" occurred both in Houston and across the nation. The neighborhood recovered in the nineties, but it took longer than in most neighborhoods. This century saw gentrification in the area, improvements in Braes Bayou, and the realization that the lots were large and close to town. Today, the Terrace is home to many black politicians, educators, doctors, lawyers, and other professionals. French also lives there.

I had French's address from Spokeo along with the sale price, number of rooms, etc. from Trulia. A mixture of older homes and newer miniature mansions were on his street. I pulled up across the street and snapped a couple of pictures, but I didn't feel comfortable just sitting there. A white guy parked on the street doing nothing might be noticed, and the description of my truck would be a giveaway if it got back to French. Sitting in the neighborhood to monitor French would not work.

***

Back at the apartment, I decided it was time for a little science experiment. I pulled out the oval, olive green colored pill I had removed from Donovan's glove compartment while at the golf club. I'd already determined that it was Rohypnol, or at least supposed to be based on its markings, but now I had new information from Benni. I carefully cut it in half and discovered that it was a blue color inside. Huh. Apparently, that was what made it change a drink's color.

Next, I filled a clear glass with some water. Would water work? I didn't want to mess this up since I only had one pill. I dropped one half in and waited to see what would happen. Sure enough, the water took on a bluish tint, so I dropped the other half in. Blue.

According to Benni, that meant that the pill was probably a genuine pharmaceutical product, illegal to sell in the States. Who handled its sale? None other than Manny Poliakoff.

Was I happy with this fresh development or not? In a way, I would have preferred that the pill was counterfeit and that Donovan was getting his drugs from some other source. But this discovery came with a new question; was this a coincidence, or was there a connection between Donovan and Poliakoff?

If Donovan was working for Poliakoff, or someone in his organization, what did that mean? Was Donovan the shooter? If so, was he aiming for me, or Benni? If it was for Benni, then why was I targeted at the hospital? No, I had to be the target.

If Donovan is connected to Poliakoff, then that meant that he had a connection to drugs. And it was drugs that killed Rueben and nearly killed me in the hospital. There were simply too many coincidences to be ignored. Indeed, all the pieces seemed to fit together.

I carefully slid Benni's micro SD into a carrier and guided it into my laptop's SD Card slot. It was encrypted. I shouldn't have been surprised, and I doubted Benni was going to give me the key. Problem was, I didn't have a relationship with a geek who could hack into it. I knew a guy, but...

Letting the FBI or the department in on the card was risky. It might contain incriminating information about me. That wouldn't be good. No, I had to know what was on the card before I could share. Furthermore, if the card had stuff on anyone outside of Poliakoff's organization, it could come in handy. Perhaps Benni's insurance policy could now become my insurance policy. I'd need to make a couple of copies, and one of those "In the event of my untimely death" things with an attorney. Well, if I could find an attorney that I could trust.

18

In the morning, I donned clothing more appropriate for the neighborhood and went down to the heart of Benni's territory in Meyerland. I parked and walked a block to a seemingly abandoned corner grocery store; the kind that used to be mom-and-pop operations in the fifties. The place had been long abandoned before Hurricane Harvey, but the floods didn't do it any favors.

A rusted pole stood out front like a lone sentinel, its sign having been long blown off. The plywood covering the doors was so completely gray that it no longer resembled wood. The only recognizable signage was an old Coca-Cola sign, a testament to the quality of the red paint that had been used.

Shingle siding had once covered the exterior, but now they only extended down from the roof to about three feet above the broken ground. The lowest layers had rotted away from repeated flooding. Plywood or strips of rusting corrugated metal covered the bottom portion of the skeleton. I found the plywood section that was hinged, swung it open, and ducked inside.

Just inside the hidden entrance was a new wall with a door. The door was seldom locked. There wasn't a need. Security by obscurity. I opened the door and stepped into the dimly lit room with its racks of glowing LEDs.

Cricket swiveled her chair around and squinted. Although in her twenties, her hair was dyed silver. The bluish glow from the computer monitors gave it an eerie glow. Her heavy black makeup contrasted sharply with her pale skin and red lip gloss. A small silver hoop ring dangled from the cartilage between her nostrils. To make the ensemble complete, an intricate tattoo pattern of sugar skulls climbed up her left arm, disappearing under her short sleeve.

Recognition was slow, but I knew she recognized me when she sprang from her seat yelling, "You got some nerve coming here, or any place where you are known by the business."

She was right. It also spoke volumes I was less afraid of Benni's people than I was of my own department. "I come in peace." And spread my fingers in a Vulcan greeting. Geeks.

"Don't give me that. You here to arrest me, or have me gunned down too?" The ring in her nose jiggled a bit as she moved her head animatedly.

"No. I'm not going to arrest you. And Reuben wouldn't have been 'gunned down' if he hadn't been shooting at the HPD."

"What then?"

Cricket was a scrawny kid. She should have been in college, where she would have excelled in computer science. But she was too smart for college, but not smart enough to stay out of the criminal life. She didn't think of herself as a criminal, though. It was just a game, a game of who was smarter, cleverer. She was Benni's technology guru and did jobs for him, like tabulating odds on random bets or hacking into systems to influence betting. Who knew what else she did?

"I need a favor."

She started up again. "You got some nerve. You know, I could have one of his goons over here in a flash. They'd like it too."

"But you won't." I hoped. "One, you're not a criminal..." she was, "and two, you'd rather play the game." I think she tried to spit at me, but, well, it didn't make it past her chin. More like an aggressive drool. "You call the goons, and then I would have to arrest you. We both lose. No percentage in that."

She scrunched up her face into a scowl that only a twenty-something millennial can give. The nose ring rode up on the top of her upper lip.

"You still got a lot of nerve...What?"

"I need to crack a password, bypass some encryption, and leave a little present for someone." Appealing to her vanity, I added, "Simple things you could do in your sleep."

She bared her yellowed teeth. I'm not sure why. "What's in it for me?"

"A couple of pounds of beef jerky, and a case of energy drinks." Start the negotiations low.

"You got some nerve. What do you think I am?" It looked like she thought about trying to spit at me again.

"That wouldn't be all. Some cash." Despite how she lived, I doubted she needed the cash, probably got all she needed online or with advance knowledge of certain bets.

"Not how I keep score."

"An offer to work for me. Odd jobs. I can help you stay out of jail." She tried not to look interested, but I caught a glint. "Jeez, it's cold in here."

"Sixty-nine, year-round."

It would have been silent except for the whir of dozens of muffin fans.

"You get to screw with a cop, probably a dirty one."

Bingo! That got her.

"I'd like to screw with you. You're a filthy cop bastard." She hadn't quite let it go yet.

She had made a point that I hadn't considered. She might double-cross me. I wouldn't trust her with Benni's insurance card. At least not yet.

"Your little present. It's for this cop?"

"Yup. And he is a filthier bastard than I am. In fact, he might be involved in Jonah's and Reuben's deaths."

She softened a bit. "Let me get this straight. You want to screw with another cop, who you think may have killed Benni's guys?" One eye was squinted.

Cricket turned to her desk and fished out an SD card. "Keep this safe. Put it into your computer first, then get your friend to put it into his computer. After that, any time he is online, his computer will upload all of his files to your computer." She beamed a wicked little smile. "Will that do, or do you want something more destructive?"

"Oh no. That would be perfect."

"You can use this too. It is completely anonymous. Can't be traced back to either of us." She gave me a blank business card. On the back was a hand-printed email address. "You got the files you want to be cracked?"

"Not with me."

"Drop them off with the beef jerky and drinks. Some Cheetos too. The crunchy kind. Leave the files in an envelope. I don't want to look at you again, so just leave the stuff outside the inner door. I'll get back to you."

"How?"

"Really? I'll find you." Of course she would. "Oh, and don't use that email from your own IP."

I should have known that, but wouldn't have remembered. Instead of saying thank you, I said, "How stupid do you think I am?"

Cricket was answering that as I walked back through the door.

On the way back to the truck, I read the card she handed me. "Harry Bentwick@Yahoo.com." How nice. Such a cute little girl.

***

Later that night, the sniper opened his gun safe again. He pulled out the two burners and turned them on and exchanged pistols. One of the burners beeped. It was the other one, not the one that beeped last time. "Layoff Hunter for a while," it read. It wasn't the message that surprised him as much as the number from which they had sent it.

19

Curly wisps of vibrant colors. Red, pink, teal, orange, and green. They bounce around above you. You know they are there, but you can't see them. You know the shape and the reward that will follow your success. You swing wildly, not sure what you are swinging at but hoping to connect. The noise doesn't help your concentration, not that it would matter if you could concentrate only on finding the elusive prize.

Maybe you will make the connection, but maybe you won't either. Others have tried before you, and are you any better than they were? Then, suddenly, you connect. The phantom has now become tangible. You can feel that it is solid. A rousing cheer goes up as the children all around you dive at your feet. You've broken the piñata open and a piece of candy pops out.

Detective work is just like that. You grope around in the dark, following your best instincts, and when you make the connection, the case cracks open, and your reward pops out. Or sometimes you just get lucky.

"You'll never believe what has happened." Jax practically spewed the words out over the phone. "There has been a break in the case. A big break."

"Umm. Which case exactly?"

"Your case, dummy." When I didn't respond, Jax continued. "You know, the one where you were shot." There was more than a trace of sarcasm in the last part.

"Oh? Oh! I didn't think anyone was actually working that as a case." No one wanted to look inside. It was toxic.

"Well, OK, no one was digging any deeper, but then,"

Jax' tone perked back up again, "we got a break."

"Huh. What kind of break?"

"The owner of the apartment building called in."

"What apartment? You're losing me."

"The building directly across the street from Goldberg's Deli," Jax said. "He went to show a guy a vacant apartment that he had. When they go to the apartment, someone had moved around some of the stuff and he spotted a spent casing on the floor."

"What?"

"We went over and looked. The door lock had some recent scratches on it and a window facing Goldberg's was unlocked. Our lab guys went over and collected the casing and dusted it for prints. The door, window, and casing had all been wiped clean, but the rest of the apartment was littered with dozens of prints, probably from the previous owner and guests. They took the prints, but given the quantity, it will be awhile before the results come back."

"So, you're saying that a sniper was sitting in an empty apartment, right below where the SWAT guys were perched, and no one noticed." It was a statement more than a question.

"Yup. That's the working theory, anyway."

"How was it that no one noticed?" I wanted to know.

"Who would have?" Jax asked. "The SWAT guys were on the roof, the street detectives would have had their backs to the building, and the alley detectives were heads-down after getting fired upon by Jonah. You were hit in the middle of the gunfight, so nobody would have noticed one more shot being fired."

"You think anything more will turn up out of this?"

"No. I doubt it. If the guy took the time to wipe the areas where he had been, we won't find anything among the other prints. He probably left everything he didn't touch alone just to tie us up. Unless the lab guys turn up something unexpected, it will be case closed."

"I bet IA is happy," I said.

"Probably. I don't think they were looking anyway, but if they were, it is case closed for them for certain."

We talked a bit more about this development, then Jax said, "I'll let you know if there's anything else that turns up. But I wouldn't hold my breath." Then he rang off.

Wow. At least that explained why I wasn't dead. If it wasn't one of the SWAT team, he wasn't as good a shot. I guess that I'd investigated the wrong guys. But if that were true, now I had two additional problems.

Who took a shot at me? And what was I going to do about Donovan? Those questions would nag the back of my mind until I reached a conclusion. Back to square one.

20

I found myself back on Tiki Island. The discovery of the sniper's nest had changed everything. I started pulling down my research. Maps, photos, significant notes, and a timeline. It had all been a waste of time and had made me paranoid and cynical about my fellow officers.

I piled the detritus in a corner. I pulled down the photos of Donovan's drugs and stood there, frozen in time. What to do about Donovan? I knew he had a problem, but was it my problem to worry about? If it was just oxycodone, I'd assume that he just had an opioid problem. But the Rohypnol meant something else. He wasn't using it on himself, of that I was sure.

A good-looking guy in a uniform. With Rohypnol. If he were 25 years older, I'd consider Donovan a suspect in the stripper murders. Not having been born yet is a pretty good alibi.

I put Donovan's stuff in its own pile. I could still be cynical about Donovan.

In the kitchen, I mixed up some powdered lemonade in the clear glass pitcher, dumped in ice purchased at the Tiki Store, and poured myself a glass. While doing this, it occurred to me I still didn't know who had taken the shot at me.

Since the sniper's nest was discovered, I now knew it wasn't the SWAT guys, but that left me with an even bigger problem; I had absolutely nothing to go on. And that bothered me. At least when I thought it was a cop, I had suspects. I could investigate. I could eliminate and narrow down the suspect list, just as I had done with Enrique. But now I had nothing. Bupkis, as Benni would say.

And I guess Teddy was right. I had become paranoid.

One thing was certain, though. Someone had tried to execute me. It wasn't just a stray bullet from Donovan or French, and they lied about it just to cover their derrieres. Whoever it was, had tried again at the hospital and failed. Well, at least with me. Reuben didn't get so lucky. If it was a planned assassination, then I had to assume that whoever it was still wanted me dead, and that was an unsettling thought.

I felt safer on Tiki Island. Maybe I should spend more time here, but the house still had a lot of damage. If I stayed here, I'd want to beef up security. Did that make sense in the house the way that it was? Besides, a sliding glass patio door was never a powerful element of security.

I stared at the door to squad room Tiki and considered adding a double deadbolt lock and three-inch security screws, but that provided little security at all. First, the door, like most, opened inward, so someone could easily kick it in. I could resolve that by reversing the door so that it opened out into the hall, but that still didn't improve security too much. The door, a solid chink of wood, was sturdy enough, but it was surrounded by typical residential hollow interior walls. The only thing dividing the room was two sheets of half-inch drywall separated by an occasional two-by-four. A child could kick his way through the wall in little to no time, and it certainly wouldn't stop anyone.

It was time to build a safe room.

I got in the truck, crossed the causeway, and went to Home Depot. I bought a pile of two-by-fours, nails, a hammer, pre-cut insulation, a couple of rolls of chicken wire, a staple hammer, staples, duct tape, three security hinges along with a box of three-inch long security screws. I guesstimated I would need eighteen sheets of drywall; Type X firewall. Finally, I added a kit that had a battery-operated, rechargeable screwdriver, circular saw, and flashlight. And a bag of beef jerky at the checkout.

While I loaded out the truck with the help of an employee, another truck was loading out similar supplies. It bore the logo of Galveston Remodeling. Again, another cleverly named business. I noted the address anyway and drove on over.

The woman was friendly at the remodeling office. I put the wheel in motion to have them pull out all the insulation in the attic and replace it with new. Since they could get on it in a week or so, I gave them my key and headed back out across the causeway.

I stopped at the Tiki Store, collected the spare key I had left with Bob, bought more ice, and went home.

I spent the rest of the day pulling off the drywall from the two interior walls of squad room Tiki. I put insulation between the existing studs and then stapled horizontal rows of chicken wire over where the old drywall used to be. The chicken wire wouldn't prevent someone from coming through, but it would slow them down and snag any power tools they were using.

I pulled the rest of the supplies out of the truck and into the garage and called it a day.

The next day, I continued construction. I put up drywall over the chicken wire. I felt much better about the wall now. Then I framed out a wall that went all the way around the room, all four walls separated from the existing walls by a quarter of an inch. I had to stop to recharge the saw battery before I finished, but I needed the break, anyway. I made another pitcher of iced lemonade while I waited and stared off the back deck into the water by my boat dock.

When I bought the house, I had intended to buy myself a boat, but then life got in the way and I never got around to it. Maybe it was time. After all, having a house on a manmade island with a boat dock seemed naked without a boat. What was the point?

I had stuffed insulation into the newly framed wall as I went, so I finished the day by nailing up the drywall. There was no mud to cover the seams and the gray color of the paper gave the room a depressing air. Still, with another weekend's work to reverse the door, do some finishing touches, and a coat of paint, I'd have an OK safe room. Maybe I'd figure out how to get the gun safe from storage and put it into the room.

***

Sunday, I finally worked up the nerve to go to my sister's house and retrieve my new debit card.

Hannah lived in our parents' home, alone, now that dad had died. It was a rather awkward-looking house in Pirates Cove, with a view of the 12th hole of the Galveston Country Club golf course. We weren't members.

I turned past the squatty palm trees in the front yard into the dull concrete driveway. The sea green house brought back pleasant memories. The only memory that wasn't completely pleasant was the one still living inside.

Typical of the homes in the area, the ground floor consisted of garage space. Hannah and my rooms were on the second floor, and our parent's room perched on a small third floor.

Left of the garage, I put on a smile and climbed a set of stairs leading to the main floor. Despite the door always being unlocked, I rang the doorbell and waited.

Hannah looked the same as I remembered. Her tanned athletic face was crowned by brown hair, long braids slightly bleached by the gulf sun. Her brown eyes still shone atop her high, rounded cheeks.

"What a surprise to see you." Hannah stood frozen in the doorway.

"I guess I should have called first?" I hadn't had the guts to call ahead for fear of a confrontation.

After a moment of awkward silence, "No, of course not. You are always welcome. Come in."

"Look, I'm sorry that you had to bear dad's funeral alone."

"I'm getting over it. We are the only family each other has now."

"Still, I'm sorry."

Hannah led the way into the small living room and sat down on the overstuffed buff-colored couch where our dad always sat.

I followed and took a seat across from her on the matching loveseat. "Sis, I was so deep undercover that it would have been a risk to my life if I had come."

"And yet, you still got shot anyway."

"How did you know?"

"The hospital called. I'm your next of kin, remember?"

"Oh, did I miss you while I was out of it?"

"I didn't say that I came to visit." Touché.

"Dad would have understood."

"Yeah, I know. So would Great Griff." Her tone was one-third frustration, one-third mocking. "The Hunter cop legacy. I'm reminded of it often when I sit here. If I sit wrong, I can feel the .45 dig into my hip."

The 1911 Colt .45 belonged to Great Griffin. Dad kept it tucked between the couch cushions in the event of an unwanted visitor. As kids, we knew it was there and were taught how to use it but to never touch it.

"You could take it out. You want me to take it?"

"No. It gave dad a sense of peace having it there. It still reminds me of him, and that reminder gives me a sense of peace, too."

"Um, did I get an envelope from the bank?"

"Sure did. I didn't know how to reach you to let you know it had arrived."

We chatted about what had happened over the last year, mostly Hannah, since I spent my life hanging out with criminals in strip clubs. When the conversation became strained, I made my excuse, got up, and said goodbye.

Driving past the golf course on Carthegena Way, I thought, "That didn't go that bad at all." and smiled a slight smile of relief.

***

Back at my desk at 1200 Travis, I dug through two more years of cold case files looking for Hispanic strippers. I was a bit surprised that I found several. The girls had all worked at different clubs. No two had worked at the same club as another at the time of their murder. I set aside the ones where there were differences in the murders. That left me with seven similar cases. They had all been harvested on their way home after work. Their bodies were not completely naked, their panties were not found, and someone had strangled them. There was no obvious evidence at the scene.

I went to the crime lab to see if I could get the DNA against each girl run to see if there was a match. A match would prove that they had the same killer. I wanted to match all seven, but they wouldn't consider it. It hadn't popped up as a match before, so it was unlikely it would match again.

And there was another problem. Twenty years ago, the HPD Crime Lab came under scrutiny because of local newscasts that highlighted several criminal cases, including the Josiah Sutton case. Sutton had served over four years for rape based on DNA evidence. That evidence proved to be wrong. The Department requested an independent audit of the Crime Lab's DNA section. Shortly thereafter, the Crime Lab's DNA testing was suspended. For two years.

IA investigated the crime lab. Several supervisors resigned instead of being terminated. Two grand juries were held, but they returned no indictments.

To add insult to injury, nine years ago some city council members blasted the crime lab and argued that they should remove it from under police control. At that time, it was revealed that there were over 4,300 sexual assault kits sitting in the freezer of the HPD property room waiting to be tested. Some dated back to the time of my murders.

The city council got its wish when the crime lab moved

out of 1200 Travis and became the Houston Forensic Science Center in 2014. But only three years later the lab was rocked again by scandal when auditors reviewed 88 cases handled by an officer and found that 65 had incomplete documentation, including 32 with administrative errors. In eight cases, evidence had been misplaced. A year after that, they fired an investigator from the lab over a testing policy violation.

The possibilities were endless. But one thing was certain, the lab was still too backed up to work thirty-year-old cases and even if they did, how reliable would the results be if they had mishandled the samples to start with?

The only way to get it tested would be to send it to an outside lab, but how to find the funding? No one was going to provide that.

21

That afternoon, I took a drive back over to the Chrysalis Hospice Center to drop in on Ms. Dolce.

The receptionist seemed happy to see me. "Griff, it's so good to see you again."

"Is Ms. Dolce doing better today?"

"Yes. She is. I'll need to see some identification."

As I showed her my badge, she purred, "Oh. A detective."

Her welcoming smile broadened. Most people didn't respond that way when they met a detective.

"She is in room...you know what? Let me walk you back to her room."

Dolce was a frail husk with hollow black eyes. Her hair was thin and prematurely gray, probably from her treatments. I couldn't imagine her as an exotic anything.

"I'm Detective Hunter. We spoke before on the phone."

She was startled. "How did you find me? I thought it was anonymous." Quickly followed by "Show me your badge." Which I did.

"Your identity was in the file. From the report that you filed several years ago, the rape report."

A bit deflated, she could only offer a dry, raspy, defeated "Oh."

"I'd like to hear your story first hand if I may..."

She told her story.

When she was 17, she came across the border to live a better life. She found herself working at a strip club in Houston.

As a kid, she ended up with the nickname pickles. She didn't say why. She thought about using that as her stage name but changes it to Pepinillo Dulce (sweet pickle) because the sweet part went well with being a young dancer. She kept the Dulce part for the rest of her life because she like the sound of it, the melody, much better than her real name.

She didn't think of herself as an exotic dancer; she was a stripper, and she knew it and accepted it. What she wasn't was a whore. Coming from poverty, she wasn't used to having much. The tips she received, one dollar at a time, stuffed down her bra, then her panties when the bra was gone, then her garter when the panties were gone, was more than sufficient for her needs with a little to set aside.

She found her dancing experience a liberating way to prove that she had escaped the Mexican culture that held women to different standards than men. Men now clambered to see her, although most still thought of her as a whore. But she wasn't a whore, and she knew it, so it didn't matter that much to her.

She lived in a low-rent apartment, crummy by American standards, but nice compared to what she grew up in. Overall, she was happy with her new life in the states.

On her first night, she didn't receive many tips, but she observed the girls who got the most. This caused her to trim up her pubic hair. She also had to cut her long, black, flowing hair because when it moved to the front, it obscured her petite breasts. She wasn't happy about cutting her hair.

She had been on stage for three months at her first club, a seedy dive when she moved up to The Bush Monkey. The club was nicer, the clientele better, but being nicer, it was in a slightly better part of town, which put her farther away from her apartment. The club offered slightly better security for the girls than her last gig. Still, that security ended at the edge of the parking lot. Some bouncers were just that, big guys who would crack someone's head if need be, but a few were off-duty policemen, earning a few extra dollars to supplement their modest paychecks. The girls primarily looked after one another.

Pickles didn't have a driver's license. ID was still an issue, nor had she saved up enough to buy a car. Not that it mattered. She had never learned to drive, anyway. It was an aspirational dream.

On many nights, she caught a ride with one of the other dancers, but that wasn't always an option since most of them often went on "dates" after work with their admirers. Many of the girls had a steady boyfriend they dated, but with many others, the dates were supplemental income.

At the top of the list for steady boyfriends were the off-duty cops. The policemen were almost always single, because what wife would let her husband stay out until three in the morning hanging out at a strip club? That meant little chance of them lying about not being married. Furthermore, the idea of having a protector wasn't a bad thing. Security and protection are primal needs. Independent, modern woman or not, working in a strip club came with risks, and a boyfriend with a gun and a badge helped satisfy that need.

A few weeks after Pickles started working at The Bush Monkey, another cop joined the security team. Being new, he wasn't attached to any of the girls yet. Everyone called him Mick.

Mick was tall and handsome, with a full head of rich, dark hair. He was the perfect balance of polite, respectful, and playful. In a word, charming.

All the girls who didn't already have steady boyfriends eyed Mick, as well as one who had a boyfriend. Pickles was no exception. But Mick wasn't quick to get attached to any one girl based on their physical assets. Mick seemed to take an interest in the girls, finding out more about each one, who they were, and their past. Things like that.

She rested for a bit. When she had caught her breath, I prodded, "Go on."

"I just can't. Perhaps another day."

The interview was over and the only new thing that I had was a name, Mick. That and a lot of sympathy for this woman who had lived a rough life and was dying too soon.

I was miffed she wouldn't give me the last name. Then again, I understood her reticence at some level since I was having my own issues with corrupt cops.

As I was leaving, the girl at the front desk called me over.

"How'd it go?"

"Depressing actually."

"Yeah, there is a lot of that here. You coming back, Detective Hunter?"

"Yep. Still more to do. Perhaps she will be feeling better the next time."

"Don't count on it."

As I headed for the door, she added, "Don't wait too long."

22

Mick sat in near darkness in his Colonial-style home in The Woodlands, illuminated only by the alien blue glow of a nearby monitor and his memories. His manicured fingers held a Waterford snifter, which in turn held Cognac Prunier VSOP. Mick's eyes closed as he noted the rich fruity and floral aromas with notes of apple, rose, and light orange. A careful sip rewarded his palate with flavors of a taste of oak and left a well-balanced burn that warmed the tip of his tongue.

He still remembered that road trip he and his high school buddies made to Nuevo Laredo at the end of their senior year, like it was yesterday. The five-hour trip would be worth it; it would be his first time. Crossing the border was quick and easy back then and the town had a long history of looking the other way when the gringos came to enjoy the nocturnal entertainment with their American dollars. So much so that they had carved out a "zone of tolerance" known by the gringos as Boys Town.

Mick found himself and his two friends outside a rundown whitewashed cinder block building, with a garish yellow stripe, barred windows, and painted signs of local cerveza brands. Numerous arches were serving no purpose surrounding the outdoor patio, but the most prominent arch over the wooden door bore hand-painted lettering "Donkey Show Every Night."

"That can't be real," Mick said.

"That's not what I've heard." Replied Tommy, one of his friends.

"That's not what we came here for." Said the other

friend, "I came here to get drunk and get laid."

"Of course, that's why we came," said Mick. "This looks like as good a place as any, at least to get drunk."

Tommy headed for the door and Mick followed. The third one said, "I'll meet up with you later. I'm going down there." He jerked a thumb to an ugly bright purple building with a sign that simply said "Women Here" and turned up the street.

The cantina was grubby, but no one seemed to notice. It smelled of beer, sweat, smoke, and some other odor that Mick couldn't quite identify. They sat at a small round cocktail table on metal folding chairs that had "Corona" stamped into the backrest of the chair. A scantily clad senorita delivered their cerveza, leaned over the table exposing most of her breasts, and smiled alarmingly. Her breath smelled bad.

By the end of their second beer, a short, rather stocky woman with curly black hair walked out onto the "stage", which was just an area in the center of the bar with bare plywood raised on some two-by-sixes underneath with some sort of stepped platform in the middle. Music from some unknown source blared Stevie Wonder's Superstition. While the woman danced to the rhythm, she removed her outer layer of clothing. She looked bored.

It took three songs before she was buck-naked. More cerveza was served. The "entertainer" headed toward the rear of the stage. Mick expected her to disappear behind the red velvet curtain that hung there, but instead, she pulled it open. Revealing a miniature donkey. Mick and Tommy stared at each other, speechless.

This time the music blasted Cher's hit Half Breed. The

woman strutted around the stage in a small circle leading the donkey. For a full 3 minutes. They were milking it for all it was worth. Another round of cerveza.

A man appeared on stage and took the donkey's lead. The impresario of this freak circus. The woman took a position on the stepped platform as the beast was led over to the platform as well.

Tension built as everyone waited for the next song to start. Tommy looked like he was going to throw up. "Oh, man. I can't watch this." Tommy ran for the door as the man signaled the poor animal. Another cerveza.

Finally, as Gilbert O'Sullivan's Get Down started up, the donkey's front legs stepped up to the highest level of the platform. Of course, Mick couldn't tell if the donkey had penetrated her or not. He was too inexperienced to know, anyway. But it didn't matter. What did matter was that he had watched this woman defile herself.

After the show, Mick stumbled out of the cantina and found his buddies at the nearby strip club "Women Here" where Tommy was getting a lap dance. To Mick, it didn't look all that different from the donkey act, with Tommy playing the role of the donkey. He watched as that dancer defiled herself, too.

Mick had done a good job of the first goal of the night; getting drunk. They all had. If he hadn't been so drunk, Mick would probably never have been so bold. But in his current state, he walked right up to one of the naked women coming off the stage at the end of her number. "Let's go someplace more private where we can, you know..."

"Twenty dollars."

"You got it."

She held out her hand and just stood there. Not knowing what else to do, Mick gave her an Andrew Jackson. She didn't have any pockets to put it in.

"I'll go put something on. Meet me out front in a few minutes."

Mick waited out front obediently. For an hour. At first, he was afraid to go back inside for fear that he'd missed her. When it became apparent that she wasn't coming, he checked back inside, but no one knew who or what he was talking about. Selective understanding of English.

Mick sat next to the club for another hour, embarrassed at his stupidity. His anger rose the entire time. Eventually, a door opened near the back of the club and a woman stepped out into the night air. It was her. The stripper who took his money. She turned toward the alley behind the club and walked away.

Mick started to yell at her, but he didn't want his money back. That wasn't why he'd come to Laredo. He wanted what he'd paid for. He decided then and there that he was going to get his money's worth, too.

As she turned into the alley, Mick sprinted to catch up, his adrenaline rising. He had closed most of the distance before she sensed someone and turned around. They were past the club now, still in the alley. She reached into a pocket in her miniskirt and pulled out a twenty, but by that time Mick was on her. He slapped her hand aside, causing Andrew Jackson to tumble to the ground.

Her eyes showed little emotion, but she tried to scream. Mick's hand shot out and grabbed her by the throat. He followed through with the entire weight of his body, shoving her to the gravel with him, landing hard on top of her. Perhaps it was because Mick was a full foot taller than she was, or she had the wind knocked out of her from the tackle, or she simply knew that she had to give it up for another paying john, but she didn't resist.

Mick tugged her mini skirt off, followed by her panties. His jeans dropped to his knees, and he was on her. He put his hands on her neck again to make sure that she would be quiet and to control her. For the first time in the evening, some kind of emotion flickered in her eyes. As he pounded her back into the gravel, he supported his upper body weight with his hands. The ones on her throat. When she struggled, it made it feel better. It didn't take him long. He stopped pounding. She had stopped struggling. Feeling his satisfaction, he sat upright, straddling her.

Her face was still. Her eyes seemed to bug out of her head the slightest bit and looked somewhat bloodshot. As Mick panted, he realized that her entire body was completely still. She was making no effort to get up. In an instant, the intoxication cleared, and it dawned on him. He leaned back down on her to see if she was breathing. She wasn't. He studied her face carefully and, looking deeply into her eyes, realized that they were completely lifeless. She was dead.

Nick should have been afraid. Or shocked. But another wave of heat swelled up in his crotch and another wave of exultation swept over his body. The experience was better than when he had been inside her. It etched a lasting memory into his psyche. He knew she had already defiled herself countless times, but now he had desecrated her once and for all.

Mick picked up her miniskirt and dragged her slight,

limp body to the edge of the gravel and onto some sparse adjoining grass. As he turned to leave, he saw her cheap panties still in the gravel along with the twenty-dollar bill. He stepped over to the panties, picked them up, and slipped them into his pants pocket. He looked at the currency but left it. It was hers. He paid for it and she earned it.

He strolled confidently out of the alley and back onto the street where they had parked the car, where he waited for his friends to return. He had experienced a new kind of intoxication.

Now, sitting in his overstuffed brown leather chair, Mick took another sip of his cognac and, reliving the experience, let a wave of pleasure wash over him. Although the effect was exhilarating, it also left him empty, yearning for a fresh kill.

Unfortunately, a change in circumstances had made it all but impossible for Mick to take part in his pastime anymore. He had been prolific in Houston while he was in his twenties. The introduction of DNA testing had been a serious setback for him because, after all, he didn't want to be caught and publically disgraced. For a while, he relived the mounting pressure by visiting an assortment of border towns. But then the drug lords moved in and made that an unappealing prospect. Even when he was in high school, there was violence that occurred between the drug dealers and the Federales, but that rarely spilled over onto the tourists. But for the last decade, it was completely different. Rotting in a Mexican jail was nothing compared to what the cartels could do.

So, for now, he would relive that first moment with Juanita. He did not know what her name was, nor did he care, but he had given her a name for his fantasies all the same. Of course, he had refined his skills over the years, but he forgot their names. After all, you always remember your first love. As tonight's reenactment in his mind faded, Mick knew he had to come to terms with a new problem.

Griffin Hunter. With him rooting around in the cold case files. He reminded himself, *his* cold case files. With Hunter rooting around in his cold case files, Mick couldn't risk that Griff could make a connection between all of his girls, or especially to him. Oh, Mick had cultivated a mutually beneficial relationship with someone inside the department that had allowed him to make sure that there would never be a DNA match back to him, but one couldn't be too careful. Mick hadn't gotten to where he was by being careless.

No. Something had to be done. He couldn't have direct contact with the man who would eliminate Griff, which also would be too risky. Plus, it would give the man something to hold over Mick's head. And what if he didn't succeed and Griff killed his man instead?

Actually, that might not be that bad either. If his man killed Griff, then Mick didn't have to worry about the investigation into the files. If Griff killed Mick's man, then the link to the tampered evidence would be eliminated, thus reducing the risk of Griff's investigation to a tolerable level. It was a win-win situation for Mick. All he had to do was signal his man without having direct contact.

After another glass of cognac, Mick shuffled over to his safe, pulled out a burner phone, and sent a text to one of his mutual contacts. "Let someone know that Hunter has been asking about DNA results in some old cases." She would forward the message and his man would figure out what needed to be done out of an interest to protect his hide. Mick would chuck the burner tomorrow.

***

The next morning, the sniper opened his gun safe, just like he did every morning. He repeated his ritual and looked at the text message. This time, the number it came from hadn't been as much of a surprise. "Det. Hunter has been inquiring about DNA in some cold cases." Crud. This changed things.

It no longer mattered what the previous text had said. Griffin Hunter had to die. Soon.

23

He wore black pants with black shoes over black socks. His hair was black, cropped close, and combed straight back. A small black mustache hung above his lips. He moved with an air of confidence that most men never feel. Perhaps the attractive woman in the black fishnet stockings by his side made him look more confident than he was. But no, he was confident in his abilities.

The starched white shirt contrasted with everything else, especially the black tailcoat over it. From seemingly nowhere, that man produced a small red ball. It contrasted nicely with his attire, but matched the skimpy outfit the woman wore.

The magician tossed the ball up into the air above his head. His eyes intently followed the ball, causing his head to rise. His assistant's eyes followed the ball into the air as well. The ball reached the top of its arc and dropped back into his open hand, followed by his eyes and those of his assistant.

He tossed the ball up into the air a second time, his eyes trained on it. His assistant watched it rise and fall as well until it was back in his hand. The magician's eyes landed on the ball a half second later.

He threw the ball up into the air a third time. The assistant leaned slightly forward, dipping her cleavage toward the audience. He looked up. His assistant looked up. The audience looked up. But the ball wasn't anywhere to be seen. As if by magic, the ball had disappeared.

It wasn't magic, of course. He never threw the ball the third time. It sat in plain sight in his hand as everyone's eyes lifted up. If anyone had not looked up but had kept staring at his hand, they would have seen him palm the ball. For those few not following the ball, the assistant's minor movement provided enough motion to involuntarily draw the eyes toward her for a tenth of a second.

I could finally articulate what had been bothering me about the sniper's nest. I lifted my head and cleared my throat to get Q's attention. "Why would a guy leave a shell casing at a scene when everything else was wiped clean, including the casing itself?"

Q thought for a moment. "He could drop a different caliber shell to misdirect the investigation into thinking a different gun was used. Drop a thirty-eight when he used a nine millimeter. But that would only work if the bullet wasn't recovered."

"I don't think that's it. The caliber was right."

"Well," Q paused. "I suppose he could leave a calling card. He wanted you to find it."

"Hmm. Thanks."

I started looking at my murder/rape files again. One of the remaining files indicated a friend had thought the victim used to date a policeman, but there wasn't a name given in the file. A security guard could be mistaken for a policeman by most people. Cheryl and Nancy were known to have security guard friends. It was tenuous, but was enough for me to pull that file into the circle.

Despite this potential discovery, I was finding it hard to concentrate on the stripper investigation. Since my brief conversation with Q, something was churning in my subconscious that was distracting me.

I finally decided that maybe it wasn't what Q had said,

but was the unresolved issue of what to do about Donovan. To clear my head, I decided to do a little B and E. I'd break into Donovan's glove box again and relieve him of his illegal drugs.

But despite its much-celebrated use, Rohypnol wasn't even legal to prescribe in the United States. Rohypnol was developed to treat insomnia, and it certainly does a good job of that. But the misuse was so problematic that in 1998 they added a blue dye to the formula to make it easier to detect in drinks. By 2016, they had pulled the drug from Spain, France, Germany, and the UK. Of course, most roofies in the U.S. weren't real, and the counterfeiters certainly didn't put blue dye in their formulations.

Even if Donovan had a legitimate prescription for the oxy, why would he put it in a different bottle?

What would be the safest way to get at the drugs? Breaking into his car while it was parked in the department lot seemed like an exceptionally bad idea. I decided that checking the Golf course parking lot next Sunday might be worthwhile, but there was no guarantee that he would be there. Besides, I wanted to spend the weekend finishing the safe room at the Tiki house.

***

Q came back from lunch. "The buzz is that the hostage negotiator got called out."

"What else did you hear?"

"Some guy got into an argument with his wife. He cut himself on some broken glass. The wife got out but called it in. When patrol got there he had barricaded himself inside, said he was armed, and was threatening to kill himself."

"Huh." If the hostage negotiator was called to the scene, that probably meant that SWAT was there too. I normally hate Twitter, but it had its moments. I checked and sure enough, a tweet from the HPD showed SWAT had been dispatched and gave the address.

That still didn't solve the problem of getting at Donovan's car, it was still in the department lot, but if he was one of the team members included in the response, chances were he wouldn't be leaving work at the usual time tonight. The team would probably hit a bar after work to decompress and celebrate. Depending on the bar, it might be less risky than the department lot. Having a car broken into in a bar parking lot wasn't all that unusual, even if it was a cop bar.

O'Ryan's seemed like a nice enough place. The parking lot was more lit up than I would have liked, but I couldn't see any security cameras on the lot. I'd followed Donovan here once they finally cleared the shift. After a few minutes had passed, I slid carefully along the row of parked cars. I paused at the passenger side rear bumper of Donovan's car. Just as I was about to make my move, a set of headlights swept over me from a big pickup truck entering the lot. It was French's truck. Great.

I continued into O'Ryan's. someone had carefully staged the atmosphere with an Irish pub motif. I grabbed a Lone Star at the bar, then headed over to the SWAT crew. No sense in pretending that I hadn't been there at this point.

Enrique was telling a cop joke in Spanish. "El policía buscaba el ladrón de las gallinas. Cuando le veí él llama con su radio y dijo. ¡Apoyo, apoyo!"

It was a pun because in Spanish, the words chicken and help pretty much sound the same. "Hear you guys had a long day," I said.

Enrique spoke. "Long and hot. The negotiator talked to the guy for, like, an hour. Then the guy suddenly stopped talking, so we went in. He had passed out from blood loss. Sort of anti-climactic."

Skinner said, "Haven't seen you here for a while. What since the thing with Benni?"

"Yeah. But since the discovery of that nest, we know someone on Poliakoff's team is after me. Doubt he'll make a hit at a cop bar." That much was true.

One corner of French's mouth momentarily curled up into a sort of smile.

After some small talk and another Lone Star, I slipped out of O'Ryan's, got in my car, and re-parked in a lot across the street for no particular reason. "He wanted you to find it." That was what Q had said that was bothering me, not what to do about Donovan.

My mind drifted back to the sniper's nest. Our team had to set up before sunrise so that they wouldn't be spotted going into the building. They would have been scanning the street all morning as well. Anyone walking the street with a bag long enough to conceal a rifle would have caused suspicion, but nothing like that had been noted. What did that mean?

One of two things. Either someone carried a rifle in, and that tidbit was intentionally left out of the report. If that were the case, it would have to have been a conspiracy to leave it out of the reports. Otherwise, the sniper would have entered the building, or at the very least planted the rifle there before the team was in place.

How did the sniper get out of the building? Once again, anyone carrying something that could have concealed a rifle would have caught someone's attention. It would have been risky to leave it behind and return to the scene of the crime to pick it up later, and it would have been near dawn before the crime scene crew and detectives would have finally left. That meant that the sniper would have to have spent eighteen to twenty-four hours in the apartment. And that meant that he would have used the john. I'd have to check the crime scene report, but no one had mentioned it being wiped down. I'd check on that.

I needed to figure this out. Maybe the whole Donovan thing was just distracting me from something more important. Wait. That thought triggered something.

Donovan's Camaro backed out of its space and left the bar's lot. With that action, the thought disappeared from my mind just as quickly as it had flashed in.

I decided to follow Donovan anyway, even if it was a distraction. He pulled into the lot of a CVS, climbed out, and went inside. The lot was pretty empty. It was a bad idea, but the Lone Stars clouded my judgment. I was able to pull in and park next to Donovan's car.

I pulled on Nitrile gloves and slipped out of my car, ready to pick the passenger door. In the corner of my vision, I could see that the driver's door was unlocked. Nice. I quickly, but casually, crossed to the driver's side, opened the door, and slid in. The glove box was still locked but gave way to the picks quickly. I started to take the bottles, but instead dumped the contents into my pocket and left the bottles. It might take longer for him to realize that they were gone if he opened the box for another reason, or periodically checked it.

I slipped out of the passenger door, locked it, closed it, and slid into my truck. Pulling away, I saw Donovan leaving the store and approaching his car. I pulled out onto the street in the opposite direction from his home and drove slowly away. I watched in the rear-view mirror, but he didn't delay his departure, pulled out, and drove toward home.

I didn't realize how tense I was, but seeing that he hadn't discovered the theft caused a wave of relief to wash over my whole body. With that release, the flash returned. It wasn't Donovan that was the distraction; it was the sniper's nest. "Damn." It was a distraction. A misdirection planted to make me look elsewhere and close any internal investigations. That's what French's fleeting almost smile meant. French just moved back to the top of my suspect list.

Well, it was good for him to think that I had taken the bait.

24

He wore black pants with black boots over black socks. A nondescript black baseball cap suppressed his wavy hair underneath. He moved with an air of confidence that most men never feel. But this was no magician. Well, he was there to make things disappear, so maybe he was a magician after all.

Donovan walked directly to Griff's apartment door and worked at the lock. "I see you upgraded the lock. Makes no difference. I wonder if the manager knows. Probably a violation of your lease." The lock yielded, and he pushed the door open.

As he expected, the lights were off in the apartment still. He slid inside and gently closed the door behind him. He stood silently for a full fifteen seconds, listening for any sounds inside or outside. Nothing.

Donovan took about five steps inside. A dog barked. From inside. His heart jumped, but only for a second. Griff didn't have a dog, at least that anyone knew of, and this dog sounded big. Too big for a small apartment. Besides, most apartments don't allow large dogs anyway.

After recovering from the initial start, Donovan moved carefully further into the apartment, directly toward the source of the barking. The bark grew louder as he advanced, but it also sounded too repetitious. A small gray box sat on the floor. An alarm. "Nice." He raised his leg and stomped down with his heavy combat boot on the box. The barking stopped. Donovan smiled.

Griff wasn't home, of course, Donovan had made certain of that. Still, he cleared the apartment room by room, just as he did when the team entered a home on the job. Clear.

Donovan made a methodical sweep of the place. He took his time. He pulled out drawers, dumped them, and looked underneath them to ensure nothing was taped to the bottoms. He ransacked every cupboard and the medicine cabinet. He dug through every pocket in every piece of clothing. Since Donovan took part in drug raids, he looked at all the places a dealer might hide stuff; inside the toilet tank, air conditioner vents, like that.

He pulled a cheap picture off the wall. "Bingo." He removed an SD card that had been taped to the back and slid it into his pocket. It had been a fruitful effort, after all.

He grabbed the laptop and the two thumb drives sitting nearby and a few other odds and ends and headed toward the door. He paused. Griff had the dog alarm; what else did he have? Donovan returned to the bedroom and pulled the pillowcase off. He then walked around the apartment and took anything that was plugged into the wall, starting with the digital alarm clock. He pulled a chair over, rotated the smoke detector, disconnected it from the ceiling, and dropped it into the pillowcase as well. He took another circuit around the apartment for anything that could be a covert camera.

Satisfied that he had everything, he carefully opened the door, took a quick peek outside to ensure no one was nearby, then casually strolled out into the daylight, pillowcase in hand, closing the door behind him. He left the door unlocked. If he were really lucky, some dumbass would try the door, leave his prints on it, and step inside. Not likely, but it could happen.

As soon as he was out, Donovan tugged off his nitrile gloves and stuffed them into the pillowcase. The pillowcase looked slightly out of place, but since many people put their dirty laundry in one when going to the laundromat, he hoped it wouldn't be noteworthy if anyone noticed him at all. But the gloves would have been a dead giveaway.

***

That night, Donovan made the quick seven-minute trip to his Montrose townhouse. No stops tonight. There was work to be done. He turned off Alabama onto Montrose Boulevard, then into the driveway and through the security gate into the parking lot. He tucked the laptop up under his arm, grabbed the pillowcase, walked past the exercise room, and headed to the elevators.

Exiting on seven, he stood in front of his door and thought about how easy it had been to break into Griff's Northshore apartment. Maybe he should beef up his own security and do a better job of concealing things he didn't want to be discovered at his pad. He unlocked the door and went inside.

Donovan dropped the pillowcase inside the door, moved through the entryway, and set the laptop down on the wood-toned breakfast bar. He passed the two classic cruiser bicycles decoratively hung on the faux brick wall and turned down the hall to the bathroom. He slid open the white laminate drawer and pulled out the beer-colored Carbinoxamine prescription bottle, popped the top, and chugged down an oxy. Before it entered his mouth, he looked at it. Didn't want to swallow the wrong one by mistake. That would never do.

Looking right, past the long ultra-modern bathtub, he could see the kitchen through a ceiling tall window the designer had put there. He initially thought that it was weird, but it suited his lifestyle to see into the bathroom from the kitchen. If he wanted privacy, there was a white shade that could be lowered, but how to do it wasn't obvious to his usually inebriated guests.

Exiting down the hallway, he turned right, passed the modern electronic fireplace mounted into a stark white wall and stood before the sliding patio doors, and took in his view while he waited for the latest hit of oxy to kick in. The seventh floor was high enough that Donovan could see the lights of Downtown Houston over the roof of the parking garage.

He liked Montrose even though Texas Monthly had called it the "strangest neighborhood east of the Pecos." Once an enclave of Houston's gay men, it had become revitalized over the last decade as the gay population moved out to Houston Heights and the suburbs. The novel *The Knife and the Butterfly* was based on a teenage MS-13 gang member named Gabriel Granillo, who was stabbed to death just a mile from Donovan's. Now it was simply close to work, trendy and vibrant.

Donovan turned around, passed the modern white sofa, and returned to the breakfast bar. He opened the laptop and powered it on. While waiting for it to boot up, he continued into the sterile white kitchen, and pulled a Funky Buddha 'Last Buffalo in the Park' out of the fridge. The white and gold label claimed it was a porter, but it tasted more like a mounds candy bar that had been soaked in bourbon.

The laptop was password protected. Donovan wasn't surprised, just slightly disappointed. That could be resolved. He fired up his own computer and inserted the SD card he had found taped to the back of the picture on Griff's wall. It never occurred to him it could contain a virus. Encrypted. There was probably someone he knew that could help with that.

Next, he moved on to the two thumb drives. Encrypted as well. Since nothing from the electronics was going to give up its secrets tonight, Donovan dumped out the contents of the pillowcase on the whitewashed oak laminate floor and pawed through the debris. He cracked open the cases of all the electronics one by one. People had been known to hide heroin in the voids inside such cases. No heroin, of course, but inside the clock, he discovered a hidden SD card, slid into a small electronics board. He followed the wires from the board to the face of the clock. Hmm.

He pulled the SD card out of the alarm clock, slipped it into his computer and, with a couple of clicks, was seeing himself inside Griff's apartment. That rattled Donovan as much as he could remember in recent times. A long puff of air blew out between his lips. He was glad that he had taken everything that had a power cord attached to it. He replayed the excursion into Griff's apartment in his mind. Had he overlooked anything? No, he had even taken the toaster.

Donovan didn't want to think about how Griff would react if he had evidence that he had burglarized his apartment. Then he remembered the dog alarm. He had smashed it but hadn't taken the remains with him. Donovan frantically searched online and quickly found the device. It was widely available. To his relief, it didn't have a hidden camera.

He knew that he would have to go through the few non-electronic items he purloined, but was now too stressed to go on. Besides, the actual gold would be on the SD card once he figured out how, or rather, who could get past the encryption. Donovan needed to blow off some steam, so he headed down to his car.

He drove a couple of miles to a bar that he had never been to before, parked, and slid the keys into the glove compartment lock. He didn't use the roofie to get companions to go with him. It was easy enough for him to get them to go willingly and it didn't raise suspicion as it did with guys who had to practically drag a nearly unconscious date out of a bar. No, instead he slipped it into their drink right before he was confident that they would leave willingly. He wouldn't get them to his pad before it had kicked in enough so that they wouldn't remember where they had gone, nor the fun and games that had followed. He often wished that he had an attached garage to simplify getting the dates in and out, but it was what it was.

The air going down his throat made a sucking sound. The bottle was empty. How could that be? Donovan struggled with his thoughts for a moment. Had he used the last one and not remembered to refill the bottle? No, that wasn't it. Suddenly, he felt violated.

His stress had peaked at a new level. He couldn't go inside now. He had to go home and figure this out.

Sitting on the white sofa, he tried to focus. Donovan had taken another oxy and washed it down with another

Buffalo. The oxy wasn't really for stress, but it still calmed him down a notch. The parking at the townhouses was pretty secure. He'd review the surveillance tapes tomorrow. With the request coming from a cop, the property manager wouldn't resist. Still, he was sure it had to have happened somewhere else. Unable to resolve the issue in his mind, and without his planned "companionship", Donovan was forced to rely on a video that he took during one of his previous exploits.

Donovan was pissed.

25

I was pissed.

My apartment had been ransacked. Again. I stared at the crumpled pile of plastic and circuitry that used to be my doggie alarm. I turned to where the clock radio was supposed to be. Gone. That didn't seem like money well spent, either. Sigh.

I walked through the debris to the picture on the floor and flipped it over. I couldn't help but smile. "Got you." Let's hope you're as dumb as I think you are. But first, it was my turn to feel dumb. I no longer had a laptop. I surveyed the damage for another minute or two, then headed out. Nothing more to do here.

While on the drive over to Best Buy, I called Krunch. "You'll never believe it. My apartment got ransacked again...No, the new one."

"You call it in?"

"No. Do you think it would do any good?"

"Any chance it was just a burglary?" She asked.

"Seems unlikely. I may have a way to find out who did it this time, though. I'll at least wait until I see if that pans out. Do you have any suggestions?"

"Let me think about it. I'm so sorry, Griff. You gonna stay there tonight or what?"

"I haven't decided yet. I just needed to talk to someone." We chatted until I arrived at Best Buy, then clicked off.

Inside, I bought a new laptop, a couple of new thumb drives, another SD card, and a pack of recordable DVD discs. Back in the parking lot, I thought about going to the

Tiki house, but it wasn't habitable yet. Another night in a motel? No. I went back to the apartment and turned out onto the street.

I didn't do any cleanup. There would be time for that later. The highest priority would be to get the computer set up and see if the burglar had taken the bait. There would be time to make the bed while files downloaded.

While I was waiting for the endless Windows updates, I surveyed the damage. The contents of the freezer had been dumped out onto the floor, but at least he'd left the Lone Star in the fridge. I popped one open, poured it into a glass and, after finding the shaker, sprinkled a little salt in.

That day, I had re-read the crime scene report on the sniper's nest. The handle to the toilet had not been wiped down, yet the only print on it was from the previous tenant. That meant that the sniper had not spent the time in the apartment that it would have taken, or else he had Texas' largest bladder. Or he peed into a bottle and took it out with him. I suppose that could be possible.

The computer beeped. I logged in and downloaded the software that I needed from the cloud. I opened up the program and didn't have to wait long to be gratified. They had placed the SD card into another computer, and it was online. "Got you, you little worm!" With a couple of keystrokes, I had the IP address of the host computer. A few more clicks and the commands were sent to download the contents of the host computer to mine. How could I not help but smile?

I focused on the progress bar, but watching hundreds of files download is like watching grass grow. The IP address by itself wouldn't tell me who the computer belonged to. The downloaded files may or may not give away the identity of the owner, depending on what he used his computer for. As I sat there staring blankly around the room, my eyes landed on the wall outlet above the kitchen counter. I'd forgotten about it.

I went in and picked up a knife from the floor. Using the tip, I turned the off-white screw between the two outlets until the plastic cover popped off. The bottom plug didn't have power to it but instead had a slot off to the side containing a micro SD card. I pressed it with my fingernail and it sprang out of its slot. "Oh, I really got you now."

Files were still downloading, and the laptop didn't have a built-in slot for micro SDs. The burglar had taken the two adapters that were in the apartment, even though they had no cards in them. Fortunately, the SD card that I just purchased a half hour ago was a micro SD in an SD adapter. I doubted I would ever buy a standard SD card again.

After having to retrieve a steak knife to get into the packaging for the new card/adapter, I pulled the new micro SD out of the adapter and slid in the one from the wall plug. That covert camera had been expensive. But in the end, it was the only one that proved to be worth the investment.

I slid the Adapter into the laptop's slot. The download would continue in the background. There wasn't a video player installed with Windows, so I had to download one. Seriously? After installing VLC Media Player, I clicked the video file on the SD card's directory. The player started up and after a few seconds, "Hello Donovan."

My curiosity was extreme now. I was on the hunt. I looked at the progress bar for the files being downloaded from the computer at the other end of the line. It was still downloading files. Nevertheless, I looked at the directory for the files that had been downloaded. There was an assortment of documents and spreadsheets that I would pour over later. More interesting was a series of video files. What made them interesting was that most of them were encrypted. Why encrypt them if they are selfies from your vacation? The jackpot was that the file didn't appear to be locked. Either it wasn't encrypted at all, or it was being viewed at the very moment I was downloading it and the video player had it unlocked. Didn't matter, it was the easiest thing to look at for right now, so I clicked the file open.

The file started with Donovan's face right up in the camera. He was turning it on. As he pulled away, I could see that he had set the camera up in a bedroom, probably covertly, since it appeared to be a wide-angle view. Even with a wide-angle view, the room looked narrow. The far wall was brick, surrounding a rather large window with white curtains drawn. The side walls were white and only allowed about three feet on either side of the bed. The head of the bed was below the window, the foot nearest the camera. A coffee table sat up against the footboard with a throw pillow on it. The ceiling was of a concrete, open beam design, painted white. Two light bulbs dangled down on cords with old industrial-style disc reflectors above them. If it weren't for the window and the modern laminate floor, I would have thought that I was looking at a room in some kind of underground bunker.

I thought I knew what was coming, but I wasn't quite as prepared as I thought I was. A man staggered into the bedroom, supported by Donovan. The man appeared to be drunk and could barely stand, much less walk. Donovan guided him down on the bed and undressed both of them. I didn't want to watch the rest. I fast-forwarded to near the end. Just before Donovan's face returned to turn off the camera, I could see that his unwilling guest was still in one piece and appeared to still be breathing.

The video clicked off, and I just sat there. That was what he had been using the Rohypnol for.

***

Back at my desk the next day, I called Nick. "Did Krunch tell you what happened last night?"

"About your apartment? Yeah."

"I need your advice. I think the burglar might be someone on the force."

It hung there like a stench.

Nick said, "You got any proof of that?"

I did, but I wasn't sure that I wanted to talk about that yet. The covert video of Donovan being inside my apartment was golden and would be admissible in court. But if I disclosed it, IA would surely examine it. That would lead to the question about what he removed from the back of the picture. That would lead down a rabbit hole that ended with me illegally downloading the contents of Donovan's computer. I wasn't ready to go there. At least not yet.

"It's more than just a hunch." It was the best answer that I could think of.

"My advice. Do nothing. You already stirred the hornets' nest by suggesting that tactical might have been involved in your shooting. Frankly, you'll sound paranoid.

In fact, you do sound paranoid, even to me. You need to make certain you have solid proof. Who? And more importantly, why? You need a motive? If a cop is snooping around your place, he has to have a reason. Are you sure that you want IA to dig into what he was looking for? And what is he going to tell IA? He'll have some kind of story to put it back on you."

"Sadly, I see your point."

"Even if you have all of that lined up solid, you still run a better than fifty percent chance of hitting the Blue Wall. If that happens, then you need to have a plan for the blowback."

"OK. Thanks for the advice."

"It's free, but you should take it. Trust me on this."

I felt defeated. I was going to be completely on my own.

***

After a while, my thoughts drifted back to my Donovan problem. He had roofies, and he apparently used them to drug gay men and bring them back to his apartment. Combined with B&E, it was a pattern of disturbing behavior for a guardian of public safety. But Nick was right. What did that get me? No one would care about his private life. You couldn't prove the use of the roofie on the guy from the video, and the pills I took out of his glove compartment were inadmissible. In fact, that would blow back on me for breaking into his car, and that would wash even with his breaking into my apartment.

Great Griffin had said, "If you wrestle with pigs, you

get dirty. And the pig loves it." Donovan was the pig, and if I wrestled with him, I was going to get some on me, too. I would need more. A lot more.

I did a cold case search for men that had gone missing, reported a rape, or were found dead with Rophynol in their system. Plenty were missing, but virtually none had reported being date raped. But a few turned up dead. I pulled up the homicides and printed out the ones within a few miles of Donovan's condo. I'd plot them on the board next time I went to the Tiki office.

As I studied the files, one jumped out at me. Although most of the men looked similar, one guy resembled the guy in Donovan's bedroom video. I couldn't be sure. In the video, the guy's back was to the camera when he came in, and by the time you could see him on the bed, the image was pretty small and the angle looking up from his chin. Still, there was something about him that looked familiar.

26

As Donovan handed him the SD card, the technician said, "I really shouldn't be doing this." He then slid the SD card into a small box with multiple slots of varying sizes. The box was connected to a small desktop computer with a cable. That Computer was in turn connected to a larger tower computer. There was a large red sign hanging over the setup that said in white letters do not connect these computers to the network. "It may take a while to crack the password. You can come back later if you want."

Donovan's eyes darted nervously across the three large monitors on the counter, not knowing what he was looking at. "Thanks, but I'll wait." He stood in anticipation of what the card would yield, hoping that nothing would be displayed on the screens that would incriminate him. After all, who knew what Griff had been up to? He only wanted the tech to provide him the password, not look at any of the contents, but Donavan wasn't sure how such things worked and didn't want to leave the card alone with the technician, just in case.

"Uh Oh." The Technician stabbed at the keyboard. "Did you plug this thing into any other computers?"

"Why? What's wrong?" Donovan wanted to avoid the answer, at least for now.

The technician was pulling the card out of the slot. As he held it up, he triumphantly said, "This little nasty has an updated variant of the E.T. Trojan on it." Then he sighed. "Now I have an hour's work ahead of me to ghost the test machine."

"In layman's terms?"

"A Trojan, like in the Trojan Horse. The original captured keystrokes for passwords and the like, sometimes opening a back door. This version just sweeps through your directories and sends every file type they have configured it to look for."

"Sends where?"

"Home. Wherever it came from. It was called E.T. because it wants to phone home."

Donovan's gut knotted as he comprehended what he was being told. "So if this would have been plugged into a computer..."

"Everything on that computer would have been sent to whoever the card came from. Assuming that they connected it to the internet." The tech put the SD card back in Donovan's hand.

Donovan stared down at the innocent-looking piece of plastic. "Humph." He turned, flatly said "I owe you one." and left the room. He couldn't say thank you; he wasn't very thankful.

He had been sucker punched.

What did Griff have? Donovan's mind began racing as he thought about everything that was on his laptop. Each thing he thought of made him think about something even worse. It went beyond embarrassing. He had to put the genie back in the bottle. His fists involuntarily clenched.

He had to get revenge on Griff.

It wouldn't be enough to kill Griff at this point. Not yet. He needed to get Griff alone, in private.

Donovan spent the rest of the day distracted, trying to come up with ideas.

He had wanted to track Griff's cell phone, but it turned

out to be more of a problem that it was on TV. Warrants, privacy, blah, blah, blah. The group that did that sort of thing was under a different command. So was the tech guy who had helped him with the SD card, but Donovan knew him. He wasn't able to help with the tracking.

Putting a GPS tracker on Griff's truck didn't prove to be any easier. The department had them, of course, but you had to have a warrant to check one out. Fourth amendment the courts had ruled. Not that it mattered. The guys that handled the phone tracking were the same ones who did the GPS tracking.

Tailing Griff would not work either. Donovan's car stood out too much. He bought the car specifically so that it would stand out. It attracted both men and women alike.

He knew Poliakoff's men had ways, but he had to avoid letting Poliakoff know that there had been, um, complications.

Finally, with a bit of online research, Donovan discovered he could just buy a GPS tracker. There was even a store in Houston that sold them, so he wouldn't have to wait for it to be shipped to his home. Ironically, it was the same store that Griff had shopped at.

The salesman at Spy Emporium carefully explained to Donovan that he could only use the tracker on a vehicle that he owned. It was illegal to put it on someone else's car. Donovan thought that was dumb. Why else would you buy it? At the end of the day, he wasn't concerned about the legality of tracking a guy that you intended to capture, torture, and kill.

Donovan could access the tracker through an app on a phone, but the tracker itself had to be supplied with a cellular SIM card with its own account in order to transmit the location data. It occurred to Donovan that it would be better that the tracker's cell account wasn't connected to his own phone account, so he went to the nearest Walmart and bought a pre-paid phone and a card that gave him a month's use.

What didn't occur to Donovan was that the phone and its identifying numbers could be traced back to the store and there was a photographic record of him checking out with it. If anyone ever tried to trace the phone, it would eventually lead back to him all the same. It would only take longer.

Back home, Donovan donned nitrile gloves and opened the packages for the tracker and the prepaid phone. He teased the SIM card out of the phone and put it into the tracker. After testing it to make sure it worked, he set the tracker so that it would update its location every ten minutes. It would use up its battery power faster that way, but he would have a more accurate idea of where Griff was. Besides, he didn't plan on it taking too long to get Griff alone.

Unfortunately, it was Friday, so putting it on Griff's truck would have to wait until Monday. Donovan powered the tracker down and sulked. It was going to be a long weekend. No roofies. Lots of stress. That meant lots of Buffalo beer and oxy.

27

I was studying a postcard that I had received at 1200 Travis. The front had a photo of an Amish farm with the wording *Pennsylvania*. The postmark was from Pittsburgh. I didn't know anyone from Pennsylvania. I flipped the card over.

The neatly printed text said. "What do you call a good-looking girl on the Penn State campus? Visitor." Puzzled, I looked at the return address. It was from Lola. No last name. Lola's street address was given and a zip code. I didn't recognize the name or the address, but I recognized the zip. It was a Meyerland zip.

"I'm gonna head out for the rest of the week, Q. Have a good one," I said.

I drove to the address in Meyerland. It was a nice, upscale condo. Typical Houston brick. A two-story townhouse. I knocked, not knowing what to expect. The door opened and there was a moment before mutual recognition.

"Oh, I *knew* Benni would send someone for me!" Lola, in her late thirties or early forties, had pendulous breasts, and raven black hair resting on an oval face with a small mole under her left eye. "Please come in."

She motioned me into the tastefully decorated living room. "Can I get you something? A drink perhaps?"

"Um, no thank you." I had seen this woman around, but never knew her name or anything else about her, for that matter. She had been at the strip clubs, but she wasn't a stripper. She just went back to Benni's office from time to time, but never when I was in his office. I was sure that I had seen her at one of the underground game rooms, too.

"Of all the people that Benni would have sent, you are the last one that I would have ever expected." We sat down. "Uh," A huge gulp of air went in as her expression went from one of joyous surprise to horror. "You aren't here to arrest me, are you?"

"No, Lola. No." Is there something that I *should* arrest you for?

The air went back out and her face relaxed. "How is Benni?"

"I'm sure that he is fine." I wasn't sure Benni had sent me, or that I was even supposed to go here. Time to go fishing. "I assume I am here because Benni trusts me."

"He did trust you. It seems funny that he would still trust you. Wait, you *assume*? What does that mean?"

"Um, well, I got your address sent to me..."

"You didn't talk to Benni directly? Where is he?"

"I don't know where Benni is. The Marshalls have him stashed somewhere for his safety. They wouldn't tell me even if I asked."

"So if you didn't talk to Benni directly, then why *are* you here?" Lola had a slight Yiddish accent.

I had no idea. "You said that you knew he would send someone for you. Why?"

"To take me to him, to protect me from Poliakoff, to protect me from, well, you." She meant the police, not me personally. "Maybe to protect my income in the event they seized his assets."

Oh, she was his mistress. What am I supposed to do with the mistress of a crime boss under witness protection? They sure didn't teach that one at the academy. "I can't take you to him. I can protect you from the police, assuming you aren't entangled in his, um, activities of the business."

"Oh, no. I'm not. My relationship with Benni is personal. What about Poliakoff?"

"Do you know anything about Benni's insurance?"

"I think he had a policy for me, in case something happened to him. I'm sure he had a policy on his wife, too."

Wrong kind of insurance. At least she knew of Benni's wife. "No, I mean, do you know of anything that he might have kept to incriminate Poliakoff? Did he give you any papers or computer files to keep safe?"

"No. Nothing like that. Why do you ask?"

"If Poliakoff doesn't believe that you have anything like that, then he shouldn't have reason to bother you." That wasn't complexly true. Poliakoff could do something to her just to get at Benni. That they hadn't ransacked her place gave some credence to the idea that Poliakoff didn't think she had the goods.

"Did Benni give you any kind of number? Or a combination of letters and numbers? Maybe between eight and thirty-two numbers long?" The key to decrypt his memory card.

"No, nothing like that."

"What would you like me to do?" What I wanted to do was search her apartment.

Lola sighed. "If you are certain that you can protect me from Poliakoff..."

I wasn't. I couldn't even protect myself from Poliakoff assuming that Donovan and who knew who else was on his payroll.

"Then it would mostly be about money."

I gave her a quick smile. "I'm sure that the process to

seize Benni's assets is in the works. Unless the feds want to keep his operation going as a part of rounding up Poliakoff. Do you think they will discover all of his assets?" I wanted to ask her how much she got each month, but that didn't seem very gentlemanly.

"Hmm. Probably not. He thought of himself as a businessman. As such, he probably, what do they say, diversified his portfolio."

Which almost assuredly included offshore bank accounts. "Do you know Cricket?" That reminded me. I had stuff in the truck to drop off for her.

"Cricket? Cricket who?"

"Never mind." I figured if they knew each other, then maybe Cricket could ensure her income stream. "You might want to take a brief vacation, just to be safe, while I look into things a bit more. Do you, um, have enough to do that?"

"Yes, I am not hurting right now. Benni's been good to me."

"OK. Do that. Let's stay in touch, but only if anything changes." We exchanged phone numbers. I gave her my burner number to be safe.

I was worried about my own life. Now Benni had given me another life to be responsible for. Thanks a lot, Benni.

***

Cricket's corner store was a short distance away. I pulled out the sports drinks, jerky, and Cheetos along with the envelope containing a copy of what I needed her help with.

I ducked under the false door and stood in front of the

inner door. It was locked. And there was a new palm scanner jutting out next to the door. I guess she didn't want to see my face again.

I left the stuff and headed toward Galveston.

On the way, I called up Iverson. "Hey Ivy, I had a hypothetical question for you."

"OK."

"Let's say, someone, someone in Wit Sec, had a mistress..."

"What? Benni has a mistress. And you didn't disclose that?"

"No. I didn't say that. We are talking hypothetically, remember?"

"Uh-huh." Ivy sounded skeptical, to say the least. "Go on."

"If someone like that *did* have a mistress, what would you do about it?"

"His protection wouldn't cover her. We'd probably bring her in for questioning and put her on the stand if she could contribute anything. Before that, I'd come after you for leaving that tidbit out of your reports."

"She is not in my reports, because we are speaking about a hypothetical case. Assume that in this hypothetical case, the detective didn't know that the mistress existed," I said.

"Uh-huh. You would still tell us when you found out, though. Wouldn't you?" A statement, not a question.

"If she had nothing that would incriminate the people that the guy was ratting out, and the guy had immunity for his illegal activities, then why would you put her on the stand?"

"We probably wouldn't. No reason to."

"And if it turned out that this hypothetical person had incriminating information on Poliakoff or anyone else who didn't have immunity, would you cut her a deal?"

"Depends. She would have to have something that we can't get through Benni, umm, the guy, and it would have to be worth it. Does she have anything like that?"

"No. She's just a woman on the side. Doesn't know anything. Hypothetically speaking."

"Is she pretty?"

"Nice try Iverson."

"Griff, if you *do* find anything like this, then I need to know before Justice or anyone else finds out. You don't want to get caught in the ringer over this."

"OK. Thanks for your perspective."

28

The guys from Galveston Remodeling had been to the house during the week and had ripped up all the carpet and padding and presumably pulled all the nasty insulation out of the attic. As a result, the house only smelled bad, but not completely revolting.

I went downstairs to put my truck into the garage but was disappointed when I opened the door to find that the carpeting I had previously removed from the office, now safe room, was still there. I guess I didn't tell them it was down there, so they didn't know to take it. I still didn't know how to dispose of old carpet.

Back upstairs, with all the windows and sliding door open, I started to work. A week ago, I had hoped that I would work on renovations so I could get the electricity back on, but instead, I stared at the two piles of research that I had pulled down. At least I hadn't thrown it away.

I left the bigger pile of stuff that applied to the other members of the SWAT team in the corner on the floor. It wasn't apparent to me that they were any threat to me at this point. Instead, I picked up Donovan's pile. I was right to have segregated it.

I started putting everything that I had previously gathered on Donovan on the wall. The original research wasn't that much to go on, but today I would supplement it with all the data from the homicide files that I had pulled.

I dug through the other pile, the one in the corner, until I found the large map of Houston, and posted it on the wall opposite the door, then went to the kitchen to retrieve a Dr. Pepper before starting work in earnest.

I spread out the copies of the files that I had brought down for Houston on the table in the center of the room and sat in my chair facing the map with the table in front of me.

The first file I went for was a guy named Ross since he was the one that resembled the guy in Donovan's video. Ross's body was discovered on the edge of Buffalo Bayou Park, between Lost Lake and the Waugh Drive Bridge, known for its colony of Mexican free-tailed bats. The body was barely obscured by some trees next to the parking spaces on Allen Parkway.

The park is a century-old, 160-acre park along the banks of the Buffalo Bayou, just west of downtown. Buffalo Bayou was named after a fish, not a bison. It is now a collection of parks and attractions that offer something for everyone, including a place to dump bodies. In fact, they have discovered bodies most years in recent history in, or next to Buffalo Bayou, with two being found in 2020. The Houston Police Officers' Memorial is also in the park, an irony if Donovan had really dumped a body here.

The report showed that Ross died from blunt force trauma to the head. Toxicology reported that he had been drinking a lot and had Rohypnol in his system. The report didn't note any DNA evidence had been collected. There were no other clues to go on, and the case had received little follow-up.

The report stated that it appeared that they had killed him at or near the location. However, this was an easy spot to dump a body as long as you didn't care if it was found. You could drive right up, drag the body from the passenger side or trunk a mere twenty feet, and be done. There are no surveillance cameras to spy on you, and if done in the middle of the night, few cars passing by, at least that would notice you.

I put a pin in the map. Then I put a pin at Donovan's address. Less than a mile away.

The next file was a guy named Roderick. He was discovered in Cherryhurst Park under some trees, a few yards off Ridgewood Street. Although Cherryhurst Park had a community center, it was on the opposite side of the park, and the location of the body couldn't be seen from the center because of the copse of trees.

The report showed that Roderick had also died from blunt force trauma to the head. He had been drinking a lot and had Rohypnol in his system. Again, the report didn't note any DNA evidence had been collected, and the case had received little follow-up.

Another pin in the map. Less than a mile away from Donovan's and less than half a mile away from where Ross' body was found in Buffalo Bayou Park.

At this point, I realized I might want to pull the files by location later, so I pulled the pin and replaced it with a different color pin, and marked the color on the file.

Another file. This guy was found in a large vacant lot between Richmond and Main. While this wasn't a park, it was as large as most of the parks in Montrose and was lined with trees on both Richmond Avenue and W. Main Street. They discovered the body behind a bus stop shelter on the Richmond side, across from a laundromat. Although this guy had alcohol and Rohypnol in his system, the cause of death was listed as a drug overdose. The brief investigation had concluded that the individual had probably gotten off the bus, gone behind the shelter, and then taken too much oxycodone, dying on the same spot.

The cause of death was different. There were trees present, but there weren't enough of them to obscure the body. In fact, they barely obscured it at all. While not a match to the MO of the first two bodies, I put a pin in the map and moved on.

The next one was in Baldwin Park. Technically, not part of Montrose, but only a block over the line. Like the guy in the vacant lot, this guy had alcohol and Rohypnol in his system. They listed the cause of death as a drug overdose. Another pin.

Three more bodies. Another park, a dog park, and a baseball field. All guys with alcohol and Rohypnol in their systems, varied cause of death. No DNA evidence was collected, scant details, and not much in the way of follow-up.

All seven bodies were within a mile radius of Donovan's apartment. All seven had been roofied, but other than that, not enough evidence that you could prove a serial killer was on the loose.

***

Monday found me back at my desk bouncing ideas off of Q. "I found seven cases in a small geographic area with similarities over three years. It seems to me that instead of turning into seven cold case files, someone should have picked up on it and been investigating the possibility of a serial killer."

"What are the similarities and are there differences?"

After I highlighted the alcohol and roofie, Q said, "Seven women date raped and murdered in three years? Yeah, I'm surprised no one picked up on that either. That does seem strange."

"They are guys, not women."

Q blinked twice as he processed what I had said. "Gay guys. OK, now I'm not so surprised."

"So a dead guy's life counts less than a woman's?"

"No, of course not...but, even in this day and age, there is still a stigma attached. With the rise of Chemsex parties, there is also a feeling that if someone willingly engages in risky behavior, it's more like a natural consequence of their choices."

"Chemsex?"

"Yeah. Chemsex parties are where gay men have intentional sex under the influence of psychoactive drugs," Q explained. "These parties can last for days with multiple sexual partners. The term originated in the UK, where they use a different combo of drugs."

"Huh."

"So to your case, it's more like if a guy goes to an opium den and ODs, it just doesn't get a deep look."

We talked a bit more about my cases.

Q observed, "There isn't a strong enough case to warrant a diagnosis of a serial killer. You would have to find a common denominator in three of the cases to get the traction of a full-scale investigation. Even then, you'd still have some resistance."

After the conversation dwindled off, I researched Chemsex on the web. In a major case in the UK, Reynhard Sinaga was convicted of 159 sex offenses, including 136 rapes against 48 men. The experience of being drugged and raped is so frequent in gay culture it has almost become commonplace.

Another article by Reuters covered a TV documentary, a joint investigation by BuzzFeed News and Channel 4 Dispatches, which found that drugs were regularly used to "sexually assault gay men" with footage of the rape broadcast live on the dark web.

Had Donovan broadcast his escapades on the dark web? If so, could they be recovered or captured?

"Hey Q, I'm gonna' go look at some crime scenes. See you tomorrow."

29

My first stop was at the vacant lot. I figured it was most unlike the other six, so maybe I could easily rule it out. There was no place to stop on the street without blocking traffic, so I had to park across the street, in front of a convenience store in a strip mall next to the laundromat. The reason that the investigator assumed the victim got off of the bus was that there was no abandoned car nearby and that there wasn't a good place to stop and drop someone off on Richmond Avenue without blocking the street.

I got out and walked around the park anyway and got a feel for the location. The lot was exposed on three sides, and there were no places to park on the surrounding streets. Indeed, anyone dragging a body into the park would have to take an enormous risk, even at night. Transporting a body on the bus would also be a non-starter.

With no other references to other cases, I would have come to the same conclusion as the investigator. The guy simply got off the bus, chugged a few oxys, and OD'd behind the bus shelter.

Fifteen minutes after arriving, I walked back across the street, into the convenience store, bought a cold Dr. Pepper, and got into the car, ready to drive to my next stop.

***

A few miles away, Donovan's phone chimed. He had set the GPS tracking app to alert him when the tracker was within a geographic area roughly 2 miles from his condo. He had only slipped the tracker into the wheel well of Griff's truck a couple of hours ago and wasn't expecting any activity so soon.

Donovan stared at the map, showing the location of Griff's truck. He squinted, blinked, and squinted again. He stared dumbfounded at his phone. What was Griff doing there? It rattled him to his very core. He needed to make an excuse to go somewhere else; some place where his reaction would not be observed. For now, he headed to a men's room stall.

***

Mendell Park was only a block away from the bus stop, but since it was on the opposite side of Richmond Avenue, Griff decided to visit it on the way back and continued on. In retrospect, Griff realized he could have walked to Mendell from the convenience store parking lot.

It was only two blocks to the Evan Chew Dog Park. Griff parked on Dunlavy Street and strolled under the shade of the trees along the sidewalk next to the park. He had to walk to the opposite end of the park to find what he was looking for; a small yellow brick maintenance building with a faded blue door.

They had ditched the body next to the building on the back side. As it turned out, the building wasn't actually in the dog park, but between the dog park and the adjacent Bill Webber Baseball Field. The baseball field was next to I-69. Not that it mattered much.

As he stood in the location, he realized he had approached the dumping spot from the wrong location. Only twenty-five feet away was the dead end of another street. Griff walked back to his car, drove past the baseball field and over I-69, made two consecutive right turns, and crossed back over I-69. Four hundred feet later, he turned right again onto Norfolk Street and drove down to the orange and white barricades at the end of the street. Right there was the maintenance building and places to park on either side of the street. Although there was an apartment building to the north of the dog park, Griff didn't see any street lighting that would illuminate this entrance to the park. Furthermore, a constant rumble from the interstate would muffle out most sounds twenty-four hours a day.

***

Donovan watched the icon on the map stop, then move to the other side of the park and stop again. He rapidly stood, turned, doubled over, and vomited into the toilet.

***

Griff left the park and continued westbound on Richmond Avenue. His next stop, Levy Park, was technically outside of the Montrose district, but it was less than a mile away from the dog park. This time, Griff circled the entire park before getting out of his car to walk to the spot where the body had been found.

The similarities between Levy Park's and the Evan Chew Park were obvious. Levy Park also had a dog park and plenty of parking on opposite sides of the park where anyone could drive up next to treed areas, dump a body, and leave with relative ease. Levy Park was surrounded on three sides by apartments of various types, and the dump site would have been the same distance to I-95 almost to the foot. Both were family-friendly.

This was something that you couldn't get from looking at files in an office. You had to see the locations to see the parallels. Whether it was Donovan who dumped the bodies in these two parks, the two had to be related.

There were, of course, differences between the parks, too. Levy was more modern and had a vast playground instead of a baseball diamond. At least the body hadn't been dumped in the playground. But the biggest difference was the height of two of the buildings next to the park.

The Avenue Grove was a luxury, eight-story apartment building sitting directly across from where the body was dumped. At first glance, it would seem risky to dump a body next to so many windows. However, when Griff stood in the spot, the trees blocked the view of where the body had been. Furthermore, the architecture of the building, with a third-floor plaza and swimming pool extending out toward the park, blocked the view of the parking spots from all but a few apartments. Ultimately, fewer windows could see the activities of the killer than at Evan Chew despite the building's height.

***

Donovan was completely unraveled. Griff's first stop could have been a coincidence. The second stop made it likely that Griff was onto something, but three in a row had to mean that Griff had the goods.

He left work sick. He was sick, after all. Sick to his

stomach, sick with worry. Sick in the head, but that didn't register.

***

Heading back east on Richmond Avenue, Griff turned right on Mendell Street and drove past the park. It was a small community park, with little tree cover, and didn't have any parking. Instead of stopping, Griff ended up back on Mendell Street, headed north. A few blocks later, he turned right on Sul Ross Street and circled Menil Park.

Menil Park covers two blocks, but an art museum occupies one block. Griff parked on Branard Street under the shade of a stately oak tree and walked the few paces to where the body had been discovered. Across the narrow street were well-maintained craftsman-era homes. Other than that, there wasn't as much to see here as at the two dog parks.

Menil Park is home to the Rothko Chapel. The chapel is a frequently visited work of modern art on the National Register of Historic Places. Since Griff had never been and was effectively there, he decided to take a look. An outdoor reflecting pool featured an obelisk dedicated to Martin Luther King Jr. The sculpture had originally stood in Washington, D.C., and was offered as a memorial to stand in front of Houston City Hall. Houston turned down the gift, and it ended up being donated to the chapel.

Inside, Griff took a seat on one of the 16 minimalist benches. Each of the eight walls of the small octagon room featured black paintings, which incorporated other dark hues and texture effects. Griff understood why visiting tourists often asked, "Where are the paintings?" Even so, the effect was both calming and peaceful.

Griff found himself lost in thought, a meditation of sorts, involving the crime scenes he had just visited.

All five locations were within a mile of each other and were on, or within, two blocks on either side of Richmond Avenue. All the victims had died of overdoses and had alcohol and Rohypnol in their systems. Had anyone taken a serious look at the cases, a larger investigation would have probably followed.

On the other hand, there seemed to be two distinct sets of locations. The two dog parks with all of their similarities, and the remaining three. Of those, two had no real parking nearby and were more exposed despite not being as close to residences. One could argue that Menil wasn't part of that grouping since it had some parallel parking on the street, but its proximity to the other two made it seem to fit better in that group.

As Griff thought about it, it would be difficult to get an investigation opened using all five sites. While he thought that there was a common denominator, Donovan, he couldn't very well use that in his official reasoning. No, he had to build a case that would ultimately implicate Donovan without the use of any guilty knowledge. And without that common thread, it would be too easy to tear apart the commonality unless someone wanted to see one, and that wasn't likely to happen.

In the end, Griff decided he could build a strong enough connection between the two dog park cases to continue an investigation. That would be good enough. He only needed to pick at a solid thread to get people looking in the right direction. With a little luck, someone else would connect it to Donovan. But then again, that wasn't too likely to happen.

Griff exited the chapel, having lost track of time. Squinting into the fading afternoon sun, he walked casually past the reflecting pool back toward his car, unaware of the eyes that were following his every footstep.

30

The University of Saint Thomas was two blocks away from the Rothko Chapel. The drab three-story brick and concrete parking garage was empty at this time of day. A lone black car sat on the rooftop level, which was as hot as a cookie sheet, fresh out of the oven.

Donovan glared through his binoculars at Griff as he exited the chapel. He lost sight of him for a minute when the view was obstructed by the Guinan Residence Hall, but Griff reappeared as he got closer to his truck.

Donovan wanted to be closer, but having seen Griff circle the blocks surrounding the park on the GPS tracker app, Donovan decided it would be too risky to park his car on the street anywhere near where Griff might drive when he left.

Of course, Donovan would have preferred that Griff never left unless it was in a body bag, but there was still daylight remaining. Besides leaving Griff's body at the same place they had previously found another body would surely get someone's attention. And a dead cop would get a lot of attention. No, it would be better if Griff's body was never found, was killed in an accident, or by some criminal thug who got caught.

Donovan's frustration was driving him into a rage. Several years ago, when he was fresh on the force, someone much higher up the food chain discovered his sexual orientation. Although discrimination against gay men was technically not allowed in the HPD, it was still at a time when being a gay cop would be a barrier to his advancement. The officer had let Donovan know he could be helpful to his career. Donovan was quick to make a deal with the devil.

Donovan, in turn, had befriended other gay cops on the force and leveraged that knowledge to develop a network of cops who would do things for him, either willingly, or under blackmail when Donovan created incriminating videos of them in his apartment. He was fine with blackmail when it benefited him.

The officer had gotten Donovan onto the SWAT team, and Donovan was grateful for that. In return for his help and support within the force, the officer called upon Donovan to use his network to do certain things for him. The officer wasn't so pure himself.

Among his contacts, Donovan had someone in the crime lab who he had used to gain access to samples and files and had swapped DNA in specific old cases. On a whim, he had even substituted his semen in a couple of cases that predated his birth. The discovery and identification of his DNA in victims raped before he was born would destroy any case that ever came up for prosecution.

But once Donovan had crossed over to evidence tampering, he was under the thumb of his "helpful" officer. He could no longer deny requests to do other favors. He felt blackmailed, even though it didn't seem like it at the time, and he went into the arrangement willingly. He didn't like blackmail when it didn't benefit him.

Still, if it had stopped there, he would be happy with his situation in the HPD. But things had gone from bad to worse.

His proclivities had enticed him to buy Rohypnol. He

started by procuring a small amount from a house that they had raided. He liked the idea of drugging men and taking them home for fun and games but hadn't started out wanting to kill them, just use them for toys or blackmail if they turned out to be important enough.

Unfortunately, the drug was counterfeit, and the strength was variable. He ended up accidentally killing a guy with an overdose. He had dumped the body not four blocks from where he was standing.

Donovan hadn't planned on murder, so he'd propped the guy up in the front seat of his Camaro and started driving around, looking for a place to get rid of the body. He was driving carefully down Richmond Avenue in the early morning darkness, growing more nervous about getting caught with a corpse in his car. When he realized that there weren't headlights in any direction as far as the eye could see, he stopped his car in the traffic lane and looked carefully around at the empty street. Seeing no one, Donovan had simply pulled the guy out and propped him up behind the bus stop next to him.

For the next week, Donovan couldn't sleep. He was expecting a knock on the door, followed by handcuffs, and the perp walk. He took a few oxys out of a co-worker's locker and used them to help calm his nerves. The oxy was good, and it helped, but he wanted his own supply. After the accidental overdose, he didn't want street drugs for himself. He had learned that lesson at a high price.

After a couple of weeks had gone by, Donovan realized that the case wasn't getting any attention and that he had gotten away with it. That realization caused a strange sense of euphoria within him and gave him a sense of invincibility. But he still needed better drugs.

It wasn't hard to find out that the "good" drugs came through one of Houston's crime figures, Manny Poliakoff. Through one of his departmental contacts in vice, Donovan got the name of one of Poliakoff's lower-level dealers and where to find him.

Donovan had made a few buys and was happy with his new source of roofie and oxy. Then one day the sky came tumbling down. Somehow, the dealer had identified Donovan as a cop. When Donovan went for his next buy, instead of the dealer, one of Poliakoff's henchmen was waiting and "escorted" Donovan to a nearby car, where he met Manny himself.

Poliakoff had already determined that Donovan wasn't a narc, and he didn't care about what Donovan was doing with the drugs. Instead, he would be all too happy to supply Donovan with his drugs, in exchange for intel from within the department. Poliakoff liked blackmail when it benefited him too.

Fortunately, Poliakoff wasn't too demanding. Donovan couldn't figure out why, but didn't care. Then again, it was the biggest tip that he had given Poliakoff that had led to his present situation. Donovan had found out that Griff was an undercover agent working deep within Poliakoff's organization. He knew that tidbit would endear him to Poliakoff. Instead, Poliakoff had given Donovan orders to kill Griff. And that had proven to be harder than expected.

Donovan was miserable, at least as miserable as a sociopath can be. He had become a serial rapist, escalated into a serial murderer, and was being blackmailed by both a senior officer in the HPD and a crime lord.

Donovan was no longer invincible. Now Griff had taken over that attribute and was hot on the trail of uncovering Donovan's secret life. His vanity had been shattered. To make matters even worse, it felt like he was being blackmailed by Griff, although Donovan would have been relieved if Griff only wanted to blackmail him.

No, Griff knew he had burgled his apartment, probably suspected him of the attempts on his life, and was not likely to be satisfied until he had taken Donovan all the way down. Down to disgrace and a jail cell.

This had to end. The only acceptable outcome would be with Griffin Hunter in a body bag.

31

After a restless night, I was in the office early. If this were a proper investigation, I would put up a map, photos, and little factoids on an investigation board like the one at my Tiki house, but the tiny space they crammed us into didn't have room for such niceties. I thought about doing it at my apartment, but given that Donovan had already broken in once before, I didn't want my hand so out in the open. It would be better if he didn't realize that I was investigating these cases.

Q strolled in, and after the usual morning pleasantries asked, "How did your field trip go?"

"I'm glad that you asked. I wanted to hash some things over with you. I think that I have the three linked cases we talked about yesterday."

Q's eyebrows arched with a mix of surprise and interest. "Go on."

"First there was this guy. They found him at the Evan Chew Dog Park." I continued with the details of that scene.

"Then there was this other guy. They found him at Levy Park near the dog park area." I filled him in on the proximity to each other as well as I-69 along with the easy access and surrounding apartments.

"From the way you describe it, it seems likely that the two scenes are connected." Q asked, "Why do you think no one made the connection before?"

"There were two different detectives, so neither one saw both scenes. Even if you reviewed both files, you wouldn't see the similarities pop out. You had to see both scenes in person, or at the least be very familiar with both parks."

Q, "That's some fine detective work there."

"Not really. That's the reason that I want to bounce it off you. I haven't been a proper detective in over a year."

"Don't sell yourself short. You put together two pieces that no one else saw." Q paused, then said, "You said that there were three..."

"This other guy, Ross, was found at Buffalo Bayou Park." I didn't feel that the connection was as obvious as it was at the other two locations, but Q was right, that if I wanted a serial murder investigation started, I'd need three. "Like the others, Buffalo is a big park. It borders a busy, noisy highway, contains the Johnny Steele Dog Park, and has easy drive-up access. And, of course, the toxicology is the same." I had rehearsed this part to make sure I covered all the key points.

Q pressed three fingers and his thumb to his forehead and squeezed a bit. After a moment's thought, "Wait." His hand pulled away. "You said the toxicology was the same. Was the cause of death the same?"

"Well, not exactly. Ross had head trauma."

Q's hand returned to the desktop, and one side of his mouth curled up a bit. "Well, that breaks your connection. The dog park could be coincidental. Buffalo has everything. Plus, it is double the distance from the nearest other location." Finally, "Allen Parkway is hardly the interstate and the distance to the nearest interstate is too far to make his escape plan involve the freeway."

After a momentary pause, Q asked, "What's the timeline like?"

My silence said it all. I hadn't worked the dates on the

various cases against their locations. I felt a little deflated. Perhaps if it were on a board, I would have done that. But then again, I hadn't done it on the board at Tiki either.

"On the positive side, I think you may be on to something in the first two locations. Try digging deeper into those."

"That's good feedback. I respect your opinion." I was trying to butter him up for the next part. "Since I am a bit rusty, I was wondering if, now that the connection has been made, you would like to take the case over." I wanted someone other than myself to be the one to "discover" that the malefactor was Donovan.

The proposition hung in the air like the odor of a dead skunk on a hot day.

Q made a belittling face. "Now, why would I do that? Besides, how did you come up with these files, anyway? They wouldn't have been in our priority queue."

I didn't have an answer for that.

"When you decide you want to include me in what's going on here, we can talk about it some more. Until then, you are on your own."

There wasn't much more to say. I looked back down at the files, Q looked back at his monitor, and we worked in silence for a while.

I'd have to give some thought to Q's question about why I was looking at these files in the first place. If anyone else asked, I had to have an answer. Hopefully, something would come to me. Finally, I decided that trying to garner more support for linking the two cases would be the best way to build some interest.

I rode the elevator up a couple of floors to track down

the detectives who had worked those cases. The first detective was out on an investigation, so I would have to circle back to him later.

The second detective was sipping a Diet Coke at his desk. "Hi, I'm Griff Hunter." As I stuck out my hand.

He reached out, then a glimmer of recognition passed over his face. "Oh, yeah, you're the guy who got shot." My notoriety had preceded me again. "Please, have a seat."

"I'm stuck working some cold case files until they clear me for field duty again."

The detective's eyebrows lowered. It wasn't quite a scowl, but it was on its way to becoming one.

I had prepared for this. Like most people, detectives rarely like their work second-guessed. "Oh, no. I didn't want to ask you about a case of yours." His facial muscles relaxed. I probably would ask later, but this little deception might be forgiven if he connected the dots to the two cases. "I am working on a case that bears a great deal of similarity to one that you had, and I was hoping to get some insights from you. After all, it's been a while since I did any actual detective work."

"Sure, anything is better than this." He glanced down at his desk and made a sweeping gesture with his hands. His desk was a minefield of paperwork.

"Yeah, there had to be a ton of paperwork after I got shot, but most of it got done while I was in the hospital. Other than my statement, I managed to avoid paper purgatory."

"What do you need?"

I handed him the homicide file from Evan Chew. "This case. It occurred in another dog park nearby. The same cause of death. I was hoping you could share your insight based on your experience."

The detective started leafing through the thin file. "Oh. Yes. This is like a case I had." Oddly, you remembered the ones that you didn't solve better than the ones that you did. "My case was at Levy Park."

I didn't want to offer any prompting because I didn't want him to ask how I knew so much about his case.

After the gears turned in his head a minute, "Evan Chew. That's just down the way from Levy. I haven't been there in a while, but if I recall correctly, it's very similar to Levy. I wonder if there is a connection." Like music to my ears. "Can you make me a copy of the file? I'd like to think about this a bit more and look at my case notes."

"That would be a great help, if you don't mind." I had already copied the file, and he was holding the copy. "You can keep that file. I'll get it back from you the next time we talk. Perhaps over a beer or two."

"I'll hold you to it."

My spirits had greatly improved since my talk with Q.

***

That afternoon, I found the other detective. I did the same thing with almost similar results, only I gave him the Levy Park file. He didn't make the leap that the other detective had, but he took the file and agree to take a look at Evan Chew for me. I hoped that once he was on the ground there, the similarities would pop for him as they had for me.

32

The next day, I got a call from the Levy Park detective to come on up to his desk. When I got there, the Even Chew detective was standing with him at the desk. I smiled. What else could I do?

The Levy detective, "Guess who I bumped into at the park?"

After a moment of awkward silence, "I told you I was rusty detective-wise."

"Oh, we think your detective skills are just fine. You think like an undercover guy, though." The Levy detective did all the talking. "We don't like how you got us there, but we agree with your theory that the two cases are probably related. If either of us had landed both cases, we would have made the connection on our own."

I tried to push past the awkwardness. "So, which one of you is going to take over the cases?"

The Evan Chew detective grunted.

"Huh? They are your cases now." The Levy park guy suggested.

That wasn't the answer I was hoping for. I tried to act surprised. "What? A chance to close two cases. I figured you guys would fight over them."

The Levy Park guy glanced at the other detective. "Evan, do you want 'em?"

How ironic, the Evan Chew detective's name was Evan. I seriously wanted to make a witty remark, but, well, it wasn't the best opportunity.

Evan grunted again and snorted, "No." He kind of dragged out the "o" at the end.

I looked at Evan, then back at the Levy detective, then put my hands out, palms up.

"If they were good cases, then, yeah, we might want them. The thing is, nothing in either file adds to what we had originally. They are still the same cases, even though they are probably by the same guy. But there is nothing to pull at, so they are probably still going in the same direction. Becoming cold cases. Since you already have them, it is best for us if we just let you keep them."

I shrugged. "Well, I'd still like to buy you guys a beer for your trouble." As I turned to leave, "If you think of anything that might help..."

***

That evening found me at the no-name bar, alone with my thoughts.

I knew Donovan was drugging and date-raping other men. My instincts told me he was also killing some of them, even if I couldn't prove it. I was in a position where I couldn't bring up anything against him, and now I was running out of options to get someone else to point the finger in his direction.

I could leak information to the detectives who originally had the park cases, but it would be too obvious that it had come from me. Too much chance of it backfiring, and they might not want to go up against the blue wall either.

I could leak incriminating information to the press, but in today's climate, they might not care. A black, gay guy might get a free pass. Besides, I'd almost always done things by the book and didn't have any respect for cops who leaked.

The only thing that I had going for me was that Donovan didn't know I was investigating the murders. At least that was something. I even considered for a fleeting moment that I should just drop it and move on, but that would be against my code, too.

Of course, I could continue my investigation, but even if I came up with something solid, what was I going to do with that information? What if it was too hot for anyone to handle?

I looked for the answer in my glass of Lone Star.

***

The next morning I got some additional wisdom from Q. "What are the options when you have a solid suspect? You are sure it's him, but just can't get the proof you need to get it in front of the DA?"

"Well, in the olden days, we would either frame them or beat a confession out of them."

He had said it deadpan, so I wasn't sure if he was joking or not. "That's not my style."

"Bring him in as a person of interest and sweat him in the interrogation room. It's amazing how many criminals will implicate themselves for us."

That would not work with Donovan. I couldn't just try to interrogate him. "What if he lawyers up?"

"Another technique is to find something, umm...through non-conventional methods. Something inadmissible in court, then work backward from there to 'discover' it in a legal way." He did air quotes around the word discover.

That was exactly what I had done with Donovan. "Anything else?"

"Yeah. Bluff. Make him think you have him dead to rights, then wait for him to make a mistake. Otherwise, keep investigating till you find more."

Hmm. The bluff might work. What could possibly go wrong?

***

After entering Donovan's name and address into Spokeo, it rewarded me with his email address, Facebook, Instagram, and a variety of other tidbits. Email would be good.

I found an internet café that advertised anonymity, with no cameras. Apparently, it thrives off those seeking to view porn. It was dark. Each workstation had a divider between the next one so that you couldn't see your neighbors' screen. It was creepy. It was expensive. It was perfect.

The email was brief and to the point, "I know what you have done. Save yourself some humiliation and turn yourself in before I send the evidence to the police." For good measure, I attached a still frame from the bedroom video and hit the send button from the anonymous email account that Cricket had set me up with; Harry Bentwick@. What a nice girl.

The corners of my mouth were turned up high as I stepped back out into the evening air.

***

The next morning, I was shooting the bull with Q before heading out to Chrysalis to get more information out of Ms. Dulce, aka Pickles. At least that was the plan until my desk phone rang.

"Would you be so kind as to come up to the Chief's office?" She said.

Like I had a choice? "When?"

"Now would be good."

No, that wasn't good. Grunts rarely got called to the chief's office, and it was never for something good. If the Chief wanted to give you something good, it would happen in a public setting.

As I rose from my chair, I said, "Been summoned upstairs."

Q frowned.

The elevator seemed to take forever as it rose to the twenty-eighth floor. Had they discovered me breaking into Donovan and Skinner's cars? No, I would have been called into IA. What then? *Ding.* I was finally there.

The...what was she? A secretary? A receptionist? A bodyguard? I just didn't know. Anyway, the officer showed me directly to a conference room door. No waiting. That couldn't be good either.

Geez. Everybody who was anybody was there. My boss, his boss, the boss's boss, The Chief's aides, the Chief. As if that wasn't bad enough, the DA, an assistant DA, and an investigator from the DA's office were there, too. They glared at me as only prosecuting attorneys can do. To finish the cabal, there were three note-takers inconspicuously tucked in the corners. And Special Agent Iverson. I don't think they would have assembled this much power if I were Al Capone.

The heavy mahogany door closed behind me. "Have a seat," the Chief offered. About half the people in the room were seated. Mostly the minions, scribes, and the Chief. No one from the DA's office was seated. But seated or standing, everyone was clumped together by their allegiance. Except for Iverson. She sat alone, next to her scribe, like a leper.

I offered a weak smile and a thank you, but remained standing all the same. I made eye contact with Iverson. She winked. That was probably a good sign, so I relaxed slightly. Unfortunately, too soon.

"What the hell?" The DA Roared. And so it began.

I had no clue.

"You worked two years on this. Everybody here had skin in the game." He shot a look at Iverson as he said, "Almost everyone." I had only seen the DA on TV. This definitely wasn't a face he put on for them or the courtroom.

OK. About my undercover work. I still had no idea. Had I done some material damage to the case by visiting Benni's Cadillac in impound? They caught me off guard, but one thing about that much undercover time taught me was to remain calm, emotionless, and not give anything away.

"You got shot. Two men got killed."

And why are you mad at me for getting shot?

"Your job was to get information to bring Benni Sokol down."

I glanced at the Chief. He looked serene, expressionless.

I looked at my chain of command and gave a slight, calculated shrug. No help was going to come from them.

"Who granted you the right to bargain for the DA's office?"

"What?" I didn't figure it was my turn to speak, but I was genuinely confused.

"You. You offered Benni a deal to turn state's evidence in return for Witness Protection." Veins were sticking out on the DA's massive forehead.

In my defense, I wanted to tell him I didn't offer Benni a deal. But the simple word, *what*, hadn't gone over well. There was no point in trying to speak, at least not now.

"Who put you up to this? Iverson, Sokol himself? Who? Who?"

He sounded like an owl. I think Iverson caught it 'cause she smiled slightly.

"We're waiting?"

Was that my cue to speak? "I, umm, didn't..."

"If it wouldn't ruin the case against Poliakoff, I'd have your badge." Apparently, it wasn't my turn to speak.

The Chief rolled his eyes. The DA couldn't take my badge. Everyone in the room knew it. It was political theatrics. Of course, the DA was experienced in theatrics. Honed by years in the courtroom, it was what he did best.

"The FBI," there was a note of distaste in the DA's voice, "the Justice Department, and the Marshalls will take over the case from here."

And there it was. Instead of being happy that a bigger fish was in the net, they were ticked off over turf; who got the notch in their belt. Iverson's expression gave nothing away, but her eyes sparkled.

The DA continued to curse at me for a while, but he said nothing new. Well, except for a not-so-veiled threat that he would remember this betrayal, and that after they put away Poliakoff, we'd finish this. That and that the FBI wouldn't protect me, they weren't loyal to me, and would just use me, then spit me out.

I wasn't overly worried about the DA. By the time the Poliakoff trial and appeals were done, the DA would be dead if he couldn't control the rage he had shown. Pop a gasket. Unless the rage was just an act. Could be.

Eventually, I was dismissed after everyone felt I had been dressed down sufficiently. Most of the minions left with me while the power brokers stayed behind. It was a quiet ride down the elevator as it stopped at various floors, showing the importance of each man as he got off.

***

"You been reassigned to construction duty?" Q asked.

Construction duty was where you sat in a squad car as the LEO presence during night highway construction. Just ... sitting ... there.

"More like meter maid on a bicycle." I hoped not. Only time would tell.

"Ouch."

Q and I went to lunch together, and I rehearsed the whole thing for him.

He reassured me, "The DA was right about one thing; anything that smacked of discipline would hurt the prosecution of Poliakoff. You'll be OK." He'd been around long enough to know.

When we returned, the guy on front desk duty waved me over. "Here." He reached under the counter and pulled out a fruit basket. The price tag was still attached; Forty-nine dollars, just under the limit that we could accept as a gift.

"I didn't realize that you knew who I was." I didn't think that I'd ever talked to the guy.

"Once you get shot, everybody knows who you are."

"Thanks." I'd have to note that. My anonymity was gone. Cops who saw me coming and going would know I was someone other than just another face in a sea of faces. Not good for snooping around.

Once back at my desk, I opened the little envelope stuck in the basket. *Thanks* with the letter *I* was all that was on it.

I bit into an apple. Huh.

As I ate the apple, it occurred to me I should go visit Benni one last time to see if I could shake anything else from him. I called the HPD's Airport Division to set things in motion, but was told Benni was gone. The Marshals had already taken him away.

It had turned out to be a disappointing day. I thought I couldn't be any more surprised. Then my desk phone rang again.

"Detective Hunter."

"Hey Griff," it was Jax. "You know anything about Donovan?"

My mind said "Yes. He is a serial killer.", but my mouth said nothing. Then, don't incriminate yourself. "Um...what do you mean?" If it wasn't for having worked undercover, a sense of panic would have set in.

"Nobody can find him."

"What? What are you talking about?"

"He didn't show up at O'Ryan's last night, then didn't show up for his shift this morning. No one could reach him by phone, so they sent a couple of uniforms over for a wellness check. They said it looked like he left in a hurry."

"That's odd." I thought about asking why he would ask me, but decided that some things may be better left unsaid. "I don't have a clue where he is." I wish I did.

33

I had planned to go to Galveston the next morning, but considering Donovan's disappearance, I was afraid to spend the night in my Northshore apartment. Donovan knew where that was.

Instead, I drove back to Webster. This time I stayed at a different hotel, though. It felt like I had some unfinished business here, so it was a logical place for me to send a message. Both figuratively and literally.

After a sleepless night, I surveyed all three Starbucks in town and settled on the one that seemed to have the least video surveillance from surrounding businesses. I pulled into the lot, but not too close to the coffeehouse, and opened up the laptop. No signal. I re-parked closer and did the same. Still no signal. On the third try, I was close enough to get a weak signal, and still not be sitting right outside.

I didn't know what Donovan was up to, but it didn't look like he was going to turn himself in. To turn up the pressure more, I attached a short snippet of the one decrypted video file that I had downloaded off his computer. Another gift from Harry Bentwick@.

No sooner than I got back on the Gulf Freeway, my burner rang. "Hello."

"Griff? It's Lola. I just wanted to let you know I'm going to take a trip to Israel. I've always wanted to go."

"That sounds like an excellent idea."

"I'll let you know when I get back."

"OK."

"If you hear from Benni, give him a kiss for me.

Thanks."

I would not be kissing Benni any time soon. Or ever, for that matter. But I knew what she meant.

I crossed the causeway and headed to the Tiki house.

34

After working at the house all day, I was hot and tired. I drove into town and checked into the Motel Eight. It wasn't as nice as the other places that I had stayed in, but I was staying down here quite a lot lately. Since I was spending most of my time at the house, it didn't matter all that much. Soon, I'd have the house whipped into good enough shape that I'd be sleeping there, anyway.

After checking in, I drove over to the G Spot, pulled into the parking lot, and took the space closest to the alleyway.

Inside, the stripper pole looked as lonely as ever, but the place had enough people in it that the guy behind the bar kept busy.

After a couple of Lone Stars, I went to the men's room. I looked bad. The stress was catching up with me. I needed to get back to my motel, take a shower, and get some rest. I threw some bills on the counter and slipped out.

As I passed the big pickup parked next to mine, I was tackled low. My head hit the gritty ground, narrowly missing a soggy cigarette butt. Before I could react, I was dragged by my feet between the trucks.

"Where's Donovan?" French hissed.

"What? What are you talking about?"

"Donovan. Where is he? He disappeared and I know you're connected to it. Where is he?"

"I don't know what you're talking about."

A knife glistened in French's left hand. "Get up!"

As I scrabbled to my feet, I said, "I don't know what's

going on, but you still have time to walk this back…"

It was French's voice and face, but the hair was wrong. A semi-short afro.

"You forget, I'm the one with hostage negotiation skills. Yours suck. Get in the truck." He flicked the knife toward his pickup.

There was no way I was getting into that truck. Even if he stabbed me right there in the parking lot, my chances were better. I might get medical attention in time. Once you let a bad guy take you somewhere else, your chances of survival dropped to near zero. I needed to buy some time.

"You look ridiculous in that wig."

"You're not helping yourself. Now, get in the truck." Another gesture with the knife.

"At least tell me why?"

I didn't expect an answer, but Afro-French surprised me; "When Donovan missed you, it became my job to find Benni's insurance." He growled. "You prevented that." He emphasized the "you." "Now YOU got him so tucked away so that I will never get at him. Poliakoff is pissed. Now, get in the freakin' truck."

Right on cue, he flicked the knife to the side again. I turned toward the door and extended my left arm toward it, reaching toward the handle. Less body surface exposed this way and my ribs would offer some level of protection for my internal organs. I looked at the door handle and leaned toward it slightly. Like a magician's audience, French's eyes followed the movement.

In a desperate move, I lunged my whole body into French, deflecting the forearm, holding the knife outward as best as I could. We stumbled a little dance a foot or so backward. As the space between us spread, French dipped the knife below my blocking arm and swung it between us, his elbow bent, his hand close to his body, the tip pointing upward between us. In that position, the blade's edge was parallel to our bodies.

I punched the knife's hilt as hard as I could. French's grip on the handle was too tight. Instead of the knife dropping out of his hand, the point pivoted inward, hitting him just below the sternum. His eyes popped open with surprise. In that moment of hesitation, I was able to hit a second punch on French's hand, driving the blade in.

He gasped and toppled backward, past his truck, and into the parking lot. A scream emanated from the front of the lot.

Another voice. "Someone call 911."

I kneeled between French and the spectators and made like I was checking on his condition. I'd seen that knife before, in my motel room in Webster. "You bastard." I jiggled the knife handle around. A group of people gathered, and I saw someone coming. I stood back up and stepped back between the trucks. One pair of men looked wildly between French and me.

"He attacked me. It was self-defense." I held my hands out so that they could see that I wasn't armed.

When the flashing lights of a squad car reflected off the nearby wall, the strangers turned toward the entrance.

A uniform appeared, weapon drawn, flashlight in my face. "Freeze. Hands where I can see them."

I complied. "I'm a cop. He attacked me. It was self-defense."

"Keep those hands where I can see them."

"Radio Rusty. Ask him if Griff Hunter is a cop." Rusty was the Chief of the Galveston Police and a former partner of my dad.

"Hands behind your head. Interlock your fingers. Walk slowly this way."

Of course, I was going to comply. Doing otherwise would be suicide.

An ambulance pulled up behind the squad car, which was blocking the entrance to the lot. The second set of flashing lights lit up the otherwise dark parking area like a disco.

"Walk slowly to my car." The uniform was behind me now. "Around to the front."

A second police car arrived, along with more onlookers.

"Spread your legs. Now slowly put your hands spread apart on the hood. Don't reach for anything."

One of the new cops on the scene came over to help. "Frisk him." Said the first cop to the second cop. In the background, I could hear a third cop telling people to back up. Every cop on duty would be here in another minute.

"I'm a cop. He attacked me. It was self-defense."

"You have any weapons on you? Anything that I could stick myself on?"

"Yes. As a cop, I am armed. Nothing to stick you with. Check my ID. Call Rusty. My shield is in my right front pocket."

I felt my wallet being removed. The second cop paused while he looked inside. "Keep your hands where they are. Don't move." He reached around and weaseled the leather shield holder out of my front pocket, followed by another pause. "You understand I'm going to finish frisking you and remove your weapon."

"Yes, sir."

After he was done, "You can stand back up Detective Hunter." Cop one still had his weapon drawn. "Please have a seat in the back of the car."

I slid in the open door. Being undercover, this wasn't the first time I had sat in the back of a squad car, but it still wasn't a good feeling. The door closed. Most people think that a jail cell would feel confining, but do not know that the back of the car feels much, much worse. At least they didn't put the cuffs on me. Being in the back of the car with your cuffed hands between your back and the hard plastic seat is almost inhumane.

The scene outside followed the normal progression of any homicide. A crime lab guy showed up, all the bystanders were interviewed, the barkeep was led out to look at me through the window of the car, strobes of bright light flashed from cameras, etc.

It seemed as if I was in the back of the squad for an eternity. The wait was a good thing. It gave me time to mentally prepare and rehearse the statement that I would have to give.

I saw a familiar face push through the small crowd. A flash of a badge and she was inside the police line.

"How they hangin' cowboy?" Krunch said with an impish smile.

"What are you doing here?"

"I heard about it and came on down. Thought you could use some moral support. Or bail."

"How?"

"You're joking, right? Every cop on duty knows, half the ones at home know, and by morning, every cop in Houston will know."

"Hmm." She was right, of course.

"What happened?"

"That's what we want to know." It was a Galveston detective who had slid up behind Krunch. "Would you please step over there, ma'am?" He pointed back toward the police line.

"Sure, I understand." She flashed her badge. "Mind if I go take a look?" She nodded to the back of the parking lot.

"Sorry, ma'am. Active crime scene. Still being processed."

Krunch shrugged and walked away.

"Detective, umm, Hunter is it? You could come down to the station tomorrow to give your statement, but I'd rather have it now. While it is still fresh in your mind."

"No, I'd rather do it now. Get it over with."

"You want a Union rep here?"

"No. I've got nothing to hide." That was a whopper.

He pulled out his tablet and a pen, then looked at me expectantly.

"I came out of the bar and was going to get in my truck. He came out of nowhere and tackled me to the ground. We struggled. He pulled his knife. We struggled some more, and somehow in the struggle, he got stabbed. He went down. I tried to render aid, but he was already gone."

"Ya. Do you know the victim?"

"Well, I was the victim. He attacked me." The more you repeat the mantra that he attacked me, the more they believe it in their own minds. "The attacker is Ferrel French. He is an officer in the HPD."

"So you knew him then?"

"Yes. Not closely, but that is correct."

"What did he want?"

"Dunno." I turned my palms up and shrugged. "Maybe...I dunno."

"Why would he want to kill you?"

"I'd like to know that, too. But this isn't his first attempt." I didn't tell him that Poliakoff had sent him.

The detective thought for a minute. "Your statement seems consistent with the evidence and witness statements. Rusty says you're probably OK, so I'm releasing you on your own recognizance pending further investigation. You can't leave town yet. Where are you staying locally?"

"The Super eight on sixty-first." I nodded to the back of the lot. "My truck?"

"Given its proximity to the body, we can't allow you to move it yet. They may or may not take it to the impound yard. If they don't need to, do you want us to leave it here?" He sounded more sympathetic now. "You need a ride to the motel?"

"I think I have a ride, but thanks. And yea, leave it here."

"One last thing. Wait for the officer to give you a breathalyzer test. After that, you are free to go."

35

I had to repeat my story as Krunch drove me to the Galveston motel. At one point, she turned and looked at me. Her eyes were squinted a little. Maybe my story wasn't as good as I thought it was. But she said nothing.

She pulled into the twenty-four-hour Walgreens on 61st, just a few blocks away from the hotel. I grabbed a cheap bottle of aspirin while Krunch pulled a bottle of wine out of the cooler. I followed her over to the cosmetics. She studied the bottles for a bit, then pulled out a little bottle of Revlon's finest. Odd time to be picking out cosmetics I thought, but hey. We checked out; I paid.

Instead of dumping me off at the curb, she parked and followed me back to my room. Not knowing what else to say, I said, "Care to come in?"

"That's the idea."

Inside the door, I turned into the bathroom and ran water into a paper cup. She followed me in, rummaged through the Walgreens bag, handed me the aspirin, and took out the rest. "Take off your shirt."

"That's the best offer I've had all day."

"The day's not over yet." She replied.

Huh. I pulled off my shirt. Krunch drew nearer.

"Let's see how well this matches." She said as she opened the black and tan tube of Revlon. Its coolness of the crème felt good against the raw flesh on my face and forehead. It didn't feel as good once she started smearing it around. "Not bad."

I'd been admiring Krunch's hair as she worked, so I had to swivel my head toward the mirror to see what she had done. The scrapes and the start of bruising were well camouflaged. "Wow. That looks great. Looks like I owe you yet another one." If someone was close enough or looked hard enough, they could see the makeup. But from a few feet away, no one would notice.

Back in the main room, Krunch opened the wine bottle. "I was so worried about you when I got the call." She poured a glass into the motel paper cup, then sat on the edge of the bed.

"I can't begin to thank you enough for coming down to rescue me."

"I think I should stay the night and keep an eye on you." She flashed a coy smile.

While that was a thought that had crossed my mind many times before, I had a serious problem working in my mind. I groaned inside at what I had to say. "Umm. I'm not sure that I know how to say this carefully enough."

The smile disappeared.

"Any other time, I would jump at the offer. I like you. A lot."

She started to speak, but I held up my hand. "Please let me finish. My mind is whirling, I'm in pain, and I might just puke. I've just been through a trauma, and to some extent, you've shared that trauma with me. I want to do this, but I also want to make sure it is for the right reasons...for both of us. It's not you, it's me. Just for now."

Krunch looked a bit embarrassed. "Is it going to be weird for us now?"

"No. No. It wouldn't be any weirder than if we slept together, would it?"

"Well, no, I guess not."

"I'd like a rain check." I gave her my most endearing smile.

"A raincheck!" she huffed. "This isn't like some…"

I cut her off. "No, not like that. I didn't mean it that way. What I mean is tonight just isn't right. I'd like another chance when we can make it right."

I couldn't tell if she was angry, hurt, or embarrassed. A moment of awkwardness passed.

Finally, she said "It's late. I hate to drive back to this city at this hour, and I'm exhausted too. Can I just crash on the other bed? Sounds like I should be pretty safe from you making advances during the night."

That hurt a bit, but what else could I say? "Sure. If you'd like, I could spring for a separate room."

"That would be a waste. Let's go to bed." She wandered into the bathroom, closing the door behind her.

While she was gone, I stripped off my clothes and crawled under the covers.

The toilet flushed, the door opened, and the bathroom light went out. Krunch came out in a lacy red bra and matching panties, and strutted right past my bed, to the one beside it. She was well-toned with smooth skin. In the dim, dappled light I thought I glimpsed a tattoo. I was regretting my decision as she turned out the nightstand light.

****

Across town, a white Sprinter commercial van with stolen plates drove quietly through Riverside Terrace, directly to French's house. It backed into the driveway. Four men, dressed in black from head to toe, including the balaclavas over their faces, slipped out.

They lined up outside the front door, jimmied the lock, and filed through the door. They proceeded directly upstairs and burst into the master bedroom. Two of the men subdued the drowsy Loretta French as gently as they could, then secured her wrists and ankles with zip ties. They treated her as if she were their own wife, for indeed, it would have been if they were the one who'd been killed. They carried her to the bathroom, closed the toilet lid, and set her down.

By the time they were done, the other two men had finished clearing the upstairs. As expected, no one was there. They went back downstairs, three sweeping the rooms while one went out to the van. House empty, they congregated in front of the gun safe. The fourth man returned from the van dragging an industrial-strength refrigerator dolly.

It was tough getting the heavy safe onto the dolly. The three most brutish ones rocked the safe the best they could until the smaller man slid the edge of the dolly under the beast. One man moved to the dolly to back up the smaller guy. The remaining two brutes pulled the safe forward, its lower back edge scraping the wall behind it on its inevitable tilt forward.

After they had settled the safe onto the dolly and the balance point found, the men hauled it to the back of the van and muscled it inside, flat on its back. They were going to hurt when the sun rose. Two men secured the safe inside the van. They would worry about opening it later.

One man stood in the shadows, a sentry, watching the street. The smaller man went inside and swept the house for anything that they might have accidentally dropped, and finding nothing, returned. He left the door open a quarter of an inch.

Eight minutes after it had arrived, the Sprinter pulled away. The men inside felt sorry for Mrs. French. Sorry that they had to frighten her and tie her up, but she wouldn't be tied up too long. Soon someone would arrive to inform her of her husband's death. They felt sorrier for her for that. What else was to be done? It was a pact that they had all made with each other.

The Houston Commander of Tactical Operations didn't like being awakened in the dead of night. He disliked being awakened for this kind of call the most. The call had been from French's supervisor. The Commander had gotten dressed, been picked up at sunrise by the supervisor, and after a long, silent drive, pulled up to French's home.

He went to knock. They both saw that the door was ajar. The Commander barked with authority, "Call for backup. And I want detectives on their way here, now!" They both instinctively moved to the sides of the door.

He quickly but carefully pushed the door wide open and took a quick look through the portal. Dark inside, nothing moving that he could see. He nodded at the supervisor, who nodded back, then went through the door first.

After clearing the first floor, they headed upstairs where they eventually found Loretta French unceremoniously sitting on the throne, bound, with duct tape on her mouth. "Mrs. French. You're safe now. It's HPD." Neither man had anything to cut the zip-ties. The first of many patrol cars pulled up as they peeled the duct tape from her mouth.

"Police." The voice called out from downstairs.

"All clear. Bring a knife up here." Called out the Commander.

Loretta French gave her story for the first of many times, but there wasn't anything to go on. They turned lights on with gloved hands, more officers arrived, and it became apparent that something had been removed. The scratches on the wall, the permanent impression in the carpet.

"His gun safe was there," Loretta said. When asked what he kept in it, "Guns." She didn't know about anything else.

It was hard to keep control of the house as a crime scene with so many officers wanting in, but it wouldn't matter, anyway. There wasn't going to be any evidence to be found.

The detectives conferred with the Commander. A routine robbery for the guns. Highly unlikely, considering French's demise only hours before. What was in the safe? That would be the motive, but no one was willing to offer their thoughts out loud. Who would have done it? No one offered their thoughts on that either, but it had to be someone with some connection to the department, or HPD, to have known so soon...before it was public information.

Ultimately, the Chief would declare it a job for IA to investigate and, of course, that investigation would go nowhere.

***

When I awoke, Krunch was gone. It was probably less

awkward that way. But it meant that I had to walk back to the G Spot to retrieve my truck. Fortunately, it hadn't been impounded. The morning sea breeze was refreshing, and the walk gave me time to think about all that had happened.

36

Tiki Island itself had the peaceful vibe of a small, remote community resting under a pale blue sky that was warmed by a friendly sun. Except in hurricane season.

Before last night, I thought of my house as a sort of disaster zone; a work still in progress. But as I pulled into the driveway today, it took on the aura of a safe haven. A Garden of Eden from the evils that surrounded me. It was now my place of refuge. Smaller than most of the homes on the island, it was more intimate, womb-like.

I examined myself in the bathroom mirror for a long time. I didn't like what I saw on either the outside or the inside. Outside, I looked like hell. I tried putting on the makeup Krunch purchased for me, but it didn't look good as when she had done it. Washing it off was painful. The wound site from my gunshot was hurting again, and I had scrapes, swelling, and some skin discoloration from my skirmish with French. I also had a bruised ego.

I went to the kitchen and considered the Pop-Tarts. Cherry or Brown Sugar? Eventually, I decided on a Lone Star. It was a good day to have beer for breakfast. If I had thought about it longer, I would have opted for the Pop-Tarts with an oxycodone chaser.

I thought that I was happy when Donovan went to ground. I hoped it had meant the end to my troubles and that my life could return to normal. After French had attacked me, I realized Donovan was not acting alone. A revelation that destroyed that line of thinking.

French's attack came out of nowhere. I hadn't been expecting it even though I knew there was a bullseye on my back. It was just plain luck he hadn't killed me. The attack destroyed any sense of security I might have had. Not in the way that was "normal" for a victim of a crime, but this was something deeper, more unsettling.

Donovan was still out there. Somewhere. Just as French had popped up in the darkness, Donovan could still do the same, like some ghastly creature in a Halloween spook house.

Donovan had burned me to Poliakoff, who subsequently wanted me dead. Donovan was AWOL from the department and would need a good explanation to get back in. His career with the HPD was probably over. Did that mean that Poliakoff now had full control over Donovan without the counterweight of French or the department? I had no way of knowing. He had taken my bluff too seriously, and now I had to deal with unintended consequences.

For that matter, did Poliakoff still want me dead? Even if he no longer cared, what if Donovan wanted me dead for revenge? If so, I would have to look over my back for Donovan for the rest of my life. That would not do. Donovan was a wounded animal. He might be unpredictable now. Even deer and bunnies turn vicious when cornered, and Donovan was no little bunny.

But what could I do? At least when Donovan was on the force, I could somewhat keep track of him. Now, I didn't know where he was. Was he still in Houston? Was he still in Texas? Was he even in the country? I simply didn't know.

The one thing I knew was that this would not be over until Donovan was dead or behind bars, and, as it currently stood, I was the only one that was going to make that happen.

My biggest problem at the moment was how to find him. Well, that and the fact that he might come from nowhere and kill me.

The guy who was most likely to know where he was would have been French, but aside from being dead, he didn't appear to have known.

The other guys on the SWAT team? They certainly wouldn't talk to me. If French didn't know, it was unlikely that any of the other team members would know either.

Poliakoff might know, but what was I going to do, ask him? Could I make a deal with Poliakoff? Trade Benni's insurance for my safety. That was a thought. But it depended on Cricket unlocking Benni's SD card.

I felt I was on the defensive. Was there anything in my favor?

I opened the patio door to let the sea breeze in. I had become accustomed to leaving it open all day. The repetitive harmony of the gentle slap of water against the docks had a calming, almost subliminal hypnotic effect. The breeze that wafted through the screen not only brought the temperature down, but helped remove the faint residual odor that lingered in the house like a faint haze that was not really seen, but was still there. As I poured my beer into a glass, I realized even when the air conditioning was back online, I'd probably prefer to leave it off except on the hottest days, preferring this hint of nature to the sterile, mechanical environment that the AC created.

I needed to become more optimistic and get past the funk I was in. To take greater advantage of the peaceful surroundings, I eased out through the screen door to the small deck, perched on stilts, and positioned myself in a lone, lightweight canvas chair. Across the channel, a Brown Pelican, with his unmistakably long bill, sat unceremoniously atop a piling of the neighbor's dock.

I went back to considering my situation. What *did* I have going for me? French was dead. That was something. At least that meant that there was only one assassin after me, well, at least that I knew of. I had thought that there was only one assassin after me before French popped up out of nowhere, so, no, it would be a mistake to assume that Donovan was the only one I had to worry about. That realization called for a long swig from my glass.

I had time off from work. Again. That meant that I could keep a low profile. As far as I knew, Donovan didn't know about my place on Tiki Island.

I could hide out here until I figured out how to find him, or build a case strong enough for the HPD to find him. I didn't like the idea of hiding out. Tiki Island would be my base of operations for locating Donovan. I liked the sound of that much better.

Oh, one other thing. I was going to need to get better at my situational awareness when coming out of bars.

Then came the ugly realization; Donovan was a sniper. I might never see it coming at all. Time for another Lone Star.

Eventually, the pelican departed with an ungraceful takeoff, and I went back inside.

I had a two-pronged plan. Locate Donovan and keep track of him, thus preventing a bullet from materializing out of nowhere. At the same time, I needed to build some kind of case against him that the department couldn't ignore. A case that didn't implicate me.

At that thought, something Q had said shook me deeply. Once you had the proof through "dirty" methods, you could go back and "discover" it through legal methods. I knew when he said it that it was what I was doing, but now I realized I was quickly becoming that guy. The guy who cheats his way to a bust. In my mind, I was never that kind of guy, nor was I ever going to be one. Yet, here I was with few alternatives.

I went online to get some ideas about where Donovan might have gone. Normally, as a detective, I would have some sources to press for information. But I had been undercover for so long that I didn't have any CIs to call on. The contacts that I knew were in Benni's org, and they might not be far enough removed from Donovan to be of much help, anyway.

Cricket might be helpful if she was in the right mood. She had a copy of Donovan's computer files, but was she working on it? The problem was that I didn't know how to get in touch with her. Perhaps I'd risk a trip into the city, but there was no guarantee that she would even let me in the door.

With the help of another beer, I got distracted looking at ads for boats. Having a boat was something that I had always promised myself I would have. I rationalized that getting one now could not only help with my rehabilitation but would give me a place where I could relax, out in the Gulf, without having to be on the lookout for Donovan. I liked that.

By that afternoon, I had located the boat that I wanted.

It was a 2001 Century 2900 with a center console. Its deep V hull and shallow draft would be good for the Gulf. Twin 250 HP Yamaha engines would give it enough power to get around quickly. It even came with an array of expensive electronics. The only problem was that she was in Port Isabel, near Brownsville, a 6-hour drive away.

I made an appointment with the owner for 11 a.m. the next morning and used the rest of the afternoon to get a cashier's check from the bank.

***

After an early rise, I made the convoluted drive south, skirting Houston's south side on the Sam Houston Tollway, joining I-69 until it petered out at U.S. 59, and eventually turning onto U.S. 77 on the outskirts of Victoria.

The long drive was refreshing and gave me time to think, but after four and a half hours, I needed a stop. After I checked my mirrors again for a tail, I pulled into the Sarita Rest Area. The rest area, nestled between the northbound and southbound lanes, was a complex of clean brown buildings, separated from the highway by a row of scrub oaks. After a bio-break and a chance to stretch my legs, it was back in the truck again.

Shortly after leaving the rest stop, I passed by a Border Patrol inspection station funneling northbound traffic, barely visible through the scrub. Although more than an hour north of the border, it was a strategic location. It would add over an hour and a half to someone's journey to bypass it.

Port Isabel turned out to be a rather small place, a

jumping-off point to the actual destination, South Padre Island. Padre Island, a long spit of sand, offered protection to Isabel. Being closer to the Gulf of Mexico, it was home to a variety of marinas and other amenities for boat owners.

The marina I wanted turned out to be on the end of a small man-made peninsula. The entire neighborhood was very much like Tiki Island; rows of houses on tiny lots, with private boat docks behind each one. The houses weren't as upscale as most on Tiki, and many of them weren't raised on stilts to let flood waters flow beneath them. This was primarily because of the area not suffering a hurricane's full fury since 1967 when Beulah came ashore.

I met the owner of the boat at a marina. At five foot ten, he was three inches shorter than me. A likable guy with reddish blonde hair in a white knit shirt. He was selling the boat because he had learned that he had Hodgkin's lymphoma and wouldn't be getting much use out of it for a while.

We took a test run together, and I fell in love with the boat. The only issue was that I had wanted a trailer so that I could bring it back behind my truck. It hadn't occurred to me that the boat was in the water and didn't have a trailer with it.

The lack of a trailer wasn't a deal killer, so we concluded the sale. I planned to shop the area for a suitable 3-axle trailer, staying overnight if need be, and hauling the boat home the next day.

The allure of a new toy overtook me, and I quickly found myself out on the water, passing through the jetties extending out from Brazos Santiago Pass into the Gulf. Since I didn't know where the territorial waters of Mexico were to the south, I headed up north following the low, sandy coastline of Padre Island. Before I realized it, an hour had passed. "Screw the truck." Where was I going to park the trailer, anyway? Half my garage still had a skanky carpet in it.

In a hasty, ill-conceived plan, I continued to cruise north with the idea of navigating back to the dock behind my house, arriving sometime after midnight. I would stop at Corpus Christi for fuel and could decide there whether to continue on, or to spend the night on the boat in a marina, or even rent a hotel room.

37

Orange hues jutted across the Rio Grande Valley as the sun settled below the western horizon. The valley had seen its fair share of bloodshed, first between indigenous tribes, then several wars for independence. The fighting finally subsided in 1916. More recently, the drug cartels had resurrected violence and bloodshed in the area.

Donovan wanted to see more blood on the valley's soil. His black Camaro raced down palm tree-lined highway 77 with his burner phone attached to the air conditioner vent on a little plastic clip. The GPS app was displayed on the screen. Griff hadn't moved in over 6 hours, so he had this chance to catch up to him.

As he neared Olmito, a Dr. Pepper billboard appeared in Texas Spanglish; part English, part Spanish. There were plenty of fruit stands as well if it had been light enough to see them.

This is what Donovan had been waiting for. The opportunity to get to Griff outside of Houston.

He had watched Griff spend time in Galveston, but after French was killed there, Donovan wasn't so sure that Galveston would be the place to get to Griff, either. He knew it was superstitious, but Griff had come out alive and cleared by the local cops.

Another plus was that Griff was parked a mere 25 miles from the Mexican border. He could kill Griff, then slip away and hang out in Matamoros until he saw if he had gotten away clean. If so, he could return. If not, well, he could keep going south.

Donovan realized he was seeing a lot of Border Patrol

cars. They were as common here as any other vehicle. Donovan had never worried about being pulled over by cops before. Being a member of the HPD was sufficient to get you off with a warning, but he wasn't sure of his status now. If HPD were looking for him, he couldn't risk getting pulled over. He eased back on the accelerator a little.

As he neared Port Isabel, Donovan had to pull up directions on the burner. His regular phone was locked inside a metal pistol safe under the front seat. He didn't want it pinging off of any cell towers while on his expedition.

Although he had seen where Griff's truck was on the app, getting there was another matter. It was on a part of the island that had many little peninsulas jutting out into the water. These "fingers" had been dredged out in the twenties to form a "modern Venice." You just couldn't get from one point to another as the crow flies.

When Donovan had figured out which "finger" Griff was on, he faced a new dilemma. Not only did he need to scout out the area and locate Griff without his car being seen, but he also had only one route of escape until he connected back up with the main drag, Highway 100.

He pulled into the nearby Walmart Supercenter to think and plan. Finally, Donovan drove up the spine of the peninsulas, Island Avenue, and turned right onto Pompano Avenue. It was the street and "finger" before the one Griff was on, Tarpon Avenue. At the end of the street, he pulled into Pompano Park. A chunk of asphalt, really; not much of a park. From there, he could see across the canal to where Griff's truck was parked. Since it was dark and the park was unlit, Donovan was confident that Griff could not identify his car.

Griff's truck was parked in a marina of some sort. It was illuminated by the lights. Donovan could sit and wait for Griff to return to his truck and then pick him off with his rifle. There were two problems with that plan. First, the marina presented a lot of clutter between him and the pickup truck's driver-side door. Even if he got a clear shot, there would be an unmistakable report of the gunshot. If he had a better route of escape, he might risk it, but with only one way out, it would be *too* risky. Donovan wished he had a suppressed rifle, but AR15s were next to useless with a suppressor. Sure, the suppressor would cut down on the muzzle blast, but the round would still have a supersonic crack. To reduce the speed of the round to subsonic sound, the round would arrive at its target with less impact than from a .22 LR.

Donovan chose to sit tight and wait for Griff to leave. Then he would follow him until they were in a more deserted area, somewhere on the road back to Houston. In the end, this didn't prove to be a successful strategy.

***

Sunrise on the southern Texas coast is glorious. Clean air and an unobstructed horizon over the Gulf allow the heavenly hues to creep from crimson to orange, then to yellow, until eventually, the sun's orb rises out of the eastern sea.

This particular sunrise was unwelcome by Donovan. He had been up for 23 hours, had driven four hundred miles, and had nothing to show for it. With daylight's return, his Camaro would become more obvious. He begrudgingly retreated to the Walmart parking lot. Assuming that Griff turned west when he left the "fingers" he would pass by. After another hour of waiting, it was too light for Donovan to mask his car by having the headlights on, shining into Griff's rearview mirror. Donovan gave up and started driving back north. He did not know what Griff was doing, or where exactly he was on Tarpon Avenue, but it didn't matter anymore.

***

The same sunrise also illuminated Port Aransas, one hundred twenty-two miles to the north. It was here, at Hampton's Landing, that Griff ended up spending the night.

Even though the distance between Port Isabel and G Town was considerably shorter by water, the sun had been setting as Griff approached Corpus Christi for fuel and desperately needed food and water. As he passed through the channel between Mustang Island on the south and San Jose Island to the north, Port Aransas was right there. Why bother to go the extra distance inland to Corpus Christi?

After Griff had secured a slip for the night, he went to Mickey's bar and grill for a bite and a beer. He was surprised at how thirsty being out on the water had made him. It was while he ate that he realized how impulsive his boat trip was. He didn't know how to identify the San Luis Pass in the dark. The GPS on his phone had drained his battery before he made it to Mustang Island, and he didn't have a power adapter and cord on the boat.

The boat was set up for fishing, not for sleeping. There weren't any sleeping bags, etc. on board. There was no cabin. Sated by his meal, Griff decided that spending the night in a hotel was his best bet.

Despite the comfort of the hotel, Griff didn't sleep well. He was in one place, his home somewhere else, and his truck in yet another place. His mind worked on how he would get his truck back if he continued north. Alternatively, he could go back south to Port Isabel, shop for a trailer, and then drive back to Galveston. That was the original idea, anyway. But doing that would be to admit how foolish an idea this had been in the first place. Damn the torpedoes, continue on. He could get someone to drive him back to Port Isabel. Who exactly he didn't know. Maybe take a bus. He'd figure it out on the cruise northward...and a name for the boat, too.

He would have liked to sleep in late, but he still had a lot of distance to cover and wanted to make it to Tiki Island before sunset. Still, by the time he had rounded up a nautical chart, charger and cord, ice, Dr. Pepper, and bottled water, it was ten o'clock.

***

Donovan was leery of going through the Border Patrol checkpoint, so he circled around the long way. Long after Griff cleared the Aransas Pass Jetty, Donovan passed Corpus Christi back on highway 77. Both continued north, unaware of their proximity to each other.

Donovan arrived at Victoria, a squatty town with little to recommend it other than its location at the crossroads of Corpus Christi, Houston, San Antonio, and Austin. It was here that he decided not to continue north on highway 77, but instead head northwest on highway 59. Donovan had decided that he would go check out the Galveston locations that the GPS app had logged. One thing for certain was that Griff wouldn't be there.

At Edna, he exited 59 and took a series of lesser roads that eventually led to Galveston. His phone app showed it was the slowest route, but the quickest way would have taken him in and out of Houston. He didn't want to go there.

It was early evening when Donovan arrived in the Galveston area. He drove past an address on Tiki Island that turned out to be a residence. Huh. He drove past a Motel Eight. This caused him to wonder; If Griff stayed in a hotel, then who lived in the house? If Griff stayed in the house, then who stayed at the hotel with Griff's truck parked outside overnight? It was becoming increasingly apparent that there was a lot about Griff that Donovan didn't know.

Donovan cruised past the address listed on Griff's driver's license. The biggest mystery was why Griff spent so little time there.

He drove past the G Spot. This must have been where French was killed. That thought caused his anger to rise again. French had been a mentor to him. It was also French that had passed on the assignment to eliminate Griff. His anger turned bittersweet but didn't extinguish itself.

Donovan circled the block and pulled into the G Spot. He couldn't help himself. Even if it came up later that he had been there, he reasoned he could explain it away as visiting the spot where his coworker died, and that it wasn't related to him hunting down Griff.

After pacing around in the parking lot, he went in. Over a drink, he got the bartender to tell him what he knew about the incident in the parking lot, then went back outside and stared at the pavement some more.

He was exhausted and not thinking clearly. He had been up for over thirty-three hours straight. It wasn't smart to be cruising around Galveston while it was still light. He was too far from where he was temporarily living, and staying in Galveston didn't seem like a good idea, even though he had given a passing thought to staying at the Motel Eight to see if he could glean anything about Griff's stay from the night clerk. Ultimately, he headed back out of town to Camp Wallace road to find a seedy hotel that wouldn't ask, didn't care, to see any ID.

***

Griff regretted not having brought more supplies before he cruised up the gulf coast again. He had decent cell reception for the trip since he was seldom out of sight of land. That was something. It gave him a source of music, but more importantly, let him look up the manuals for the boat's electronics.

The boat had come with a West Marine VHF 580 radio, a Raymarine C120 radar, and a Raytheon ST5000 autopilot. Griff wished he had known about the autopilot and how to use it yesterday, but at least for today, the longer of the two days, it allowed him to relax a bit more. He also watched a couple of online videos on how to use navigational charts.

The sky was turning to what photographers call the golden hour when Griff crossed under the Bluewater Highway's San Luis Pass Bridge. The water was shallow here, but the boat's draft was less than two feet, so there was little chance of getting stuck if he stayed between the channel markers. Red Right Returning. Keep the red markers to the right. He still had to motor northeast in the West Bay between the mainland and Galveston Island for another fifteen miles. He knew he would reach home now, not that he had ever really been concerned.

Griff pulled into the slip behind his house at dusk. He tied up the boat, left everything as it was, trudged up the stairs, through the sliding glass door, and into the kitchen for a quick stop. He was hungry, thirsty, and tired. He took care of the first two items in the kitchen, then headed to the bathroom where he discovered he had, not so amazingly, developed a mild sunburn from being on the water for so long. Upon finishing up in the bathroom, he flopped down on the bed, not bothering to pull back the covers, and fell fast asleep.

38

The dawn came and went. Sleeping from pure exhaustion, neither man arose early.

Griff got out of bed and headed to the shower. Being on the saltwater had left his skin and hair in need of a good cleaning. He would have stayed under until he ran out of hot water, but his sunburn, although mild, was irritated by the heat. After pulling on some fresh clothes, he padded out to the kitchen and grabbed a cherry pop-tart for breakfast. As he waited for it to leap skyward in the toaster, he admired his new boat through the kitchen window. Warm pop-tart in hand, he went through the sliding door, down the stairs to his boat dock, and unloaded from his journey. As he did, he began to take a mental note of additional supplies he needed to stock on the boat, especially some suntan lotion.

Fifteen miles away, the motel manager pounded on Donovan's door. "Check-out time buddy. You stay longer, you're gonna have to pay for another day." At this motel, they weren't used to guests staying more than an hour or two, and certainly not until check-out time.

"Gimmie' a minute," Donovan replied. The knocking had woken him up. He cleared his head, then glanced at the GPS app on the burner phone. Griff's truck was still in Port Isabel. After a quick trip to the bathroom, Donovan headed to the office, paid for another day, and headed back to bed. There wasn't anything he wanted to do in Galveston during the daylight, so sleep now, and prowl once the sun went down.

After getting gear from the trip squared away, Griff decided he was ready to go into town for some lunch. Once he stepped out the front door, he was confronted with not having a car; his truck was still in Port Isabel. Oh yeah, that was a problem that he still had to resolve.

After sulking about lunch for a few minutes, it dawned on Griff that he had been in many seafood restaurants, like Mickey's, where the windows looked out over a boat dock and onto the water. Not being sure how that worked, he went online and searched for eateries that he could take the boat to.

Then minutes later, Griff was back on the water, circling Tiki Island, and heading northeast toward G Town. A few minutes after that, he motored under the Causeway and old train bridge. The boat had opened up a new world for him. Perhaps that is what he should name the boat; New Life. Maybe not.

A few minutes later, he passed under another causeway leading to Pelican Island. After motoring past several industrial ship docks and the cruise ship dock, Griff finally pulled up to Willie G's. He tied up and climbed the steps leading to Pier 21 and surveyed the establishment. It had two stories with a large, steeply pitched roof with four gables looking out onto the Galveston Channel. The lower story was brick and the rest corrugated metal sheets. It gave the feel of an old dockside warehouse, but the brick looked too new to be authentic.

The interior was not anything like an old warehouse. All the support timbers were beautiful wood, oak perhaps. The walls were cream in color, and the trim, and tablecloths were white. Griff ordered and while looking out over his boat, realized he had never been to this part of town before. Pier 21 was like an oasis in an industrial wasteland. Either side had commercial wharves, chemical plants, a variety of industries, and a railroad yard. From the land side, you had to cross over the railroad tracks to get here, and even though his storage unit was less than half a mile away, he'd never ventured across the tracks.

Although the food was spendy, it was delicious, and the atmosphere was calm and relaxing. As he finished his meal, he called Krunch. Maybe he could talk her into taking him to get his truck. He didn't think that she would, but if it worked out, it would give them a long ride together to get to know one another away from the work environment, and perhaps open the door to the missed opportunity the night French died. If it went well, he might be able to enlist her aid in tracking down Donovan.

"Hey, Krunch. Griff. You'll never guess what I just did..."

"Kill another cop?"

Ugh. That was awkward. Griff couldn't tell if she was trying to bust his chops or what. It was like something Cricket would have said. After a few seconds of silence, he continued, "I bought a boat."

"Wow. That's great, Griff. You can take me for a ride on it sometime."

"Sure thing. There is a funny story that goes along with it."

Krunch cut him off. "Hey, listen, I'm in the middle of something right now. Can I call you back later?"

They said goodbye and clicked off. Griff wasn't sure if he had just gotten the cold shoulder or not. Where did he stand with her?

The marina that Griff had previously visited near

Corpus Christi had fuel, supplies, and a bar and grill. Undoubtedly, there had to be similar services here. He would need to find out where to fuel up the boat, etc. After a quick search on his phone, the closest one was just past Pier Ten, less than a mile away. The others tended to be on the far side of the Island in Offatts Bayou.

After paying the check, Griff returned to the boat. His boat. He motored north past a huge offshore drilling rig that was now a museum and several industrial docks. As he rounded Pier 10, he could see the marina. The massive University of Texas Medical Branch complex, just to the right, a block away, dwarfed the marina's two-story bar and grill.

Griff fueled up, surveyed the menu for future reference, shopped the store, and chatted up a couple of the employees.

Heading back home, he replayed the call with Krunch repeatedly in his mind as he made his way out of the Galveston Channel, under the bridges, and back into the West Bay.

Back home, Griff settled down to spend the rest of the day working on his other problem. Donovan had disappeared, and Griff didn't have the resources to find out what had happened to him. He still needed to get enough evidence surreptitiously to the right people to ensure that Donovan was on HPD's most wanted list.

His phone rang again later that day. Unknown caller. Griff's day instantly became brighter. It was Cricket letting him know she had decrypted the files he had left her; Donovan's laptop files. "That's some messed up stuff there. Especially for a cop. It's up on the net now."

"That is great. Thank you so much."

"Even though it was you that asked, I enjoyed doing it to screw with a cop." Cricket was still holding a grudge.

"I think the guy in the videos, Donovan, may come after me. Would you be able to track him down and monitor his movements for me?"

"You realize that keeping you alive is not a high priority for me?"

It was a long shot, but Griff had to try. Returning his attention to the decoded files, he said, "I'm not sure that the department would investigate this, even if the files came to their attention. If you wanted to seal that guy's fate, you could somehow make sure that the Texas Rangers know about the files." The Rangers were tasked with investigating the police if need be. Not a single dirty cop, but corruption at a department level. Still, it seemed like another way to kick the hornets' nest, so to speak.

Silence from Cricket.

"Hey, I got a new boat. You should come take a ride sometime." The line went dead.

The plan wasn't coming together. Having the files decrypted and published by Cricket was a good step, but Griff didn't need to put any more pressure on Donovan. He was already under so much pressure that he had popped his cork.

39

As evening fell, Donovan came out of his hidey-hole at the no-tell motel, grabbed some fast food, and headed toward Galveston. He planned to investigate/burgle the residence listed on Griff's driver's license.

He made his way to the correct street, turned, and passed a white octagon house that resembled a lighthouse that had been squashed under a giant's footstep. As he cruised past the target house, he noticed a light on upstairs. No car in the driveway. The light could be on a timer.

There wasn't a good place to park, except on the narrow street. Since the black car didn't stand out too much at night, Donovan risked parking in the driveway where it would be less conspicuous than parking on the street where passersby would *have* to see it.

Donovan wore camo patterned BDUs, black nitrile gloves, and even though the weather was too warm for it, a black watch cap. He checked for oncoming cars, slipped out of the Camaro, eased the door closed, and deftly moved to the base of the stairs, where he paused again to look and listen.

Not sensing any danger, Donovan slithered slowly up the stairs, testing each step to see if it would creak underfoot. Near the top of the stairs, he paused. He grabbed the door handle, planning to pick the lock, but to his surprise, the handle turned. It was unlocked. You certainly didn't leave your door unlocked in Houston.

He hadn't planned to turn the handle, but since it had already moved in his hand, he was committed to continuing. He cracked the door a few inches to take a peek inside. To his dismay, only a few feet away, a young woman was peering over the top of a book, looking directly at him.

Donovan quickly said, "Oops. Wrong house."

The young woman dropped her book and swiveled, reaching for the phone sitting on the end table next to her. But the black gloves and watch cap didn't work for that narrative.

Donovan bounded through the doorway and closed the distance in less than two seconds. The woman had no time to react before Donovan batted the phone away.

As he pulled a knife, "Don't do that. Who are you, and what do you have to do with Hunter?"

The woman twisted back in her seat, dropping her phone hand to the sofa. "I'm Hunter. What do you want?"

Donovan, slightly off guard, snarled, "Not you. Griffin Hunter."

"You've got the wrong Hunter. Get lost."

Donovan was up close, in her face with the knife now, brandishing it threateningly. "And I want the right Hunter. What does he do here? When's he gonna be back?"

Donovan hadn't noticed when the Hunter woman's hand had slid between the sofa cushions, but he noticed it coming back out, gripping a pistol in the left hand.

Donovan slashed across the front of Hannah Hunter, missing her neck, but cutting into the outer side of her pectoral muscle and the front of her right deltoid. Hannah screamed, and Donovan panicked.

As the gun continued to rise, Donovan struck again, this time swinging toward the gun, but missing. A deafening roar filled the room as Hannah, still raising the gun, fired a wild shot in response.

Donovan, knowing that the next shot wouldn't miss, plunged the blade into Hannah's chest. Her eyes and mouth flew wide open, but no scream escaped. Both stunned, they were frozen in time for a moment, then Donovan withdrew the blade and slashed the hand holding the gun.

As the gun dropped to the floor, Donovan dashed back out the door, careened down the stairs, and with his ears still ringing, raced the Camaro into the night.

***

My phone rang again. What is it with the calls tonight? "Hello."

"Griff. This is Rusty." His voice was serious and determined.

A sense of foreboding washed over me. I hadn't been cleared of the death of French yet. "Yeah Rusty, what do I need to do?" Then it occurred to me that if they were going to arrest me, they would be at my door, not on the phone, and the foreboding dissipated.

"It's your sister. Hannah. She is headed to the hospital."

"What? What happened?" The foreboding returned in full force.

"We're not sure yet. Looks like she was attacked at home. Figured you would want to know as soon as possible." Rusty paused, then said in a voice that cops recognized well, "You should get down to UTMB. They are going to need you."

If she was being transported to the University of Texas Medical Branch, it had to be bad. It was Galveston's level one trauma center, with 12 ambulance bays and two helipads. They would pass two other nearby hospitals to get there. "I...I'd like a ride if you could arraign for that."

"That's ok. We have a unit already on its way to get you. I wanted to give you a heads up, so you'd be ready to roll when they arrive."

"I'll wait out front." With nothing else to be said, we clicked off.

***

The ride was quick; lights, no siren. I got to sit in the front seat this time.

We pulled right up to a ground-floor entrance, courtesy of the flashing lights. I scrambled out and dashed inside, where I was met by Rusty. I did not know what became of the officer who drove me there.

"What happened?"

"We are still piecing it together. Hannah's in surgery right now, and probably will be for a while. We'll talk as we walk." As we headed upstairs to the waiting room, Rusty said, "We got a call from a neighbor. Reported a gunshot. After interviewing the neighbor, our guy went up to your sister's door to investigate. Found the door open and Hannah slumped in a ball on the floor. Lotsa blood."

One thing about a cop telling another cop, they didn't sugarcoat the details.

"Our guys who are there say it looks like she got a shot off, but since there is not a blood trail, the attacker might have gotten away clean."

"What was her condition when they got her here?"

"From what I understand, it was a knife attack. She had multiple cuts and a penetrating stab wound to the chest. I'd suspect a Pneumothorax." Rusty paused.

We stood in silence as I processed what he had said so far.

Rusty, putting on his investigator hat, asked, "Do you have any idea who would want to do this to her?"

"No. No one. She doesn't have an enemy in the world as far as I know." Then a thought entered my head and apparently crossed my face.

"But what?" Rusty inquired.

"Well...You know the guy that had a go at me?"

"French, the HPD guy, right?"

"Yeah. He, umm, had a buddy."

"Wait. Are you saying that there is a second cop who hates you bad enough to kill your sister?" Rusty sounded incredulous.

"Not my sister. Me. I can't be sure, of course."

More silence. Then Rusty, "You gonna' give me a name and some details?"

"As I said, I can't be sure. It was just a thought. Let's hold off until we see what your guys turn up. I don't want to jam a guy up if he isn't involved." Well, I did, but I had to think of the ramifications of involving the Galveston police, too.

"You want us to post a guy at your place in the meantime?"

"Naw. If it is someone after me, and they went to Pirates Cove, they obviously don't know where I live. I'll be OK."

Rusty hung out for a few more minutes, but there

wasn't much to say and nothing to do but sit in uncomfortable silence, so he said, "I'm going out to the scene to get a look firsthand and see what they've come up with. Call me if anything changes."

One never wants to hear their family's house referred to as a crime scene.

*****

Donovan was panicked. As a sniper, he was always hidden, and in control. When he had killed his "dates" he was in control. They were drugged and posed no threat, didn't put up resistance. The pleasure of killing those men was completely absent from this encounter. He had been surprised. He had thought that he was in control, but that was taken away from him by a woman. She had not only resisted, but could have killed him, and almost certainly would have shot him if she had any more time to do it.

He had allowed himself to be in a location with very limited avenues of escape, not unlike Port Isabel. Galveston was on an island. There were only two ways off, and only one major road to get to either of them. If the local cops acted fast enough, he could get caught, or at least identified as having been in the area, an area where he had no business being.

As he drove, Donovan mulled over what he would do if he were pulled over. He realized that his best course of action would be to be calm, say nothing, and go quietly until he could get a lawyer and find out what the charges were.

Not getting caught tonight was his top priority. As he realized that, he slowed down to the speed limit. Going north toward central Galveston, he passed a southbound police car. No lights or sirens. That gave him hope that he had time to escape.

The Camaro cruised up Seawall Boulevard, then turned onto Sixty-First Street, passing the Motel Eight. As he was preparing to turn left onto Broadway and the entrance to I-45, he stopped breathing momentarily when he heard sirens and saw the flickering red and blue strobes lighting up the dark like fireworks on the fourth of July. A line of two police cars and an ambulance turned in front of him, from Broadway onto Sixty-First Street, and continued South. Donovan blew out a heavy breath and made the turn that led him onto the freeway and off of Galveston Island. He drove into the night's comforting darkness.

***

The emergency waiting room was pleasant enough, in a sterile, industrial, sort of way, but it offered no comfort for anyone who had ever had to sit there for hours on end. So it was for Griff. He sat for hours, fidgeted, paced, and scanned the magazines. He tried to avoid introspection, but it was inevitable.

***

Another crisp sunrise was breaking through the horizon when Rusty walked in. They both nodded to acknowledge each other's presence, then simultaneously asked each other the same question, "Any news?"

Griff, "No. Someone popped out twice to tell me she

was still in surgery, the best of hands, and the like, but no actual information."

As Rusty parted his lips to speak, the door between the surgery corridor and the waiting area opened. Both men turned to face the oncoming doctor.

"Mr. Hunter?"

Griff raised his hand like he was being sworn in at a courtroom hearing. "That's me."

"Your, umm, Hannah, is out of surgery now and has been moved to ICU."

"What's her condition? Can we go see her?"

"It was touch and go for a while, but, barring any complications, she should pull through. She lost a lot of blood, had some damage to her left lung, will have a few scars, and may need some rehab. It's a good thing she was brought in when she was. She wouldn't have lasted too much longer."

As Griff processed this information, Rusty said, "I'm with the Galveston police. We need to talk to Ms. Hunter as soon as possible for our investigation."

"That's going to be a problem." The doctor stated flatly.

Cops were used to that as a response. Leave my patient alone until they have a chance to recover. Blah, blah, blah. In the meantime, the most critical hours of an investigation were passing.

As Rusty started to say something, Griff gave him a gentle nudge. "That's fine. I just need to see my sister." He could get the details from here as well as Rusty could.

"You can see her now, but...there's something that you both need to know. She has been heavily sedated. She won't know that you're there or be able to respond to anything that you ask." The doctor turned to face Rusty directly. "That's the reason it would be problematic to question Ms. Hunter." Turning back to Griff, "Come with me."

They both followed the doctor to the intensive care unit, were introduced to the charge nurse, and were shown into her room. It was what they had expected to see. Hannah was in the bed surrounded by IV pumps, bags on poles, monitors, etc. She had bandages over her throat and a cannula in her nose.

It looked and smelled all too familiar to Griff. "I'm here, sis." He turned to Rusty. "What do you know?"

"Basically little more than we initially knew. There were no signs of forced entry, no fresh prints except yours and hers. Nothing appears to be missing, no actual sign of a struggle. The only weapon at the scene was a .45 with your sister's prints on it. The knife wasn't left behind. The gun had been fired once, slug in the kitchen floor. Lots of blood, but it appears to be Hannah's. There was a slight blood trail leading to the door, but that turned out to be Hannah's as well, so we believe it had dripped from the knife. No witnesses, no security video in the area that was of any use." Rusty shrugged. "The crime scene guys are done, but we are going to leave it sealed off in case we need to go back. What we need is to talk to Hannah to get a description of the attacker."

Rusty changed his tone along with the subject. "Look, you've been here all night. You look terrible. You can't do anything here until she comes around, and that sounds like it's going to be a day or two. Let me take you home so you can get some rest."

Griff nodded silently, took one last look, and turned toward the hallway. At the doorway, he turned for a last look, then was hit by a thought, a memory. Turning again, he made his way directly to the nurse's station and spoke to the charge nurse. "I was recently in the hospital and someone killed the man in the next room and tried to kill me by spiking our IVs. There is a slight chance that the person who did it could also be the one who attacked my sister."

The nurse was taken aback. With a slight bit of indignation in her voice, "that could never happen here." Then she quickly added reassuringly, "But I'll make a note in the chart for every IV to be double-checked and carefully examined."

"Thank You."

***

The fresh, damp morning air was calming to Griff as they stepped out of the doors and headed to the parking ramp.

Rusty said, "You know, I have to ask, especially since yours were the only other prints at the scene...where were you last night at the time of the attack?"

Griff halted, falling a couple of steps behind. He shouted to Rusty's back. "What?"

Rusty turned to face Griff. "C'mon. You know I have to ask. For the record." He shrugged.

Griff blew out some of the anger inside. He knew Rusty was doing his job. Family members were always suspects. He had never considered how callus the question was, or the impact it had on those being questioned before.

Still irritated, "You know where I was. I was at home. On Tiki Island."

"You have anyone who can collaborate that?"

Griff glared. "You. You are the one that called, informed me, then moments later, one of *your* cars picked me up."

Rusty shook off the hostility. It was common, and he had gotten used to it over the years. They started walking back to the car.

Griff continued, "It takes twenty-five to thirty minutes from my house to hers. You think that from the time the gunshots were reported until you called me, I'd been driving from her house, got home, and changed clothes?"

"No. I don't. I just have to put in the report that I asked. You said no, and that you had a plausible alibi."

They drove out of the parking garage in silence. Neither man could stand the sixteen-minute drive to Tiki like that.

Rusty broke the silence. "You want me to put a guard on Hannah's door?"

"Thank you." Griff appreciated the offer. "But I don't think that it would help. In Houston, the place was flooded with cops, and I had one outside of my door. It didn't work there, so no, I'd rather see your guys doing what they can to get the attacker."

"Ok. Let me know if you change your mind. You'll let us know as soon as they bring your sister around?" Rusty knew there wasn't much his guys could do until they talked to her. "So, what were your prints doing there? I thought that you and Hannah had a falling out after your dad's passing?"

"Well yeah, that's true. She couldn't comprehend why I couldn't make it to the funeral," Griff explained. "I went by the other day."

"How'd that go?" It was the cop in Rusty that was asking, not the friend.

"Better than expected. I think we buried the hatchet." It was an awkward turn of phrase under the circumstances. "Umm, made up. We realized we were the only family that each other had."

"You know if she had any female friends that might be angry enough to do this?"

"No. I still don't know that much about her personal life over the last couple of years. Why a woman?" Griff asked.

"The knife. On the street, I'd say a guy, but in her home like that, I dunno, it seems more...feminine." Rusty continued, "Just a thought. Why a knife?"

***

The knife.

As soon as Donovan had made it back to the motel, he washed the knife off in the sink best as he could, and let it soak in there overnight. He didn't have any bleach and considered getting some, but he suspected that a good forensics guy could pull something off of it no matter what he did. He couldn't get caught with the knife in his possession.

Between his hours being swapped night for day, and the tension followed by fear, Donovan wasn't able to sleep all night. He didn't bother to try. He sat near the door, listening, expecting to hear a cop car pull up at any moment, but one never came.

By the time the office opened in the morning, exhaustion had replaced fear, mostly from the realization that no one was coming for him. At least, he hoped that was the case. He was still paranoid about going out in daylight, so he went to the office and paid for another night. Although he'd rather wait for dark, Donovan knew he would have to venture out to get rid of the knife.

He headed out from the motel and stopped at some random gas station with a Subway inside. He filled the Camaro, grabbed some beer and chips, and a copy of the Galveston County Daily News. From there, he drove over the bridge where Lost Bay joins Chocolate Bayou. There was a car behind him, so Donovan pulled off into the public boat ramp, let the car go by, then did a U-turn, back onto the bridge. Halfway across, he threw the knife out of the window, over the railing, and into the muddy waters below.

He returned to the hotel, drank a beer, and tried to sleep. Donovan hated getting rid of the knife. French and most of the guys he knew who were beholding to Poliakoff all had identical knives, all with a unique engraved pattern on them. It was a token by which they could recognize one another even if they had never been introduced. Sort of like a challenge coin. Of course, that life didn't matter anymore. His only concern now was survival.

****

I, too, tried to get some rest, but it wouldn't come.

My phone rang. It was Krunch. "How are you holding

up? I heard about your sister."

"Ok, I guess. It's harder than I would have expected. How'd you find out?"

"Rusty called to let us all know. Instead of us all calling, I was nominated to call. Everyone sends their best wishes. How about I come down there for a few hours to keep you company while you wait?"

After a moment's consideration, I said, "Yeah, that would be nice. If you can spare the time."

"No worries. What's the address? I'll be there in an hour." And she was.

During that hour, I took a hot shower and took down and hid all photos of Donovan, the other SWAT guys, and their houses from my safe room.

Krunch arrived at the door wearing a short-sleeved red, white, and blue plaid cowboy shirt pulled up and tied just below her ribcage. She had dark red leather cowboy boots that came up just below the knee, with an ornate gray stitching pattern. In between, she wore a pair of moderate-length denim shorts held up with a dark red leather belt. The silver buckle was of medium size adorned with a gold longhorn steer, similar to a man's buckle, but with engraved flowery filigree all around. The belt was adorned with matching silver and gold Conchos.

She had earrings that matched the Conchos. All custom made no doubt.

Her lips sported a pleasant shade of lipstick. She never wore lipstick at work.

I hadn't seen Krunch in non-work clothes for over a year. She looked sexy, but not in a country music trashy sort of way. It was much more authentic and refined. Perhaps I should have taken a cold shower instead.

"Are you going to just stand there, or are you going to invite me in?"

Without saying a word, I stood aside to let her pass by. I was trying to think of the most appropriate thing to say about her appearance as she entered. The pockets on the back of her shorts were adorned with small sequins in an American Indian design.

"Aren't those pockets uncomfortable to sit on?" was the best I could muster. How humiliating.

"I hadn't planned on riding anything today. Did you have other plans?"

I was without a witty answer. There was nothing I could say that would not shove my foot farther in my mouth.

As I showed her around the barren house, Krunch playfully observed, "I like what you've done with the place." When they got to the safe room with maps and pictures of the cold case gay murders on the wall, she added, "Especially this room. Such a homey feel."

I felt my face go flush and stuttered. "It's some cold cases that I am working on and think that they might be related."

"All work and no play makes Griff a dull boy."

We moved out onto the small deck overlooking the docks. "Is that the new boat?"

Now it was my turn for a playful reply. "Yes. With those keen powers of observation, you won't be a junior detective much longer."

Krunch made her pouty face. "The other day, you said you'd take me for a ride."

I wanted to say something about her not planning on riding anything today, but thought better of it. "I'd love to. But not today. I want to stay close in case anything changes with Hannah. Can I give you a rain check?"

"What is it with you and rain checks?"

"That was harsh. Maybe true, but harsh." I tried to put on the equivalent of her pouty face, but it didn't work for me.

"Yeah, maybe. But this raincheck I want to cash in on." Krunch quickly added, "The one for the boat ride, I mean."

We went down the steps from the deck, and I gave her a quick tour of the boat.

After that, she said, "Why don't we go to the hospital to check on Hannah in person?"

"That's a great idea. We can grab some lunch too. Would you mind driving?"

Krunch had a cherry red mini cooper with a pair of white stripes running up the hood and over the roof. The rear window had two white stickers on it. One was the silhouette of a woman riding a galloping horse with her long hair flowing in the wind like the horse's tail. The other was lettering that said, "Don't flatter yourself cowboy I was looking at your truck." She did not have to open her mouth to be snarky.

Inside, on the back seat, there was a buff-colored Stetson with a dark red leather band and a Concho attached to the front of the band that matched her others. I realized why it was on the back seat instead of her head. The car was short on headroom. I concluded Krunch did not shop for her clothes at Walmart.

I'd never been in a car that small before. On the one

hand, its short wheelbase made it handle like it was some kind of kiddie car. Being low to the ground, pickup trucks felt intimidating when they pulled alongside. On the other hand, those same characteristics seemed like it would be fun to drive. The only thing that I could decide on was that it wasn't the right car for me.

***

The visit to intensive care was brief. The only new development was that the doctor said they were dialing back her sedatives and that she would hopefully regain consciousness soon.

Afterward, I directed Krunch on how to get to Willie G's. It was the nicest place I knew of and was pretty much on the way back to my place.

Our table was next to a window with a great view of Pelican Island, just across the Galveston Channel. The only problem was that Pelican Island wasn't that great to look at. The view primarily consisted of an industrial facility where offshore oil rig platforms were repaired. Interesting, but not scenic.

"Your sister is pretty," Krunch observed. Then, in her playful manner, "Hard to believe that you came from the same parentage."

I didn't know how to respond under the circumstances.

"Too soon? Sorry?"

After a relaxing lunch of small talk, grilled shrimp, and sour cream potato purée with charred broccoli, Griff genuinely felt much better. "I can't thank you enough for coming down today. I think I needed a woman's touch, a woman's perspective to pull me out of the funk I was in."

Krunch didn't know how to feel about being called a woman. She was never called that at work. It would have been taboo. There she was, Krunch, a detective, or on rare occasions, dismissively, a girl.

After the drive back to Tiki, we both agreed it was time for Krunch to go.

"I'd like to do this again sometime. Soon." I was testing the waters.

"So would I. It was great to get to know each other better on a personal level. Besides, you still owe me that boat ride."

We both smiled. Then she was gone. I hoped that our relationship had turned a critical corner. It was ironic that the attack on my sister had brought us closer together.

***

I spent the rest of the afternoon sleeping peacefully. Krunch had brought a glimmer of hope into my otherwise chaotic life.

The reality of my world came back into focus when I woke up. I called the hospital to check in, but there was still no change. I thought about calling Rusty, but deep inside, I knew that there wouldn't be any change there, either.

Had Donovan been the one to attack my sister? I couldn't see it any other way. Although I didn't know about my sister's recent life, I knew her personality, and that made it unlikely that it was anyone she knew personally. It was too much of a coincidence for it to have been a random attack or a home invasion gone wrong. No, it had to be Donovan.

After a quick snack, I went into the safe room and began adding photos of Donovan back to the crime board. I had to connect Donovan in some meaningful way to the murders.

As night fell, I sat in the chair at my makeshift table, staring at the board.

Donovan. How to tie up Donovan?

***

Donovan came out of his hidey-hole at the no-tell motel and grabbed a subway from the gas station. He had originally planned to get back to highway 77 and head north, back to the place he was staying in. But, as he ate his foot-long BMT, he checked that tracking app. Griff's truck hadn't moved in all this time. What was Griff doing? Or had he sold the truck to someone else who had driven it down there? Or had Griff discovered the tracker and was setting up a trap for him?

He scanned the local newspaper. It mentioned the attack, but there were no details of a suspect mentioned. Perhaps he had gotten away clean. But the woman, apparently Griff's sister, had seen him. Really well. She could describe him. Really well. He started weighing the risk and rewards of trying to finish her off in the hospital. The IV thing wouldn't work because he didn't have the fine-needled syringe and the Fentanyl. He might be able to scare those up in the hospital, but that would be too risky. Was there another way?

Ultimately, Donovan decide he had to make one last

trip to Galveston before leaving the area for good. He wanted to go tonight, but he had learned the hard way that being hasty could lead to serious consequences. It had all of his life. This would be a good time to change that pattern of behavior. Instead of going into town, he would lie low, let things cool off, and spend the night planning his next move.

He passed the time doing reconnaissance with Google maps and street views. He looked at various escape routes and the times to traverse them. He was still going to be on an island. There was no way around that, but if he got in and out quickly, he should have enough time to get off the island before the alarm was sounded.

40

Morning arrived with a tapestry of broken red clouds above. What was it they said? Red sky in the morning, sailor take warning?

The color of the clouds inspired me to choose the Cherry Pop-Tarts today. My breakfast was interrupted by my phone. I still needed to change that annoying default ringtone.

"Mr. Hunter?"

"Yes?"

"This is Kendall, at UTMB. I wanted to let you know. Hannah is starting to regain consciousness. Hopefully, she will be alert in a couple of hours."

"That is great news." It was the best news I'd had in quite a while. Then I remembered that I still didn't have a car. That was getting to be a real pain. I had to retrieve my truck soon.

"It may take me a while to get there."

"Oh, don't worry about that. You still have an hour or two. Besides, if she wakes up early, your niece is already here."

"My niece?"

"Yes, she got here during the night and has been keeping vigil."

"Uh-huh. OK. Thanks."

The problem was, I didn't have a niece. I was about to call Rusty when I realized the ICU didn't allow anyone but family in. If it was someone who had bad intentions, she would have already had sufficient opportunity to do something. No doubt, Krunch must have come back and passed herself off as my niece so she could get in.

I thought about taking the boat. I could motor up to the marina, dock at the bar and grill, and walk the block to the hospital. I also thought about calling Rusty, updating him on the new development, and asking for a ride, but I didn't want him to realize that my truck wasn't here. It would be embarrassing to explain my rash decision to leave the truck down south.

Uber to the rescue.

***

I was ready to talk to my sister this time. I was not ready for what I saw as I entered her room.

There, hunched on a chair, was a young woman in a short red and black plaid skirt. She had her feet pulled up to her chest, her heels resting on the seat of the chair, revealing that she wasn't wearing anything underneath.

Her face was buried in her kneecaps, but her silver hair was unmistakable.

"Cricket?"

Her head popped up. Her black makeup was smudged like she had been crying.

"Oh, Woody...um Griff, I'm so sorry." She made no effort to put her feet down.

"What are you sorry about?" I was bewildered.

"This is all my fault. If I would have done what you asked; If I would have tracked that creeper cop, then we would have known where he was. We could have warned your sister."

There were so many things to ask. "How did you even know?"

"What? You think because I'm a geek, I don't follow what's going on?"

"No, I'm just surprised to find you here."

"It was that cop, right?"

"I think so." I could relate to the guilt she was feeling. "This wasn't your fault."

We talked for a while. Cricket seemed to relax and came out of her fetal position.

Eventually, looking for something else to say, I asked about her tattoos. She perked up immediately.

"The skulls pay homage to Dia de Muertos, the Day of the Dead."

Her arm tattoos disappeared under the cap sleeve of a low-cut, lacy black top with red trim.

She ran her finger up the line of skulls. "At the top are the Marigolds." she tugged at the shoulder of one sleeve, pulling it down to reveal a line of large gold flowers running inward from her shoulder. "Sometimes they are referred to as the flower of the dead."

"Hmm." I tried to appear interested.

Without hesitation, she tugged the other sleeve and pulled her blouse down below her breasts, revealing the rest of the body art that ran down her cleavage and a pair of silver hoops that matched the one in her nose, piercing through her nipples.

Evidently, Cricket didn't believe in either underwear or modesty. Once again, I found myself speechless. Not that I was unaccustomed to naked women, it was just that the setting seemed wildly inappropriate. I didn't understand this generation.

After she ran out of things to say about her tattoos, she said, "I wish there was something that I could do. Do you still want me to track down that cop?"

"I think that my sister will be able to give the police a description. That should start them looking for the guy. Better that they go looking for him than us."

It felt like we had gotten past the baggage associated with the shootout. I needed to trust her now. "You *could* break the encryption on another SD card for me. It would help Benni." It would help me more. I studied her eyes as she answered.

"Sure."

I reached down and wrestled my boot off. I peeled the insole up, revealing a small cavity I had made into which I had secured the micro SD card. As I retrieved the card, I said, "Just one thing. You cannot reveal what's on here to anyone. That would endanger Benni's life. Will you agree with that?"

"Yeah, sure."

A groan rumbled up dryly from the direction of the hospital bed. Hannah was waking up.

"I have to go now. I'll get back to you with the stuff." And with that, Cricket stood, turned, and left.

"Would you let the nurse's station know that she is making noises?"

Eventually, Hannah's eyes fluttered open, and her placid expression turned to one of confusion. "What...?" She tried to move, but was quickly punished for the effort.

No sooner than I told her she was in the hospital than the nurse appeared, setting off an all too familiar chain of routine events.

Between the nurse's interruptions and Hannah's bewildered questions, I asked, "Tell me about your attacker."

Hannah blinked twice. "I was sitting at home reading a book. That's the last thing that I remember." Her face contorted into utter befuddlement.

An hour went by. Hannah was tired and was drifting back to sleep.

I called Rusty. "My sister is awake. The thing is, she doesn't remember the attack. The doctor says it's not unusual to have some temporary memory loss after trauma. He doesn't believe it's permanent. She will get her memory back. Just not today." Rusty sounded as disappointed as I felt.

***

I spent the rest of the day at her bedside. Hannah slipped in and out throughout the day. They brought me a dinner tray when they served her. It wasn't great, but much better than I expected. As the sun was setting, the nurse told me to go home. Hannah needed her rest. She was out of danger. They would call me if anything changed. They would probably move her out of ICU tomorrow. Like that.

I took an Uber back home. Realizing that it was still up to me to find Donovan, I returned to sit at the table and stare at the pictures on the wall. I wished I had told Cricket to track the vermin down.

41

Donovan left the Camp Wallace motel, drove short segments on Highway 6 and I-45, then exited at Virginia Point Road. Turning onto Tiki Drive, he passed the Tiki Food Mart and into the neighborhood. He had realized that an attack in the hospital was simply too risky. Instead, he had decided to investigate/burgle the residence he passed yesterday to see of what importance it was. And, if Griff had sold the truck, maybe get lucky and kill Griff at his home. Unlike last night, he would be prepared for someone being at home this time.

Donovan had briefly driven through the neighborhood before and was now armed with his research on the area. It would be less conspicuous if he could drive directly to his intended destination, stop and get out instead of cruising back and forth. That is just what he did.

The house for rent was just on the next block from Griff's. Donovan's black car wouldn't stand out too much in the early evening darkness. Neither would his camo BDUs.

Donovan moved from point to point, just like he was on a SWAT mission. *If* anyone spotted him, it would look suspicious but, it was how he was trained. It was how he was comfortable. The distance he had to cover consisted mostly of empty lots. Where there were houses, he had to go through the front yard. There weren't any real backyards. The houses were set back to the rear of the lots, and just beyond the house were boat docks. Methodically, he closed the distance to Griff's house.

There were two lights on, one in the backroom by the

patio and one in what he assumed was a bedroom. Donovan rightly assumed that this meant that someone was home. Instead of diagonally, crossing the open lot next to Griff's to get around back, he went to the front of the house, then slid along the side of the house for better concealment from the floor above. He waited at the bottom of the stairs to the back deck and listened patiently.

Silence.

Donovan took the next part slowly. He wanted the element of surprise, not the shock and awe that SWAT relied on. He took the stairs one by one, his combat boots making stealth a bit more challenging. When his head was just below the deck, he paused, took a breath, then poked his head up far enough that he could peer into the patio door, hoping not to see a pair of eyes looking back or worse yet, a looming gun barrel. Seeing neither, he relaxed a bit and scanned the path to the patio door for obstacles. Donovan smiled. The patio door was open.

He wished he had his knife. If he was quick enough and went for the throat, there wouldn't be any sound to alert the neighbors. Instead, he'd have to rely on a spare bootlace.

With the bootlace readied, Donovan slithered up the remaining steps and across the few feet to the edge of the sliding door. He listened, then did a quick peek around the edge. Seeing nothing, he put his head around for a longer look. The door was between the dining space and the kitchen. Beyond was a darkened living room. There was no furniture to be seen. Whoever was here must be in the bedroom where the other light shone. Its light spilled from the hallway into the living room.

Donovan made his way through the screen door,

across the empty dining area, and over to the entrance to the hallway. Once there, he repeated the pattern. Listen, quick peek, longer look. He had a clear view of the room directly across the hall. To Donovan's amazement, Griff was facing away from the door, his back facing Donovan. Donovan gripped the ends of a black bootlace in his hands and coiled for the strike.

The moment of truth had arrived. Donovan catapulted across the hallway and through the threshold of the room. Griff heard the movement behind him and stood, turning as he did so. He was too late. Donovan had closed the distance and draped the bootlace over Griff's head before Griff could react defensively. Griff had seen Donovan's face, but it didn't matter at this point.

***

Hearing a rustling of clothes behind me, I sprang from my chair and started to turn. As I did, the view of my attacker was blocked by the gloved hands near my face. My hands were on their way up, but not fast enough. As my assailant lowered his hands slightly, I glimpsed Donovan out of the corner of my eye. In that same instant, a sharp pain was around my neck.

Strangulation is most unpleasant. It strikes fear within you at a primal level. Like almost every victim, I raised both my hands to my neck and scrabbled to get a hold of the...whatever it was cutting into my flesh.

"I'll let you live if you tell me where my files are." Donovan's voice was menacing. It was a lie, of course, and we both knew it. But it had to be said all the same.

I tried to speak, but it was impossible while being strangled. He was slightly off to one side, probably because of my having started to turn. His left foot was out of range, but I tried to stomp down on his right foot. No luck. He was ready for that one and had his foot back far enough. I caught the toe, but since his boots were steel-toed, nothing happened.

"You don't get it. I'm in control here and you can't change that. I want my files."

He jerked, either to avoid my action or just to punish me for the attempt. I didn't know which, and it didn't matter. I knew I couldn't last much longer before I passed out. I forced myself to quit struggling and dropped both of my hands down to my side. It wasn't an attempt to make him think that I had passed out. He wouldn't buy that. Besides, he'd probably keep the hold longer anyway, possibly until I was dead.

But. When I relaxed and dropped my hands, he involuntarily relaxed the slightest bit too. I could only suck the slightest bit of air into my burning lungs. I still couldn't speak.

I swung my right hand back behind me, the short distance to Donovan's crotch. As he tugged the rope tighter, I tightened my grip hard. I thought my eyes were going to be squeezed out of my head, but apparently, Donovan must have had the same reaction. The pain in his scrotum had distracted him enough that he let up his grip a bit. I doubted that would last long, so I loosened my grip ever so slightly so that I could get a good grip on a single testicle. Then I crushed down as hard as I possibly could. My life depended on it.

Sure enough, Donovan released his grip and emitted a high-pitched gurgling noise. Not a little girl scream, just something almost otherworldly. His hand went down as he collapsed to the floor in agony. I can't say I felt sorry in any way.

For the next three seconds, we were both frozen in place, both inhaling a huge gulp of air. My head was light, and I felt as if I were going to pass out. I bent over and put my hands on my knees, not by choice, but because I had no other choice. I opened my mouth to say something snarky, but my voice still wouldn't work. All I could do was cough.

Donovan had moved his hands down to his crotch. Then he passed out from the pain.

I didn't know how long he would be out of it, but I didn't want another battle when he came to. Struggling through the burning in my lungs, I rounded up some duct tape, zip ties, and my handcuffs.

First, I put a strip of duct tape over his eyes. He couldn't hit me if he couldn't see me. Then I handcuffed his ankles together. With that done, I searched his body and removed his assortment of weapons. He was still out cold. Good.

I tried to pull his limp body up into my chair. Although he was slightly smaller than me, I couldn't manage it in my present condition. I gave up and went to Plan B. I pushed my chair over onto the floor and positioned the chair and Donovan's body so that it was like he was sitting in the chair, only laying on his side on the floor. Removing the handcuffs, I zip-tied his legs individually to the front legs of the chair, then wrapped multiple wraps of duct tape over the top of the zip ties. Unless you have police/military-grade zip ties, they can be broken out of if you know how. Donovan would know how, but the tape would prevent that from happening.

I grabbed the arm that was positioned toward the ceiling and pulled it back behind the chair. I zip-tied it in place the best that I could. That would have to do since I couldn't get the arm that was against the floor behind the chair.

With Donovan attached to the chair, I grasped them both and gave a tug. The chair wobbled upright. It was difficult, but easier than the sack of potatoes that Donovan's dead weight represented. Donovan groaned. That motivated me to finish trussing him up.

With a quarter roll of duct tape wrapped around his chest and the chair back, and his hands cuffed behind him, I breathed easier. I put a strip of tape over his mouth just so that I could have the pleasure of ripping it back off later. Finally, I took his knife and cut off all of his clothes. I had read somewhere that stripping someone naked made them less aggressive. Or maybe I saw it in a movie.

Fifteen minutes passed.

That gave me a chance to clear my house in case he was not alone. I locked all the doors and windows. Then I went into the kitchen and made up a glass of instant lemonade. My throat hurt and was screaming for refreshment, but I didn't dare take the time until now. I didn't know what would happen next either. I needed some time to think it through. The powder dissolved into the water as I stirred.

Then it hit me.

I went back into the office and teased out Donovan's

drugs. The ones that I removed from his glove box. Donovan was making low groaning noises. Didn't care.

Back in the kitchen, I crushed up a Rohypnol between two spoons. No, better make it two. I put the lumps in a glass, added instant lemonade, and water. As the powders dissolved, the lemonade took on a slightly green tint. I hoped he wouldn't notice. The coloration would help me ensure I didn't roofie myself. I didn't know if Rohypnol had a taste. I suspected it didn't or it wouldn't be as effective as a date rape drug, but I added some extra sugar, just in case.

Back in the office, I sat across from Donovan, both drinks on the table that served as a desk, and held the bottle of oxy in my left hand. He was awake enough now that he was starting to panic. "How does it feel?" I ripped the tape off of his eyes. He screamed under the tape over his mouth. A few eyelashes came off with the tape. His moist, wild eyes stared back at me. "Would you like some of these?" I rattled the oxy bottle. His eyes flashed with anger as he realized I had them, but then returned to pain mingled with worry. We both stared at each other. "Well, would you?" He gave a muffled grunt through the tape. "I can't understand you. Shake your head."

Donovan nodded. "You know the rules, no screaming for help. OK?" Donovan nodded again. I ripped the tape from over his lips. He winced, but didn't yell out.

"Bastard. You broke into my car. You took stuff off of my computer."

I cut him off. "You just tried to kill me for what, the third time? Or is it four? You trashed my apartment. And the files, you brought that on yourself by taking the SD card out of my apartment." I suspected we could have gone on quarreling like two little girls for quite some time.

"You want the oxy for the pain? I want to know who is behind the assassination attempt and why." I shook the bottle again. "Tell me and I'll give you one."

Donovan glowered and spit in my direction. Why were people always spitting at me?

We both stared at each other again for a while. I didn't expect him to tell me. I'd get it out of him eventually, anyway. What I needed now was some time to plan the next move.

"I'll tell you what. I'll show good faith here. You can have one. Once you have calmed down and aren't hurting as much, perhaps you'll see the logic of it when this one wears off." I opened the bottle, tipped one out, and reached for the glass containing his lemonade. I wasn't going to uncuff him to drink from it. It seemed too friendly and inefficient to tip it up for him as he drank. "I'll be right back. Don't go anywhere."

He was still there when I returned from the kitchen with a straw. It was a Slurpee straw that I had previously used, retrieved from the trash. I dunked it into the glass. "Open wide." I held the pill about eight inches in front of his face. "Now, lean your head all the way out. You come to the pill." I would not take the chance that he would bite me. Literally.

When his head was all the way forward, I closed the remaining inch and popped the pill into his mouth. He moved his head back, and I put the straw from the spiked drink up to his lips. He practically drained it. Our little game had made him as parched as it had made me. I didn't know how much he would drink when I mixed the cocktail, so I had added the second roofie to the mix. Now I was wondering about that. A double dose of Rohypnol along with oxycodone. How safe was that? I didn't want him to die of an overdose right there in my house. That would not be good on multiple levels.

We sat in silence for another fifteen minutes. The color was returning to his face. He had stopped moaning, and he looked a bit more relaxed. As far as anyone duct-taped to a chair can look relaxed. Time to see if the drugs would loosen his lips. Softly I asked, "So, who ordered the hit on me?"

Donovan smiled a goofy little smile.

"Why were you trying to kill me? I don't understand. Help me out here."

He made a little noise that was somewhere between a snort and a giggle. His smile got goofier. Then his eyes rolled upward before his eyelids slammed shut. His head lolled down against his chest as the rest of him went limp.

I checked for a pulse. There was one. That was good, at least. I wondered if I should get the Narcan out of the truck. Wait. The truck wasn't here. How did he get here? I went to the front and peered out into the driveway. Where was his car? That was one more problem that I needed to think about.

Once it became apparent that he wasn't going to OD, I decided I should at least try to establish some kind of alibi. "I was home all alone." was never a good alibi, even if you were innocent. Donovan should be out for a minimum of twelve hours, maybe up to eighteen.

I took his glass into the kitchen, rinsed it and filled it up with hot soapy water, and left it in the sink. I took a garbage bag out from under the sink, went into the office, and stuffed his boots and other pieces of his clothing into it. I turned off the light, locked the office door from the outside, then did the same to the front door, and headed down to my boat, bag in hand.

My neck hurt and I had a pounding headache. Going back upstairs, I took a quick shower, put on fresh clothes, and headed back to the safe room to check on Donovan.

He was still out of it. I transferred him from the chair to the work table in the middle of the room so that he was face up, spread eagle, with hands and feet secured to each of the four legs of the table.

If my truck was here, I would have gone into town and shopped at several stores using my pre-paid debit card. If I took the boat, only one marine store would be open. I could have gotten most of what I needed at one store; a couple of shower curtains, several hand towels, four lint rollers, two five-gallon gasoline cans, and a battery that was the correct size for my pickup truck, but criminals got caught all the time by buying supplies at a single store.

I was thinking about removing the battery from my boat when my cell rang. I nearly jumped out of my skin. It was Nick. "Just so you know, the Galveston police have cleared you." I involuntarily sighed a sigh of relief. "Yeah. There's a but in there, isn't there?"

"Of course. IA still has to look at it, so you are on administrative leave again. No point hurrying back until this blows over, or they call you in for an interview."

"Thanks. I need a couple of days to get my head straight." And to deal with the guy I've got tied up.

"Yea, so how are you doing?"

"I'm in a bit of a state of shock right now. I never

figured French."

"We didn't see it coming either. You had to have been close to something or I don't think he would have taken such an obvious risk. At least it's over now."

We chatted for a few minutes and clicked off. With so much going on, I decided I needed to leave my phone turned on for a change.

By then, I remembered the alibi. Instead of removing the battery from the boat, I'd motor into town, buy one and have some dinner. I could justify buying the battery, the same size that was in the boat, by stating that the one that came with the boat needed replacing if anyone ever asked.

After taking one last look at Donovan and convincing myself that he would be out for hours, I locked up, cast off, and made the trip up the West Bay, under the bridges, and into Galveston Channel.

After buying the marine battery, I headed for familiar territory. Willie G's was much busier than it had been at lunchtime. That was ideal. While waiting on the Crawfish Etouffée with white rice, I struggled with what to do with Donovan after I had extracted all the information out of him I wanted.

What was I going to do with Donovan? Even if he was a cockroach, a manhunt might already be underway. Had he let anyone know where he was going? Not likely. You rarely tell a friend I'm going to go kill a guy, be back by midnight. I didn't want to kill him, although, after the multiple attempts he had made on my life, it seemed like it could be justified somehow. But right now, if I were found out, what would the charges be? Up to the point where I drugged him, then didn't call the cops, it was self-defense. Now what?

Obstructing justice. Kidnapping maybe. Even with a string of other petty charges, it would be nothing compared to murder. No, killing him wasn't a good option.

Turning him loose could end up being just as bad. Would he turn me in? How could he do that without implicating himself? Hmm. Probably not. He'd just make another attempt to kill me and keep on trying until he got me. Or have someone else do it. A dirty cop had to have some disreputable connections. Turning him loose wasn't a good option, either.

Perhaps I could somehow drop him off in Mexico and send him on the lam, but there was no guarantee that he wouldn't still try for revenge.

I wasn't a cold-blooded killer. Sure, I had killed French, but that was in self-defense. On the other hand, his death solved a lot of issues.

While trying to resolve this problem, my phone rang again. "What now?" I intended to ignore it, but the caller ID showed it was Chief McCormick. "Hello... Yes, Sir. No, I'm having dinner at the moment. I'm at Willie G's in Galveston." I made it a point to name the restaurant for my alibi and was glad that I had come. He wanted to talk to me in person. "Uh-huh. Yes, I can wait here for thirty minutes." He clicked off. "Damn it."

I'd finished my food by the time McCormick arrived.

I'm certain that the etouffée was excellent, but between my burning throat and the weight on my mind, I didn't notice. I wasn't there for the food, anyway. I paid with cash and left an unusually large tip. A credit card receipt would have a time stamp on it. With a big tip, I hoped the server would remember that I had been there, but not be certain of the specific time I left.

Then my phone rang again. The Chief wanted me to come outside. That would be a pretty big timestamp.

I stepped into the parking lot's humid night air. The chief's Suburban pulled up next to me. Apparently, he had already been in town when he called. The rear passenger door opened. One of his bodyguards stepped out and waved me over. I glared at him cautiously as I climbed in.

"How are you doing?"

"Fine, sir." It is what every cop on the planet said when asked that question.

"You know Rusty's not pressing charges." It was a statement more than a question.

"Yes sir."

"I have the utmost confidence that IA will clear you, too."

"Thank you, sir."

There was a moment of uncomfortable silence.

McCormick spoke. "I want to personally thank you for taking care of French. He was a bad seed and a blight on the department. The kind I was referring to when we talked last time."

"It was self-defense."

McCormick gave a big smile. "All the better, isn't it? Of course, I can't give you a commendation or anything."

We both nodded slightly.

"I don't know what happened to his minion. Donovan."

I opened my mouth to plead lack of knowledge, but McCormick held up his hand and continued, "And I don't want to know either. I, uh, heard he went to ground.

Probably since his boss couldn't protect him any longer."

"Interesting idea, sir."

"Once again, I thank you on behalf of myself, the department, and the city of Houston."

With that, the interview appeared to be over. I opened the door and turned to exit. McCormick gave one parting bit. "Watch your back. French isn't the only one of his ilk. No doubt he has friends in blue, just like him."

I stood there in the darkness while the bodyguard lumbered back into the car, and they drove away.

I thought about the week ahead. If I read the chief right, nobody had me in their sights for Donovan. I was going to have some time off.

Time to turn the phone off. I could say my battery died.

As I returned to the Tiki house, I kept checking that there wasn't a boat following me or a helicopter overhead. I had slipped back into full paranoia mode.

Once docked back at the house, I started walking around the neighborhood to locate Donovan's car. Only a block away. I had to go back home and retrieve his keys, then I drove his car back to my place. Deciding it would be much better out of sight, I opened the garage. I still hadn't dealt with the scrap carpeting, so I had to drag it out into the driveway so that I could stash the Camaro inside.

***

At about three a.m. sleeping beauty finally awoke, but he was still groggy. I stood over his naked body stretched out on the table.

Donovan's eyes flew open wide. His expression went from one of minor fear to that of major panic.

"I just talked to McCormick. The department thinks you've gone to ground after French's death. No one is looking in my direction to find you. No one."

"You're lying." He sobbed a bit. Somehow, he knew it was true.

"Now you are going to tell me all about who was behind all this."

Donovan snorted. "Why would I do that?"

"Because you won't like the pain. Eventually, you'll break, so why not go easy on yourself?" It was another one of those things that had to be said, but never worked.

After a moment of silence with no response from Donovan, I raised the ends of the jumper cable I had attached to my recently acquired marine battery. I had secured half of a wet sponge from the kitchen in each clamp.

Donovan didn't comprehend what was about to happen. When I pushed one sponge to his belly and the other to his scrotum, he jerked so hard I thought he might break my makeshift table. I expected a louder scream, but he was sucking air too hard to make it happen.

"Let's try again. Who?"

Donovan hesitated, but when I raised the jumper cables again, he talked.

"Poliakoff found out that you were inside Benni's organization. He told French to kill you. French told me to do it. When that didn't happen, then he tried and failed, too. We were waved off and told to see if you had Benni's insurance. I don't know why French came after you again. When you got into my stuff, well..." he trailed off.

"Who called you off? Poliakoff again?"

"I don't know. It went through French."

We were alone in silence for a while, each contemplating what had brought us to this point. I stood over Donovan and weighed everything that had happened over the last two weeks.

Then my heart went black.

42

I gave Donovan another serving of "special" lemonade with a roofie. I don't think he cared at this point, and relief from the pain was a welcome thought.

Donovan solved two problems for me. One was how to retrieve my truck from Port Isabel, the other how to get rid of his car.

I would have liked to have gotten rid of Donovan first. After all, having him tied up and drugged in my house was incriminating. But if I got caught driving his car south, it would be better that he was still alive. Not good, but better.

I put on dark clothes and pulled on a pair of black "Grease Monkey" brand nitrile gloves I had from the hardware store. I pulled the Camaro out, closed the garage door, and headed south.

My phone rang. I'd forgotten to turn it off. "Hey Q, what's up?"

"Something funny happened."

"Funny ha, ha or funny weird?"

"I didn't hear anyone laughing when the Texas Rangers showed up."

"The Rangers?"

"Yeah. Uh-huh. Bright shiny stars and everything. They took some cold case files. The very case files you were working on. You know anything about that?"

I was surprised. "No. Did they say why?"

"No. But it can't be a coincidence. Thought you might like to know."

"It's a mystery to me. Thanks, Q. It wouldn't be good to get blindsided."

We chatted a minute more. After the call, I turned my phone off. Suddenly I wasn't so sure that having Cricket wave Donovan under the Rangers' nose was such a good idea. It seemed like a good idea at the time. Having law enforcement look for him was good when I didn't know where he was. Now that he was bound and gagged in my house, I didn't want anyone looking for him, least of all the Rangers.

I drove past the exit to Port Isabel and continued into Brownsville. There I drove around a bit until I found the type of neighborhood that I was looking for. It had to be near the border, close to a Valley Metro blue line bus stop, and the area had to look pretty sketchy. Fortunately, in this case, bus routes and sketchy neighborhoods went together. It didn't take long to find the right spot. I parked and left the Camaro's door unlocked, windows down, and keys on the dashboard. Then I walked to the nearest bus stop and caught the bus that would take me out to Port Isabel.

***

The first ladrón to spot the Camaro passed it up. It was too good to be true. The car was too nice to be in this neighborhood and it simply looked too easy. He figured it was a bait car; a car the cops used to entrap car thieves such as himself.

The second ladrón wasn't as discriminating. The Camaro was too tempting to pass up. He considered it could be a bait car, but dismissed the idea. The cops were far too busy with the drug gangs to worry about the rampant car theft that plagued border towns. Even if it were a trap, the worst thing that would happen would be that he would be arrested, driven to the border, and escorted across by inmigración. He decided, rightfully so, that someone *wanted* the car stolen, so he might as well help them out. He took one last look around, jumped into the car, and headed for International Blvd. Less than fifteen minutes later, he rolled under a sign that read "Bienvenidos a Mexico."

Even though the distance was short, the bus ride was long. By the time Griff had arrived at the Port Isabel Walmart, the Camaro had been across the border for over an hour, sitting in a chop shop.

***

After the bus dropped me off at Walmart, I walked the rest of the way to the marina and retrieved the truck.

After leaving the "modern Venice" I grabbed some fast food to go from Whataburger and headed out of town. Further up the coast, I stopped at a big box hardware store to stretch my legs and buy a couple of cinder blocks and a fresh roll of duct tape.

The sun was going down when I pulled up in front of my house. Inside, Donovan had come to, and in a struggle to free himself, had turned the table over on its side. He was half suspended, half resting on the floor, but wholly uncomfortable.

I left him in that position as his punishment. After operating under the stress of the situation, I was tired. I needed to nap for a few hours. As I ripped the tape off his mouth again, "You look uncomfortable, hungry, and thirsty. Let me get you some more lemonade."

Donovan must have figured out that he was being drugged. "No. I'm not taking any more of your drugs."

"Well, your drugs, actually. They were good enough for your victims."

I went to the kitchen to grab a snack and returned. While eating it in front of him and sipping on a Dr. Pepper from a transparent glass filled with ice cubes, I said, "I promise, on my honor, I won't kill you while you're drugged." He wasn't convinced, but, eventually, with the temptation of more oxy, he gave in, drank the spiked lemonade, and went back to sleep.

Before going to bed, I put tape over his eyes, assuming it might reduce the risk of him trying to escape again if he couldn't see what was happening around him. Then I set an alarm for oh dark thirty and drifted off to a restless sleep.

43

The alarm was unwelcome. Still, there was work to be done before it got light outside. I went out front and dragged the carpet up the stairs and into the living room.

I gave Donovan a quick, gentle touch with the jumper cable to ensure he was out cold, then cut him loose from the table. I dragged him into the living room, secured his hands and feet with zip ties and duct tape, checked the tape over his mouth, and rolled him up in the carpet.

I secured the carpet with more duct tape on each end, then dragged the Donovan enchilada down the back stairs to the boat dock. Thump, thump, thump.

After maneuvering the carpet roll into the boat, I cast off in the predawn shadows and headed down the West Bay.

I timed the departure so that I would arrive at San Luis pass around sunrise, thus ensuring visibility for maneuvering between the narrow islands at the entrance to the pass. Once in the Gulf, I headed southeast, toward the Texas A&M buoy.

The thing with the Gulf of Mexico is that the waters remain very shallow for a long way out. I had consulted the nautical charts to find the nearest waters that were over a few hundred feet. That required me to motor out a long way to reach deeper water. From the A&M buoy, I headed due south.

The Raymarine C120 radar unit was equipped with a sonar option. This not only allowed me to be on the lookout for other boats in the area, but gave me a readout on the depth below the boat. When the depth finder showed it was deep enough, I had one last chat with Donovan. I opened the head end of the carpet enchilada and ripped the tape off his mouth. Didn't matter if he screamed out here, no one was near enough to hear.

"Your video files were finally decrypted. They've been posted on the internet. The only legacy that you'll be leaving behind is that of a date rapist. Maybe that of a murderer, too."

In the end, neither of us had much more to say.

First to go was the bag with all of Donovan's clothes and personal effects. Then I propped the foot end of the carpet over the side of the boat and attached a cinder block to it.

Although it should have been apparent, it only now dawned on Donovan what was about to happen. "Wait. Aren't you going to kill me first?"

"Naw. Then I'd have to clean up your DNA."

"Well, how about you drug me first?"

"Hmm. That *was* a courtesy that you gave to your victims." As I was tying the other cinder block to the head end, "But, I don't think so. I gave you my word that I wouldn't kill you while you were drugged, remember?"

Donovan started to wail as I pulled the head end of the carpet back over his face, then over the side. His salty tears quickly blended with the salt water of the gulf as he disappeared below the surface.

At that moment, I realized something. I needed to buy some suntan lotion to keep on the boat.

***

Back on Tiki Island, I dedicated the rest of the day to deep cleaning for any traces that Donovan had been my houseguest. I knew I couldn't guarantee that all hair, DNA, etc. could be gone, but if it ever came down to it, I'd suggest that he must have burgled my house as he had done to my apartments in Houston.

I also received the first piece of non-junk mail I'd gotten at the Tiki Address. It was a postcard, also posted in Pittsburg. Again, the text was neatly printed; "Thanks for taking care of Lola. I owe you one." No signature, no return address. How he got this address, I wasn't sure, but I suspect it involved Cricket.

It was a pleasure to have my garage back again, but the carpet had left small strands of itself on the front steps, throughout the living room, down the back stairs, and out to the boat dock. Collecting all of those pieces took some of the joy out of it.

I swapped the marine battery in the boat with the new one that I had purchased. At first, I assumed that I'd return the old one for the core charge, but ended up keeping it in the garage. It could run a small inverter in the event of a long power outage from the frequent gulf storms.

***

The following day, I took the boat to the marina to have it detailed and selected the lettering for the boat's new name. I also picked up a bright orange and blue tube of Banana Boat Ultra Sport suntan lotion to keep on the boat. SPF 30.

While hanging out at the ship's chandler, I got a phone call. "Ivy, glad you called."

"Yeah, I thought that I'd wait for the dust to settle

down after that thing with French. That was clean, wasn't it?"

"Pure as the driven snow." Well, not exactly.

Ivy got straight down to business. "Have you heard anything from our friend? Benni."

Suddenly, I wasn't as glad that she had called. "Oh, so this is a business call. I was hoping it was on a more...umm, informal level."

"Are you evading the question?"

"No. Of course not. Why would I have heard from Benni? He's not supposed to contact anyone from his old life." It was a half-truth. I didn't know for certain that the postcard was from Benni. But the timing of her call set me on edge and I passingly wondered if I just got caught lying to a federal agent.

"It's probably nothing. The Marshals called and asked if he has had contact with anyone here. They suspect he isn't following all the rules. Since you didn't have contact with his mistress, I thought maybe you didn't have contact with him either."

"I swear, I don't know how to get in contact with Benni. No address, no phone number, no email. Honest."

"Ok." She paused. "Do you think Benni might bend the rules?"

"Benni has been coloring outside the lines for his whole life. I'd be more surprised if he didn't bend the rules."

"If he reaches out to you, let us know before you make contact. Understood?"

"Yes, Agent Iverson."

"Special Agent Iverson."

They were so funny about that. "Listen. I bought a

boat recently. You should come out to the bay for a ride."

"I'd love to hear about it. Maybe some other time. I gotta run." With that, she rang off.

Apparently, all I had to do to end phone calls from women was to invite them out on my boat. It certainly wasn't proving to be the chick magnet that the boat salesmen would have you believe it would be.

44

I had to make a trip to 1200 Travis to see the shrink. It seemed to be the usual tripe. "How are you doing?"

"Much better actually." It was an honest answer, but I couldn't tell her why.

"Even with your sister in the hospital?"

"While that's awful, it has given us a chance to reconnect. So you see, some good has come out of it. The mending of our relationship is healing for me."

"I still can't clear you for duty. Come back next week and let's talk again."

With that out of the way, I rode down the elevator and stopped in to say hi to Q. I wanted to get a first-hand account of the visit from the Texas Rangers.

"Hey. How are things going?"

Q sighed. "Not great. But it's good to see you. How is it on your end?"

"I'm better. Things have gotten quieter. Tomorrow, we'll transport my sister from the hospital to a rehab facility."

Q was gathering up some things as if he were going somewhere. "That's great. I'd like to talk, but I gotta run."

"Sure, where you off to?" Cold cases normally didn't require this much of a sense of urgency.

"Over to the University. I'm going to help out on a case."

"An active case? I thought you didn't do those anymore. Why?"

He started to walk toward the elevator, so I followed.

The conversation continued.

"I got a call from a guy that I brought up, Detective Buffalo, over at Central Patrol. He needs some help and asked me to do some grunt work for him."

"What happened?"

"Body washed up at the campus."

"Yeah, I heard something about that. Topless or nude?"

"No, she had clothes on. No ID. So far, no one has been reported missing. Buffalo, his partner, and eight campus cops are sifting through the student photo database, trying to match the face."

"Ugh. They can't use facial recognition? They don't have it. You know we don't have it, so no."

It was true. HPD didn't use any facial recognition software.

The elevator doors opened, we got in and started down.

"How about an online facial match?"

"Two problems. First, the software would need to upload or have access to the student photo database. That ain't gonna happen. Ever. Second, Even if that did magically happen, if it ever became an issue in court, there would be a problem with using facial recognition since the department specifically doesn't use it. It would be problematic for the prosecutor."

"Send me a pic of the victim."

"Sure. You want to come help?"

"Can't, not cleared for duty."

The doors opened and Q stepped out.

I said, "Buffalo?"

"Talk to you later."

***

The next morning, Krunch came down to Tiki, picked me up in the Mini, and we headed over to UT Med. The plan was to get Hannah, drive to her place to pick up a few things, then drive to Webster, where there was a good convalescent facility. She would probably be there for three or four weeks before she could go back home.

We stepped into Hannah's room. "Hi, bro." Her voice still sounded weak and gravelly.

Off to the side, another voice joined in. "Yeah, Hi, bro. Good to see you again." It was Cricket.

How was the transportation going to work now? Hannah wouldn't go with Cricket, would she?

It would be awkward for Krunch and Cricket to go together. It would be even more awkward for Cricket and me to ride together.

"Cricket, I was wondering if you could do me a favor."

"I'd do anything for you, Griff."

She had softened up a bit since the attack on Hannah, but I knew she was playing to the room. Seeing if she could get a reaction from me. Messing with me. She liked that. "I need a facial recognition search done. On the QT." The last part piqued her interest.

"What does it entail?"

"Let's step outside while Hannah gets dressed and I'll fill you in." Krunch stayed behind to help Hannah. "I need to match a photo against the UHD student photo database to identify who the person is."

Cricket looked suspicious at first, then made the connection. "Is this that girl that they found yesterday?"

"Yup. They haven't ID'd her yet and are trying to do it manually."

"Wow. Your cavemen buddies are in the stone age."

"You would be helping the victim more than the cops..."

"Fine. It'll cost you thirty dollars, though."

Like she needed thirty dollars from me. "Sure thing."

"And some beef jerky."

"Fine."

"And,"

I cut her off. "Wait. You're just testing to see how high I will go." A demure expression slid across her face. "Thirty bucks and beef jerky. That's all." I'll send you the pic.

The transportation thing sorted itself out. Cricket wasn't going to Webster with us anyway, but she wanted to follow us to Hannah's apartment so that she could witness the scene of the crime. It was some kind of a morbid rush for her. After that, she left, avoiding the stop at the convalescent home.

We had small talk on the drive to Webster, with Hannah mostly listening. Once at the convalescent center, we got her settled in. My phone buzzed with an incoming text from Cricket. "She is not in the UHD database. Not a student there."

I sent a text to Q. "You're Jane Doe isn't in the UHD database. You are wasting your time there."

Q replied, "I want to ask you how you determined that, but I don't think that I want to know. Thanks though. That will save a few days for the investigation."

By the time we got Hannah all settled in, it was getting late. If we had taken separate cars, Krunch could have gone home, but as it was, she needed to drive me back to Tiki. I briefly considered spending the night in Webster instead, but the memory of my last stay there still lingered in my consciousness. Besides, I still had to get back to Tiki the next day. How was it I kept ending up in some place with no way to get back?

We decided that Krunch would drive us back to Galveston, we would have a nice dinner together, and then she would drop me off at the Tiki house.

She spent the night.

45

The bright Texas sun glinted off of the new gold leaf lettering on the white hull of the Century 2900. The water was calm; the slightest of sea breezes kept the heat from being unbearable. The boat drifted lazily in the water.

Krunch said, "If that is ever going to happen again, you need to get some furniture in your house."

"You get to pick it out."

With that, Krunch dropped the beach cover-up she had on, exposing a bright red string bikini. Its resemblance to the red bra and panties that she had on in the motel the night French died was unmistakable.

I choked on my Dr. Pepper and began coughing uncontrollably. I'm not sure why. While working in Benni's strip clubs for over a year, I'd seen so much flesh as to make me immune. Somehow, this was different.

An impish grin of amusement danced across Krunch's face. "Pull yourself together, cowboy. It isn't anything that you haven't seen before."

I tried to reply, but could only cough.

She put her wineglass back into the gimbaled cup holder. "I guess if this is too much for you, I'll have to keep the rest of it on."

While I continued to gasp for air, she laid face down on the padded cushions in the U-shaped bow, then untied her top, so that there would be no tan line.

"No, it's not that. Some of my soda went down the wrong way."

"Uh-huh. At least your jaw wasn't danglin' down." After a moment of silence, "Don't you think the name of your boat is a bit....um, provocative?"

"What? Why no. I named it in honor of my dad."

She craned her head back to look at me with an inquisitive look.

"He was a huge John Wayne fan. Donovan's Reef was his favorite movie."

"What?"

"Donovan's Reef. It was a romantic comedy about an ex-navy guy on a Polynesian Island. It had Lee Marvin and, I think, Cesar Romero and Dorothy Lamour in it." I wasn't sure she even knew who Cesar Romero or Dorothy Lamour were.

Krunch mused, "Still, it seems in poor taste considering all that has happened. Besides, you sure know a lot of details about this movie. Kinda like how a suspect who lies gives too much detail."

"No. It's not that. Being my dad's favorite movie, I had to watch it repeatedly. Try me if you want to know more." I realized I was going to have to put up a movie poster if I was going to keep that storyline up. "I don't see how it is in poor taste. No one knows what happened to Donovan."

Krunch, "humph." Seemingly satisfied, she turned her head back around and lay on the padding in silence for a minute.

"So, would you like me to keep calling you Krunch, or would you prefer Kennedy?"

Without looking back, "My friends used to call me Cat."

"Cat?"

"You know. For Catherine. But never call me that when we are at work."

"I thought your first name was Kennedy."

"That's my middle name. Kennedy works, but it sounds too formal for friends. My dad shortened it to Ken. Maybe that's where I got the tomboy streak in me."

"Catherine is nice and Cat is kind of cool, so why do you hide it?"

"Because then I'd become Cat Krunch, like pet food, or Cat'n Krunch like your lame joke in the hospital."

"Wait. That's not fair. It was the drugs they injected me with that were talking."

She glanced back with a playful smile, "Sure." She then returned to her tanning.

We sat in an easy, comfortable silence for a while. Me in my new Ray-Bans, drinking my Dr. Pepper, Krunch, tanning her backside in the Gulf sun. Out here, the air smelled fresh and clean. No scent of an oil refinery. No odor of mildew mixed in, just clean, healthy air.

Krunch raised the tube of Banana Boat. "You wanna' put some of this on my back for me?"

Afterward, I sat comfortably, admiring the view. I closed my eyes and thought, "Things have turned out right after all." I couldn't help but afford myself a little smile as I thought about Donovan almost a thousand feet below.

***

Fifty miles away, Mick sat in near darkness in his Woodlands home. His manicured fingers held a Waterford snifter, which held Cognac Prunier VSOP. Mick's eyes closed. He thought, "Things have turned out alright. Donovan's gone and has taken the clues to my secrets with him."

Of course, Mick would have been just as happy with Griffin Hunter dead. But that could wait for another day.

The hunt for Mick continues in

RELENTLESS

Griffin Hunter volume 2

By Parker Samuels

RELENTLESS

After bodies start to wash up in Houston's bayous, HPD creates a task force to track down a serial killer.

A powerful and mysterious man named Mick wants Detective Griffin Hunter to stop investigating a cold case serial rapist/killer and pulls the strings to get Griff assigned to the task force.

Hunting the killer won't be easy for the task force because there is a surprising twist that will keep them far from the trail.

While Griff works on both cases, death will follow as Mick tries to cover his tracks and dissuade the pursuit of the cold case. Not even those around Griff will be safe.

Once the task force's serial killer is revealed and the immediate danger appears to be over, Mick is still in control and won't rest until Griff drops the cold cases.

Or is dead.

1

Mick sat in his overstuffed brown leather chair, reflecting on his situation. A Waterford snifter of Cognac Prunier VSOP rested nearby. This place was the only place where he could truly think alone.

That dumb-ass Donovan had attempted to kill Griff and had failed. That failure had started the chain of events that now made Griff a problem. The shooting had led to Griff working on the cold case squad. That, in turn, had led to him examining the decades-old murders of strippers. Whores, really, in Mick's mind. Whores that he had raped and murdered.

On the one hand, he wasn't that worried about the cases being traced back to himself. Donovan's weak moral character had made it easy for Mick to exploit him, using him to tamper with the evidence in the old cases. Now, examining how badly Donovan had botched his attempt to kill Griff, Mick wondered if Donovan hadn't botched that too.

Donovan. Why had he tried to kill Griff in the first place? Mick wasn't sure. Where was he now? Mick wasn't sure of that either, but had a strong suspicion that Griff had killed him. Either that or French had killed Donovan as a way of cleaning up the mess. That is before Griff killed Donovan. No, French probably hadn't done it. There was too much evidence that Donovan was still around after French was killed. Either way, Donovan's disappearance was good. He couldn't try to implicate Mick.

Even if Donovan were still alive, he had been so disgraced that any attempts to point suspicion of wrongdoing toward Mick would immediately be dismissed.

A sip from the snifter warmed Mick with the aroma of rich fruity and floral aromas and a taste of oak.

On the other hand, having anyone dig into those files carried some element of risk, however small, for Mick. And Griff had proven to be both resourceful and resilient. After all, he had somehow managed to get the Texas Rangers to look into Donovan's crimes. The solution seemed simple enough though, get Griff off of the cold case squad. That should have already happened, but the messy business with French had reset the clock. Damned shrinks.

With the solution at hand, Mick closed his eyes. The thought of the cold cases brought back the memories. The sensations of desecrating those whores who desecrated themselves. Those sensations left him yearning once again for a new kill.

They say that rank has its privileges, but anonymity is not one of them.

Krunch said, "If you liked *Corruption*, please leave a review."

www.ingramcontent.com/pod-product-compliance
Lightning Source LLC
Chambersburg PA
CBHW071233300726
48975CB00002B/399